"HOT BUTTERED BISCUITS AND JAM"
THE MEMOIRS OF SEVEN

Bethel Bates

iUniverse, Inc.
New York   Bloomington

"Hot Buttered Biscuits and Jam"
The Memoirs of Seven

iUniverse books may be ordered through booksellers or by contacting:

iUniverse
1663 Liberty Drive
Bloomington, IN 47403
www.iuniverse.com
1-800-Authors (1-800-288-4677)

Because of the dynamic nature of the Internet, any Web addresses or links contained in this book may have
changed since publication and may no longer be valid. The views expressed in this work are solely those of
the author and do not necessarily reflect the views of the publisher, and the publisher hereby disclaims any
responsibility for them.

ISBN: 978-1-4401-4995-5 (sc)
ISBN: 978-1-4401-4996-2 (ebk)

Printed in the United States of America

iUniverse rev. date: 11/11/2009

About The Author

Bethel (pronounced Beth-l) *Bates was born and raised in Philadelphia, Pennsylvania. With family as a loving, supportive, and magnetic force in her life, Bethel was able to devote much of her time to her writings from an early age.*

In her youth, she began to explore different writing techniques as her thoughts began to take on a whole new life of their own. She carefully took note of them, keeping pen and pad near her at all times. It was very essential that she recall each monumental moment and her exact thoughts which paralleled them.

She began to compose songs by age eleven. By age thirteen she came to realize her potential and appreciation for her gift of writing poetry and short stories. Since then, she has evolved, fusing together short stories, poetry, and songs; thus resulting in the creation of novels and plays. Her writing has become more than just a past time for her, it has become a necessity. It has become life.

INTRODUCTION

07' was the year that Cadence wore many faces. She wore the face of evolution and the face of progression as it was mandated upon her life. She wore the face of fear; trepidation and apprehension accompanied the ideology of change. She wore the face of anxiety—uneasy about today and unsure about tomorrow. She wore the face of grief that settled into her spirit as she mourned the lost of trust and love. Bewilderment and despondency manipulated her expressions as she bare the burden of coping with the dread and hopelessness that each day brought.

Cadence was on the brink of a life changing break through. The faces that she wore were many and diverse. Nobody could wear them except her. She tried to disguise the faces, camouflaging them as she had done for so long. Cadence had come to the crossroads in her life where there were major decisions that needed to be made. Which direction would she choose? She had grown weary of masquerading her reality, always pretending; but who was she really?

She wore every face accept her own. Because to wear her own would come with consequences; consequences that meant having to confront herself. It meant coming to terms with her circumstances and the possibility of having to walk away forever. And if walking away was her only means of accomplishing that thing which she had never been able to realize thus far—she would accept the fact that it could very well be her only alternative.

She knew that she had come to herself, arresting everything that had been haunting her, freeing herself up from all that had held her captive; She'd become at ease with the reality that, abandoning a life that had never been hers to begin with, would prove to be a most challenging and subsequently taxing task. It would be the most difficult thing that she would ever have to attempt in the whole of her life.

She had rehearsed it over and over again in her head, playing out every scene, word for word and line by line. She had become comfortable with the scheme of disassociating herself with the lot of it; disconnecting herself from all of which she no longer desired to be apart of and that which no longer desired to be a part of her.

She understood that to abandon those unconstructive things which she had become so toxically accustomed and familiarized with in all her journey, would be nothing less than life changing. But even more than that, it would be life saving. Her life had been consumed by an evil force. Yes, it was evil in every sense. It was harmful; planting its seeds of despair and anguish into her mortality. It was evil and it came to rob her of everything God intended her to have.

But Cadence had to acknowledge the crucial role that she'd played in what had taken place in her life, whether she was a willing or non-willing participant. Whether she was aware or not aware; she inadvertently gave her permission. She gave her consent, to all critical and censorious persons, places, and things, to sabotage and disrupt every good thing in her life.

As a result; a long term relationship with her husband was DEAD. Her house couldn't stand. Her savings had been EXHAUSTED. Her credit had been SIFTED like wheat, and yes, even her pride was DIMINISHED. There was no place for pride when it came to matters of the heart. What was left of her was merely a lump of clay. She knew deep down, in what was left of her delicate spirit, that something had to be done about her life; a life that was fading before her very eyes…….. but what?

Dedication

This book is dedicated to everyone who has had a profound effect on and in my life, good and bad alike. All of which have grown me into who I have evolved into today.

To God, I thank for being a healer and a revealer; for being my true and factual source of inspiration—you are my everything.

To my parents, Rose and Bennie; thank you for being the vessels in which God used in order to introduce me to this world. Your strengths have gone unprecedented and unmatched.

And to my children, Marsharelle, Diavah, Cambriae, and Frederick; thank you for always loving me.. and loving me more. You have been the greatest gifts of all; because of you I will never be the same.

SPECIAL THANKS

To Pamela Tolbert, for giving me back, that which had been lost. How could she ever know?

"Hot Buttered Biscuits and Jam"
THE MEMOIRS of SEVEN

Bethel Bates

"Lord give me valor—the boldness to face the giant that pursues me at every turn. Shield me as I am under fire. Lift me and my martial spirit in my search for the truth and certainty that will make me whole—as I carry the cross that bears my name. Amen."

Cadence prayed as she knelt in a small section of the church, her head bowed and her hands together, as the New Year approached. She thought about all that had transpired in 07'. She thought about everything that her family had endured in the past 12 months and just how long the year had truly been in all its twist and turns. This time last year, things were a little bit different as she lay in a bed down the hall from her bedroom. She laid wondering what the next year was going to bring to her life and to the life of her family . Never did she imagine the misfortune that would ultimately take place.

Chapter One

||||||||||||||||||||||||||||||||||||||||||||||||||||||||||||||||||||||||||||||||||||||||||||||||||||||||||||||||||||||||||||||||||

Keep your head Up

It was the last Thursday in June. It was a pretty dreary and lackluster day, as the winds were high and the rain commenced to pounding the sidewalks endlessly. Cadence stood outside of the Kinkos, across from the funeral parlor where she has been employed now for the past seven years. She didn't recall the forecast mentioning rain. So with no umbrella, she tried to shelter herself from the torrential down pour, armed with a plastic bag, which she had used earlier to hold her peanut butter and jelly sandwich, and the Philadelphia Inquirer she proceeded to stand and wait patiently. It was the third time this week that Halstead had been late picking her up.

She had just gone to the hair dresser the day before and her pin curls were surely suffocating and sweating out underneath the plastic bag. She watched as at least a dozen people had gone in and out of the Kinkos. As she waited she studied their shoes, their style of dress, but mostly the expression on their faces. She was good at determining so many things by the expressions people had on their faces. Couples were her favorite. She could tell just as much by their body language—whether they were really happy, just holdin' on til' something better came along, or absolutely fed up.

Cadence, dressed in a purple ruffled top, black high waist bubble hem skirt with belt, suede ¾ length coat trimmed in fox, and three inch leather black pumps with purple trim— looked across the street and down the long block to the next hundred to where the nearest phone booth was located. "O.K. girl," she told herself, "let's go." She started to run for the light, when her feet became entangled with another and came from under her. Embarrassed, she scurried to collect all of the items that flew from her bags and on to the street before the light changed. She looked around and saw an older guy standing at the corner drinking coffee. She got up and realized that she had broken the heel of her left shoe. Her right knee was bleeding and her stockings were torn. She limped across the street as quickly as she could. She was beginning to lose feeling in her fingers and toes due to the freezing rain.

She found her way to the phone booth where there was an out of order sign placed in front of it. She went inside the mall, two blocks to her right. There she saw a phone booth that was seemingly operable. She reached in her pocket only to find two dollars and fifty cents in change. She placed one quarter into the slot, waited for a dial tone and began to dial Halstead's cell phone. His answering service picked up, "Yeah it's me. Who is this? Naw I'm not available at the moment to take your call. Either I'm taking care of some business or I just don't wanna talk to you right now. But either way, I'll hit you up later. At the beep, you know what to do." "The least he could do is answer his phone", Cadence thought to herself

She couldn't decide whether to walk back to the opposite corner or stay right there and try and wait for Halstead a little longer, or cross over and take the next bus. "Thank God it's pay day tomorrow," she spoke out loud to herself. Bothered and frustrated, Cadence started to reflect on so many times in the past when Halstead would leave her stranded—at times he would never show up to pick her up at all.

Her head became heavy and her face began to heat up intensely as her mind began to race. She felt her bags trying to slip off her shoulder. Her heart began to pounce as she held her head down. It became difficult to hold her, I won't be defeated smile in place. She thought about the words that her mother would say to her when she knew that times were getting tough for her. "Always keep a smile on your face and hold your head up high; regardless of what's going on in your household. Nobody has to know your business but you and God."

For the most part, she did good following her mother's advice. But on this particular day, her tears had their own agenda. They had been trapped inside her for so long. They wanted their freedom. She held her head down and wouldn't look up until she was able to get her bearings. But the more she wiped her tears away the more they flowed. She began to loose control of her emotions. She started to fumble around urgently through the bag on her right arm—looking for tissue to wipe her face and blow her nose. "I don't know how much longer I can continue to do this Lord, Oh God I'm so tired," she thought.

A passerby, that unintentionally witnessed her small mental break down, came over to her. "You alright Miss?" a strong and convincingly caring voice inquired. Cadence, feeling ashamed of showing a weaker side of herself, immediately found restraint when she heard him and paused keeping her head down as she studied a pair of fairly new brown oxfords that stood before her. She quickly cleared her throat and thought for a moment before she responded to the voice without a face. "Yes I am, I'm fine, thank you." Never looking up, she pulled herself together and began to walk away.

Chapter Two

||||||||||||||||||||||||||||||||||||||||||||||||||||||||||||||||||||||||||||||||||||||||||||||||||||||||||||||||||

Tanya

Half way up the block, Halstead drove up in Cadence's car like a bat out of hell, on top of being two and a half hours late. Cadence was happy to finally be able to come from out of the rain and relax her frozen tired feet and thaw out, but she wasn't thrilled at all to see Halstead. She remembered some time back when all she ever wanted to do was see and touch his face, and she could never get enough. That seemed so long ago. It was becoming more and more difficult as time went on to even look at him.

"What you doin'? You need to be where you're supposed be. I don't have time to be driving up and down this street looking for you. Get in, I don't have all day," he hollered as he rolled down the window just before he reached her. Not so much as a hello, how was your day, or anything. "Ignorance is surely bliss," Cadence thought.

Cadence got in the car and was confronted with a very distinct and intimate odor that had been poorly masked by cheap car deodorants. At the very thought of what had taken place in her car while she was at work; she began to have heart palpitations and sweaty palms just thinking about it. She tried to ignore proof of his blatant indiscretions just once. She strapped herself with the seat belt and adjusted the passenger seat that was reclined. Then she looked out of the front window with a dead empty stare as they began to drive away. "You fill out any applications today?" she asked him with an expressionless face.

"If all you're interested in is nagging me about a job, I'd rather you not say anything to me at all. I told you I was looking didn't I? Now if that's not good enough for you, then I don't know what to tell you."

Cadence shook her head in disbelief and continued to look out the window. Halstead pulled over about two miles from where she worked, and stopped in front of the Barber Shop that he frequented. "Yo Steady," one of his partners in crime yelled out.

"What it look like?" Halstead responded. "I'll be back. I need to run in here for a minute to take care of some business," he told Cadence as he exited the car. Everything he wore had to have somebody's name on it. Cadence liked to look nice too. But it really didn't matter to her whether there was a name on her pocket book or her shoes—as she was more interested in style and coordination.

For Halstead, his looks came before everything else, including the mortgage. He was 6'2", creamy milk chocolate skin, piercing eyes, with hair as dark as coal and strong bone structure. He was always dressed to the nines with some of his favorites; Polo, Ambercrombie, or Louie "V" when he left the house. He constantly reminded Cadence that he had an image to uphold.

Cadence noticed that the cell phone that was connected to the belt of his pants, had come out of its holder and fallen into the car seat. She wasn't in the habit of searching through his things. She saw no point in it. Besides, she knew him well enough to know—that the truth was never in him. But just as she had re-established her non-snooping policy with herself, a text message had been sent to his phone. She went back and forth in her mind about whether or not to check it. After all, "It could be important," she thought to justify her intentions.

She reached for his blackberry with her left hand and as she touched it to view it, she felt a coolness run up her left arm and zap the left side of her neck, as she saw short fragmented glances of unfamiliar faces, all female. She gazed expressionless as she read the text from somebody named Gabby: I'll be over my mom's until eight and no later. I thought we'd have a late dinner; maybe some Bottom of the Sea. Do what u gotta do. Handle your business and don't make me wait. I LOVE U.

Although human memory is infinitely fallible, there are certain things that it will never allow you to forget. Cadence worked a part-time job at the Rite Aid Pharmacy on Broad St a few years back. It was common for Halstead to pick her up after her shift was over. He would wait in the parking lot while Cadence closed out her register. There was a young woman, Tanya, that would come into the Pharmacy on a pretty regular basis to fill prescriptions for her ailing mother. They would always speak, sometimes even a short conversation would emerge. Tanya seemed nice enough from what Cadence could see. It would be around this time that Cadence started to receive prank calls at her home.

A few months had passed when Cadence noticed that the belly of Miss Tanya had begun to swell. Her belly wasn't the only thing that was changing. Ms. Tanya's attitude and demeanor changed significantly and appeared to be directed towards Cadence. "So how far along are you?" Cadence asked as she engaged in small talk.

"I'm almost near the end," she answered reluctantly.

"How is everything going with the pregnancy?"

"Everything is going just fine."

"Is everything okay with you?"

"Me, oh everything is great, why do you ask?"

"Just because that's all," she responded with a false-hearted smirk on her face.

Cadence continued to receive the phone calls. But now the person on other end would begin to ask for Halstead. Her voice was muffled and familiar but Cadence was unable to place it. The mysterious women would never say who was calling and refused to leave a message.

Several weeks later, Tanya came into the Pharmacy, no longer pregnant, but without her newborn baby. "Oh, what did you have?" Cadence asked.

"It was a boy," she said.

"Well congratulations," Cadence responded as she took the prescription from her hand. Cadence took notice of the name on the prescription—Tyrone Griffin. "Griffin," Cadence said. We have the same last name.

"Well Tyrone has his father's last name, my last name is Waters," Miss Tanya took pride in saying.

"Oh, okay," Cadence said with an apprehensive feeling that took hostage of her stomach.

Tanya came into the Pharmacy many times after that day, but she would always be alone—no baby. As fate would have it, Cadence ran into Tanya coincidentally while finishing up at the TD Bank located on Walnut Street. Cadence exited the bank and was just about to open the door to her car, when she caught a glimpse of Tanya walking in her direction; she was pushing a stroller. "Awl, is that him?" Cadence asked as Tanya came to a halt right in front of her. Cadence slowly bent over and peeked into the high end stroller. As she laid eyes on the child, the blood in her veins ran ice cold and a pain as sharp as a lightning bolt ran up her spine and into her throat. She could hardly speak. "Wow," Cadence struggled to get the frog out of throat as she responded. "What a gorgeous son you have."

"Yes he is."

"Well", Cadence responded, "I really need to get back to my errands. I guess I'll see you around."

Cadence got into her car. The chilling sensation that she previously felt had now been reversed as her blood began to warm. She clutched her heart while she strained to maintain her composure. She began to speak to herself, within herself. "This is ridiculous", she thought. She had looked into those eyes a million times before. The eyes of Tanya's son were identical to the eyes of her husband, Halstead.

"But how could that be?" she began to question. Was she so suspicious, doubtful, and mistrusting of Halstead that her mind would now begin to play tricks on her? She would later bring herself to mention Tanya's name to Halstead in hopes that it would spark some type of reaction.

"How popular is the name Griffin?" she asked Halstead as he stepped out of the shower to dry off.

"What?" he asked.

"Griffin, how popular do you think that name is?" Cadence repeated.

"I don't know," Halstead answered in an agitated tone. "I guess it's just as popular as any other name. Why are you asking?"

"I don't know. Someone who comes into the Pharmacy, just had a baby who's last name is Griffin. I figured they might be related to your family," Cadence explained.

"Naw, I don't have any family around here," he said. "Well how can you be sure," Cadence asked.

"I'm sure OKAY," he snapped.

"I saw Tanya today," Cadence nonchalantly pointed out. There was a moment of silence.

"Who is that?" Halstead asked in a semi stuttering voice.

"Tanya Waters, you don't know her?" Cadence asked as she studied his eyes and body movement.

"No, should I?" Halstead cautiously asked after scratching his head.

"I don't know—should you," Cadence responded and stared with eyes that could've burned a whole completely through him.

"Look, I don't have time for your games. I gotta go," Halstead stated as he grabbed his coat from the love seat that was directly across from the bed. He was lying through his teeth and Cadence knew it even if she couldn't prove it. But her women's intuition was proof enough for her.

Just as always, she swept all of her doubts, fears, and misgivings into her skeletal closet of, death, cloak-and-daggers, and inexplicable clan destined mishaps that would one day materialize and be brought to life.

Cadence found her way back to the present, just in time for Halstead to make his way back to the car. He was relieved once he laid eyes on his cell phone. "I thought I lost this in the street or something, whew," he commented, in a semi whisper that was loud enough for Cadence to hear. He looked over at Cadence and immediately saw a bizarre look in her eyes as he realized that he was speaking aloud and she was not responding.

"What's wrong with you?" he asked her. Cadence shook her head, gesturing that there was nothing wrong. Halstead began to drive off. "I forgot, um, I've got to meet up with the boyz over at the studio later on to talk over this thing we tryin' to do."

"Later on like what?" Cadence asked.

"Round about eight," he responded.

"Eight," she countered. "Unbelievable she garbled."

"Yeah, eight. I'm gonna try and be back by eleven, but don't hold me to it. You know how these meetings have a tendency of running longer than anticipated."

Cadence turned her head in Halstead's direction. "Don't worry, I won't," she mumbled.

"Did you say something?" he asked. Cadence turned back in his direction with a cynical look about her face and with no words, she shook her head no. Under normal circumstances,

Cadence would have been all over him with the evidence that had just been uncovered, but at this point, she was just too tired. She was tired in her determination to hold on to somebody that clearly didn't want to be held on to.

It was the first time in her life that she opted to reserve her energy for thinking instead of fighting. She felt strongly in her unwavering heart that Halstead would never change; not for her, not even for himself. She thought about confronting him, why not, her conscious questioned her?" It would all be such a proverbial scene, as it had been so many times before. It would always end the same—badly. Everything would be taken out of context. It would be twisted, contorted, and turned around to make Cadence into the villain.

Halstead had an uncanny way of making everything that was wrong inside and outside of his life and marriage, Cadences fault. He had been unemployed for almost five years; that was Cadences fault. His car was impounded for outstanding tickets and traffic violation and was later repossessed; but that was Cadences fault. He owed money all over town due to bad investments and poor judgment on his part; but it was Cadences fault. If it rained that day or the Eagles lost the championship, Cadence would be the blame.

He had been unfaithful for most of their marriage, and from time to time, he would even bring home something in the form of a STD, to remind Cadence how much that too was also her fault. For a man who was unemployed and never had the money or couth to take care of his own family and his household, he was always current with the kicks on his feet, the gear on his back, and the blue tooth that was permanently attached to his ear and updated every six months. Oh he kept up with all things that he thought made him look like he had it going on. Keeping up with the Jones' was a necessity for him and it was obvious that it was all that mattered to him.

Halstead dropped Cadence off at home about twenty minutes later. That's when she called me. "I'll be over in a few", she told me. Cadence was my best friend. We've been through a lot together. Cadence and I have been as thick as thieves since grade school. We went through grade school together, puberty together, we stuffed our bras together, we did our dirt together, and then we graduated high school together. We've spent most of our lives together. I consider her more than a friend, I consider her my family.

Although we both have families of our own, we have a bond outside of our families. Cadence has a family that consist of two brothers and three sisters, well three if you count me—and a host of other relatives whom she is fairly close to; but that being the case, I still have a special place in her heart. Unlike Cadence, I don't have any siblings, I am an only child. But Cadence and her family have made me feel like part of their family. Her sisters and brother's are my sisters and brothers.

It was nineteen seventy seven when I moved on Hawthorne St. towards the end of the summer. Cadence was the first person to befriend me. I was nine years old and about to start third grade. It was by coincidence that we ended up in the same class. All of the other children thought I was strange and wouldn't play with me. I remember the first time I had lunch in the cafeteria. I sat alone because I was used to being alone; with no brothers and sisters, I was very creative at amusing myself.

Cadence never ate the cafeteria's lunch. She would always bring her own lunch. She would bring a bag full of all her favorites; a turkey sandwich, chips, cookies, and a Sunkist soda for lunch. In addition, she would always have a bag full of penny candy; Coka Cola Ranchers, Kits, Now & Laters, Bit O Honeys, Mary Janes, and Bazooka Bubble Gum.

I had just come from the dentist about a month prior, where I was given two fillings on both my molars. Cadence had given me a couple of Mary Janes to hold me over until lunch. As I began to chew, I felt the filling in my right molar literally being pulled from out of my tooth, causing excruciating pain. When I got home, I was taken back to the dentist again, but this time it was an emergency visit, which would cost my dad some out of pocket money.

My dad was fumming all the way there and all the way back; asking and answering his own questions. "You know how much this gonna' cost me? Of course you don't. You don't care either, do you? No, you can't. You kids don't care about nothing, because you don't have to pay for nothing. You don't respect the value of a dollar. You're reckless and thoughtless. But you know what, you gonna' pay me back this money. You gonna' pay me back every dime that I had to put out on those seven hundred dollar fillings. You kids think money grows on trees. Well I'm not no tree and money don't grow here, is that clear Michelle?"

"Yes sir," I responded. He had just spoken to me earlier in the week about eating too many sweets and ruining my teeth. Well needless to say, I haven't eaten a Mary Jane since.

But anyway, the first time I saw Cadence in the Cafeteria, she came in alone, and she just started talking to me. I mean yes, she spoke to me around the way, but most of the time, people would treat you different in school. "Hey," she said. "Why are you sitting so far away from everybody?"

"I don't know, I don't like people much, and people don't much like me," I replied.

"Oh," she said as she sat down." "Well what's that?" she asked, referring to my lunch.

"It's supposed to be a burger, but who can tell." We looked at one another and we began to laugh.

"Wanna piece of my sandwich?" she asked.

"Okay," I answered with a great big crackerjack smile on my face. She handed me a piece of her sandwich. As I reached out to except the sandwich, removing it from her hand, she slightly jolted back with a strange reaction, like she had experienced some sort of shock. "What's wrong, you okay?"

"I'm okay," she said as she forced a smile to her face. We ate, we laughed, we talked, and that was the beginning of our friendship.

From our childhood up until now, we spoke to each other freely about things relating to our lives, our family's, and the difficulties we suffered during the course of our marriages. We eventually learned that we couldn't share every bad thing that happened to us in our lives with our families because family never forgets—and they'd never let us forget either.

We knew that our families loved us and that they meant well. Over the years they've seen the make ups and the break ups between the four of us and they knew the seriousness of our relationships and how detrimental it was to our lives. But they also knew that until we realized that very thing, there wasn't very much that anyone could do about any of it until we made a conscious decision for ourselves and for our children.

Cadences family realized that Cadences love for Halstead ran as deep as the Pacific Ocean in all its 12,925 feet and it wasn't just going to dry up over night because of a few indiscretions. And just as it had taken a lifetime for her love for him to grow to such a capacity and develop into the deep seated, fervent, and passionate love that she had for him, she knew that for the same passion and fervent love to diminish, just enough for her to see clearly; that it would take another lifetime. She had to be able to see things through a different set of eyes. But we never passed judgment or criticism on one another for not being strong enough to bring those things to pass.

Cadence knew that whatever she said to me would stay with me. And I had that very same confidence in her. She knew me better than I knew myself. Our lives were intertwined and had almost become one. Our lives mirrored each other. The most pertinent thing that we had in common was how we loved. We loved our men long and loved them hard. We loved them until our dreams dulled, our hopes were discarded, our expectations vanished, and our hearts bled; and then we love them some more.

Cadence and I hit it off almost from the very start. It usually takes me quite a while to warm up to people, but with Cadence it seemed easy. Cadence had more of a receiving personality. I guess you could call her an extravert and me an introvert. She would meet you for the very first time and you would know whether she liked you or not. Most people warmed up to her for a lot of reasons. She had a bubbly personality and sincerity about her that made you feel her realness. She had a fairness about her that allowed you to discern that she was genuine.

I'm a living testimony that Cadence could be the nicest person you would ever want to meet. But with that in mind, the opposite held true for her also. Under a different set of conditions or circumstances, she could be a person that you wished you'd never laid your eyes on. She didn't mind standing up for herself because she found standing to be easier than sitting down. On the wrong day she had a mouth that wouldn't quit and two fist to match. I think I liked that most about her; her ability to transform herself, her mood, her disposition, and her temperament, to suit the present state of affairs was awesome .

Chapter Three

||||||||||||||||||||||||||||||||||||||||||||||||||||||||||||||||||||||||||||||||||||||||||||||||||||||||||||||||||||||||||||||||||||||||

Victory for Cadence

During middle school and even through high school, Cadence was very popular, and she never wanted or asked for popularity. As a matter of fact, she despised it. She would get agitated when people made a big deal about her or any of her accomplishments. She would shy away from clingy people. But she realized that in every clingy person there was a fostering that was somehow missing from their lives, and so against her better judgment, she appeased them.

She had a reputation for fashion flair; being one of the better dressed girls, she earned that reputation early on. Completely wise beyond her years, she was one of the smartest people I'd ever known; always giving advice on one thing or another. She wasn't very social, but she was social enough in demonstrating confidence in herself that I'd seen few people have.

Her size was average. She had brown shoulder length hair, and legs up to her neck. Her face was attractive, accented with almond shaped eyes and brows that were naturally shaped to an arch; and her cheek bones were sculpted and set atop her fair brown complexion.

She would always speak her mind assertively and believed whole heartedly in equal opportunities for people, to include women and was in full support of their liberation. The first time I realized just how serious she was about that particular subject was in home economics class in ninth grade. "How come all the girls have to take cooking classes and sewing classes and the boys take up wood shop, metal shop, auto mechanics, and printing?" she asked our Home Economics Teacher, Mrs. Gant. "The boys will be equipped to find jobs when they graduate and we'll only be fit to stay at home and be house wives."

"Well Cadence," Mrs. Gant began to try and explain as she cleared her throat. "It's been a tradition. It's appropriate for all girls to learn to cook, clean, and sew. One day you'll have a family of your own and these skills will help you to adjust to family life."

"Well, why don't the boys have to learn these skills? Wouldn't that help the family if they both learned those skills? Wouldn't they both need to know how to do them?" Cadence asked.

"I suppose it would Cadence, but for the most part, the lady of the house would be more inclined towards these skills," Mrs. Gant finished.

"No Ma'am," Cadence disagreed. I'm not inclined cause I'm not gonna' be home that much to be cooking, sewing, and cleaning; especially for no man. I'm gonna' have me a career. I'm gonna' travel and I'm gonna' see the world. And if my husband wanna cook and clean for me, he'll be more than welcome."

The girls in the class were literally stunned to hear Cadence challenge Mrs. Gant in her philosophy on the traditional teachings at George Washington High school. Every female in the class began to laugh, cheer, and give each other high fives. "I'm not gonna' be no house wife either," Helen Carson belted out.

"Me neither, I'm not gonna' be nobody's slave," another voice from in back of the room sounded off.

"Now, now girls, nobody said anything about being slaves, just calm down. This is just an elective, what you do with it is really up to you.

"Well, why don't we have some say in what we elect Mrs. Gant?" Cadence asked.

"Yeah, why don't we have some say?" Gertrude Marshall cosigned.

"Yeah," the whole class yelled.

"Now look girls, you know that I don't make the policies around here," Mrs. Gant insisted.

"Well who does?" asked Cadence.

"That would be the school board," Mrs. Gant responded.

"Well maybe we should refuse to take these sexist classes until the board considers changing some things." she continued with the whole class behind her

"Yeah," the all responded.

"I don't think I wanna be here," Cadence stated as she got up out of her seat and began to leave the classroom.

"Me either," one girl after another said, as they followed after Cadence.

"Girls," Mrs. Gant resounded. "You get back to your seats this instance. I will be giving you all zeros for the day. Get back here right now. The girls continued to proceed in their walk out until every single girl had exited the room.

The principal got wind of the walk out and called Cadence to his office. He gave Cadence a one day suspension for disrupting the class and alluring to influencing others in citing a riot. Cadence was more than glad to accept her one day suspension. She was determined to have the policies and practices of the school overturned and she wanted to picket on school property to make her point.

The girls at other schools around the city got wind at what the girls at George Washington were doing and began to make their demands as well. Shortly thereafter, Cadence was brought into the office, to speak about her demands. She was promised by Principle Chappy, that he would bring the matter to the board's attention, and that he would do everything in his power to see that the board made a conscious decision to take into consideration the concerns of hers and the other girls.

This was not only a victory for Cadence and George Washington, but for all local school age girls. Some were wishing they were her. Some were inspired by her courage and her valor. Cadence had proven that she was a fighter. Most of the guys at George Washington either were drawn to Cadence because of her strengths or kept their distance as they were intimidated by them. Because of her strong stance on women's rights, some labeled her rebellious or anti-male. They knew that Cadence was not easily swayed and would not bow down to her male counterparts. So for most guys, she was more than a handful. Some of the guys were even afraid for their girl friends to be in her presence, for fear they would adopt the same mentality and be influenced by her charge of emancipation.

I was completely opposite from Cadence. We struggled with ourselves differently. I struggled with low self esteem and was uncomfortable in my own body. I didn't like much about how I looked. I was shaped funny with a disproportionate body. My skin was darker than I would like, my eyes were set too far apart with bushy eye brows, I had broad shoulders, size double D breast, and leveled backside that I hid under layers of clothing. My hair came past my shoulders but posed a likeness of my personification; being frizzy and hard to manage.

The left arm of my eye glasses was held together with duck tape most of the time, as I was very accident prone. I was described by most people who knew me as a book worm. I was pretty smart when it came to school and subject matters. But I had a deficiency in the school of life. When you're an only child, you have a tendency to be sheltered from things that could have possibly made your strengths in other areas to be more profound. Cadence, unlike me, in my view, had the total and complete package. She did well in school. She hated Math and Science but still managed to pull it off and she loved any subject that had to do with the study of history and people.

I was very much a shy and recluse individual. I felt practically invisible because I didn't feel like anybody noticed me. Sometimes I liked that, and sometimes I didn't. I didn't like not having a voice. I was often awakened by silent screams and paralyzed vocal cords; calling out for help but nobody would ever hear me. If only I could have screamed aloud. I was last at everything and I hated it. I wondered why I was last at everything and why I could never speak up for my self, like Cadence. I really had a lot of things that I wanted to say, but just couldn't figure out how to bring myself to say them. I was guilty of always second guessing myself about who I was and what was my mission of life—so afraid to fail—so afraid to succeed.

My sophomore year in high school was the most memorable for me. That was the year I became visible. Cadence was aware of all my insecurities. It was the end of July. I had gone over to see Cadence where she was preparing to go walking. "Hey CC, I thought you invited me over to listen to the new Frankie Beverly and Maze album?" I asked.

"Oh yeah, well we can do that after I get back. You coming?" Cadence asked.

"Where you going?" I asked.

"I'm going to walk around the park a couple of times. School begins in a month and I want to lose the extra pounds I gained this summer, eating all those water ices and pretzels."

"As small as you are girl, you don't need to exercise. Look at your stomach and look at mine."

"You think my stomach is naturally flat? No, I'm not that lucky. That's 'cause I do a hundred crunches before I go to bed every night," Cadence explained.

"A hundred, every night Cadence, I don't know where you get the will power."

"It's like anything else. Once you start engaging in fitness, it becomes habit. It's not that bad. Are you coming or what? Come on, you don't have anything else to do. It won't even seem like exercise, it'll be fun. Come on," she insisted.

"Okay, okay. But don't get it in your mind that this is going to be routine, because its not. This is a one time only deal," I assured her.

"Alright, whatever you say," Cadence laughed.

Needless to say, Cadence and I began to walk every day. We even played several games of tennis. I went from a size eleven-twelve to a size nine-ten in one month. Cadence straightened out my hair, cut and layered it. She arched my eyebrows, and bleached my face with ambi one shade lighter, and instead of glasses, I opted for contacts.

I would like to say that it really didn't bother me about what people thought of me. But the truth is—it did. And I can't say that it feels good to admit that. Why couldn't I love my self; my hair, my skin, my body, my face, and my teeth? Why couldn't I love me the way God made me?

We worked out all summer together and the weight came off. People hardly knew who I was when I began my sophomore year, but people began to notice me. For the first time people complimented me; it wasn't something that I was used to. I had to learn that not every compliment is a good compliment and everyone who compliments you doesn't necessarily mean to do right by you. But when you're not used to something, you don't know.

I began to attract all the wrong people, because I wanted so much to be needed. I wanted so much to be wanted, and I didn't heed as to what kind of people wanted me and for what. Then people began to talk. They began to say all kinds of cruel and malicious things about me, calling me out my name, laughing and snickering whenever they were around me. I had never experienced that before. Nobody ever knew I was in the room. They began to talk about how easy I was, and how much I liked to do it, and how much I couldn't get enough. They were all lies and they hurt.

I tried out for cheerleading practice; something that would have been above the old Shelly. Needless to say, the new me tried out and made the team. I was officially a cheerleader, who would have ever imagined. Most Thursdays I would walk home with another cheerleader named Sweets. But she didn't come to school this one specific day for some reason. It was getting late and I didn't feel like taking the long way home. I cut through the back fields and over the bridge, just blocks away from my house.

Darkness soon over took the sun as I began to pick up my pace with a slow jog, in hopes to make it home before the street lights came on. Just as I trotted around the crook in the path, I was stopped in my tracks by an arm that had extended out of no where and met my throat with a force that cut off the air to my wind pipe; then I fell to the ground in a quick rearward motion.

I was semi-conscious for an unknown period of time. I heard several voices around me as I attempted to open my eyes and focus on the objects that were surrounding me. My vision began to clear as I recognized the familiar faces around me.

It was Zelda and her gang. "Wake up muffin, come one now," she said. Still feeling faint, I sat up and looked strangely on.

"Oh my God, what did you do to me?" I asked as I coughed and reached up with my right hand to sooth my injured throat.

"Let Zelda kiss it and make it all better," she said as she came towards me. I began to push off backwards with my feet, scooting in the opposite direction.

"What are you doing?" I asked nervously.

"You're a big girl, I'm sure you can figure it out. Word is, you like boys and you like them a lot. What else do you like? You like me?"

"I need to get home. I need to get home now, before the street light comes on."

"Awl, ain't that cute. She's gotta get home before the street light comes on," Zelda repeated as her crew of about a half dozen, began to laugh.

I proceeded to get up when Zelda took her right foot and pushed me back down. "Zelda come on now, please."

"Oh yeah, I like how that sounds, say it again."

"I need to go home Zelda, what do you want?" I asked.

"I'm gonna let you go home, but I wanna give you a present first." At that point, I tried to get up and get away as fast as I could, but to no avail, I was knocked back down and held there by Zelda's crew.

"Get off a' me!" I began to kick, swing, and scream. I fought them the best that I could. "Get your hands off me right now," I continued.

Zelda's goons held my arms and legs down, one girl on each. I began to scream louder and louder as I witnessed Zelda unfastening and pulling down her pants. She straddled my body and began to squat down, positioning her body as though she were about to place her bottom on the seat of a toilet. "I want you to taste something before you go," she said. I began to move my head from side to side, refusing to succumb to the attempt of her sadistic transgression. One of her generals tried to hold my head steady as Zelda continued with the heinous act. I tried not to cry as she sat all of her foulness upon my face. I tried urgently to come from under her, as I struggled not to suffocate. I felt myself fading when Zelda was vehemently knocked off of me. I'd never been so scared and humiliated in all my life.

"Get the hell out of here, you skank hore," the guy with the familiar face said as he drew back a two by four he held in his hand. Zelda and her crew disbursed.

"She know she liked it," Zelda stated as she fixed her pants and prepared to leave. "It was good wasn't it muffin?"

Jim Albright saw the embarrassment in my face. "Don't worry, I won't tell anyone," he said to me so genuinely. He handed me a handkerchief to wipe the vaginal residue from around my mouth and my face as I constantly spat. "Come on, I'll walk you home," he said. And he did.

"Please don't mention this to anyone," I asked.

"Don't worry, I told you I wouldn't, I would never do that," he promised. After a long shower, and as I lay in my bed, I vowed to myself that I would never ever speak to anyone about that incident—not even Cadence.

I may have looked a whole lot better than I used to look before, but I didn't feel better. After that incident, I studied myself in the mirror and came to the conclusion that I liked myself better before the make over; when my hair was frizzed, my eye brows were bushy, my skin was darker, and my glasses were busted. I liked it better when I was invisible. But for some reason, I could never go back to the old way. I became like every other insecure, self-doubting, apprehensive, fifteen year old teenage girl; mixed up, tied up and lost.

I always felt like Cadence was so much older than I. It really didn't matter to her how a person looked. She really thought that beauty was over rated and that what really mattered most, was what was inside a person, not outside. In her eyes, everyone was basically beautiful; regardless of their skin color or hair texture, the size of their nose, or the shape of their lips. But deep down inside, I wondered if she would have felt the same way if she didn't have the luxury of being pretty.

Cadence could always be caught reading some type of self motivation book, books on health and nutrition, or her favorite—the bible, yes the bible. Maybe that's why she seemed so much wiser. And she knew what she was speaking about, at least most of the time. But me on the other hand, I was the total opposite. I hated to read and I didn't really want to be bothered with healthy eating, self motivation, or biblical things. I knew what I needed to know and I didn't have to read about it to remind me of it.

Oh I believed in God, that's for sure, but I wasn't convinced that I possessed him, you know like if he lived within me. I didn't feel anything inside. I mean, how does it feel to have God inside you? I wanted to feel that. I liked how spirituality looked on Cadence. I didn't really wear it well. I always equated spirituality with something whimsical and mysterious; something that some folks had naturally. Cadence was mentally stronger and intellectually set apart, due to her spirituality.

Chapter Four

‖‖‖

The Decision

So anyway, what was I saying, I get off track sometimes. A half hour after Halstead dropped Cadence off at home, she showed up at my house. Halstead and Cadence lived approximately two blocks from my home; one block up and one block over. As soon as I saw her I knew there was something definitely going on with her. She was very rational and clear in her thinking.

Usually after an episode with Halstead, it would take no less than four drinks, a few cries, and a pack of Newports to calm her down, because she would be infuriated. She would do her pacing thing, back and forth about ten times with a half burnt Newport wedged between her fingers.

But this particular day, she came in, stood very still with dry eyes and without a cigarette. I wasn't sure if I heard her right over the phone because her actions would've warranted more of a hysterical reaction. She was just too calm for me. It was almost eerie. It was as if she was there speaking on behalf of herself. The strangeness of it all struck me peculiar.

Cadence was a lover of people. She often spoke of opening up shelters for women in transition or feeding and clothing the homeless. She had a real burden for people who were less fortunate then herself, and that was one of the things that I dug about her; the fact that she cared so much. She was a lot better than I was in that area, because I couldn't really see past my own circumstances in order to care about the circumstances of somebody else.

There were always too many things going on in my own life for me to be getting involved in someone else's mess. Besides, why should I do anything for anybody anyway? That was my motto. I found out early on that all people really wanted to do was use you. I couldn't see the love so I couldn't see the need. I've seen enough of that in my lifetime to know that it's a lonely road to travel.

Cadence told me once that, it never really bothered her whether someone had done anything in return for her or not; and that everyone's state of affairs were different. She felt there was always a reason buried deep inside a person, that was camouflaged, that made them do the things they did and made them act the way they acted. And perhaps in the beginning, it was no fault of their own.

I knew deep down she was right, but it still didn't make me feel very different, I still didn't trust people. I know that we all have hardships and afflictions, and we come up differently. But there was no justification for mishandling people, especially those who tried to care for and about you. Coming from a place where I'm from, it was just hard to sympathize with any of it. I was raised by loving and caring people who were giving, but I didn't inherit a lot of that from them. For the life of me, I don't know how I've come to feel that everybody wanted to take something from me, something that I could never get back.

The way I feel is that we all come into this world, naked and with suffering in some shape, form, or fashion, whether we realize it or not. And that's basically how most of us will leave it; at least most of the people I know. But Cadence had a way of seeing her glass half full instead of half empty. She saw hope in people and in their lives. Her compassion and her heart was greater and her dreams were bigger than most.

She would tell me over and over that she would be leaving Halstead one day. That's what we did most of the time; talked about one day leaving our husbands and starting this great new adventure. But I never really thought that either of us would really do it. I didn't take her serious because I didn't take myself serious. And I knew that if by chance it were to ever really happen one day, we would do it together and never apart.

"Shelly," she said in a steady nonchalant manner. "I'm going away for a while."

"Yeah I know," I interrupted. "I mean I think I'm ready to speak to a lawyer about my options," she said.

"Lawyer," my mouth dropped open. Instantly, all I could do was think about me. "What are you going to see a lawyer about?" I asked.

"I need to decide what would be best for me and the children. Do I stay and fight him or do I walk away." Walk away, you mean like leave? You're not gonna leave me are you? How are you gonna pay for this lawyer CC? How are you gonna take care of the children by yourself? How are you gonna' afford all of this?" I asked in desperation.

"Calm down. I'll figure everything out. I have to. I'm just gonna take it one day at a time. Because I can't think about all of this at once." She began to shake her head and speak solemnly without so much as dropping one tear—and that just wasn't Cadence.

Cadence was definitely a crier. She would cry at times while watching the news. "Come in and sit down," I said to her slowly. "Let's talk about this over a glass of wine."

"No, I don't feel much like drinking," she responded. She didn't feel like drinking. Oh my; it was worst than I thought. "Besides," she said, "I have to get back to the house."

"Can't you just think about this a little longer?" I practically begged.

"That's all I've done is think for the last five years. I can't think anymore. I'm dying Shell. Everyday that I come home to that house, I die a little more. Say you understand me," she pleaded.

Reality began to set in as I turned away from her eyes, realizing the seriousness in them. I held my head down, and I held the tears back to think for a moment before I gave her my support. She looked to me to give her some sort of sign or acknowledgement that I understood. She needed that from me because it was something that only a true friend would do.

"Yeah, sure, I understand," I reluctantly replied.

"You've always understood that this has been a death sentence for me, she went on. I'm having a hard time waking up from the same nightmare everyday. But I don't need to tell you any of this, because you know. You've been there with me through it all". I began to shake my head in agreement, knowing better than anyone how hard it's really been for her. "It has got to be something more to life than all of this drama, right?" she asked as she looked to me for confirmation in justifying her feelings, and I knew that they were justified. "For once, I'm ready to stop being afraid. I'm ready to step right out there on faith. I have to do it for the children. If I don't do something now, they may grow up to hate me for it later, or even worse; they may follow in my footsteps …. I just don't think I could bear it."

Cadence saw a look of sadness come over me as I became flush. "I want you come with me—you and me, like we've always talked about," she insisted. "You can't stay here Shelly, it's not safe. Please say you'll come with me." I paused for a moment.

"You've always been the one with the big dreams and aspirations and I've always been the one in the shadows. I don't have much to look forward to in my life. This is it. I just can't leave my home CC. And I can't see how you can just up and leave yours. Is this really what you want to do?" I began another desperate attempt to change her mind for my sake.

"No. But, it's really what I have to do. That house around there," she said as she pointed. "That house is not my home. Everyday that I'm there, I feel like a stranger. I feel nothing but anxiety and stress. I can't go on like this Shelly, I'm going crazy. I can't sleep. My hair is falling out. I'm nauseous all the time. I can't continue to allow my children to witness anymore of this madness. It's not right and it's not fair. I have to try to go at life alone. I need to at least try …for them."

Cadence whispered to me with absolution. "We can do this together—you and me. We can," she said convincingly. "Think about it okay? I'll call you," she added as she headed for the door. I was simply done after that. I was speechless. I really wasn't prepared for what she told me. All I could do was shake my head and say okay. I knew it took a lot of courage for her to come to that conclusion. And I guess I was just upset that I wasn't able to bring myself to do the same thing. I began hoping that something would happen to change her mind about leaving.

I knew better than anyone, that once she decided upon something, she meant to see it through. I knew without a doubt that she would do fine out there in the world by herself—just her and her children; and I knew that I should have been happy for her; but for some selfish reason of my own, I just couldn't bring myself to embrace the fact that I would be losing a big part of my life. She would be moving on with her life without me; how could I bring myself to embrace that?

Chapter Five

Jim

I felt deprived in love and intimacy. For some reason I've always felt disconnected from truth. My parents were the greatest, and I knew that they loved me. But why was there such a void in my life? Why did I feel so destitute when I had so much? I never was a good choice of character. I guess my relationship with Jim says a whole lot about me and my choices, huh?

I did understand Cadence when she said that it was getting harder and harder by the day. My marriage to Jim was a complete charade. Yes, I married him. I guess the hardest part for me was having to accept all the bad that I saw in him and not be able to assist him in resurfacing the good in him that I knew he once possessed.

Jim had a kindness about him that most people had yet to see. Like the kindness that he showed me that night when he rescued me from Zelda and her crew. I saw it then, but that was a long time ago, before his championship game. I have to constantly remind myself time and time again, that the kindness that I saw him exhibit so long ago still exist, because I have to believe that it does. Believing in that is what help keeps me alive.

Jim was about seven feet, weighing 270 lbs, very defined facial features, proportionate body, mustache, outstanding sideburns, big hands, and big feet. He reminded me of a tall and muscular Don Cheadle when I first laid eyes on him. He looked like he could take on the world and beat it with his bare hands. If things had gone the way he planned that night, he would have made his career in Basket Ball, instead of auto sales. James Albright, # 77, Jim for short, was a forward for Chester Pike University's Chester Condors, in Chester Township.

He was a first draft pick and had been anticipated by all to lead the Condors to the

Championship that year. But the weekend before the big game, Jim was asked by his father, Reginald, to put in a couple of hours at the dealership that he owned because they were short handed. They had just received a shipment of new merchandise that had to be inventoried. Jim had just finished showing a car to a client who was ready to buy. He took the car in the back of the lot to be cleaned and detailed.

He began to walk the lot, taking careful inventory. As he approached the Vehicle Transporter he noticed that the cars were not secured by the chain that was supposed to hold them in place. He knew that the cars should be secured at all times on the transporter, until they are to be removed. As he approached the transporter, there was a small patch of oil on the asphalt that caused him to lose his bearing. As he felt his feet slip, his body shifted, his left hand's reflex responded quickly as it automatically reached out to grab hold of something; anything that could possibly break his fall.

His attempt had failed as he felt his body crashing to the ground beneath him. And just as his body came tumbling down, dazed, he looked up to see a Toyota Camry, silver in color, with brand new rims on it. It was the last car on the Vehicle Transporter. The Toyota Camry began to roll slowly out of its unsecured position on the transporter. In a daze, Jim urgently tried to pick himself up from the ground. He rolled to his side and began to lift his head. Just at that moment, the Toyota Camry picked up speed as it left the transporter and directed itself into Jims pathway.

Jim began to fear that he did not have the strength to move himself out of harms way in time; as he threw both his hands up in front of his face in a defensive reaction as the car rolled across the upper part of both his legs, crushing them on impact.

Jim's screams rang out and echoed throughout the dealership. He could be heard within a two block radius. Everyone in the dealership except Mr. Albright, who was training at another branch, ran frantically towards the sound of the shrieking screams. By the time the car was lifted from his body and he was pulled from underneath it; his screams were just a memory. The pain had stopped. He could no longer feel his legs.

Jim was taken to the Germantown Hospital, where he was rushed into surgery in an attempt to save his legs. The family was told that he had major damage to his back, pelvic, upper thighs and suffered temporary paralysis from the waist down. The doctor explained that there were many major bones that were crushed and that they would have to perform several operations and reconstructive surgeries on his lumbar and sacral vertebrae's, in addition to his pelvic, femur and hip bones. The first and most major procedure took all of seven hours. It was seven weeks before any feeling returned to his lower extremities. He was told by five international doctors that he would probably never walk again.

In an effort to grasp what had happened and why, Jim was traumatized and sunk into a clinical depression. My heart ached for him. It was as if our bodies had become one. I began to experience his pain in my legs and had trouble walking at times. I visited him everyday. It was a very difficult time for everyone, especially Jim. He hadn't spoken a word to anyone in a little more than six weeks. He began a silent therapy. After about six months, Jim began standing alone. And shortly there after, he began to walk. His recovery was astounding and nothing short of a miracle, the doctors described.

With all he'd achieved, it wasn't enough to give him back his basketball career that he'd dreamed about his entire life. It was unanimous—he would never play ball again. That Toyota Camry robbed him of any chance of that. It stole everything that he ever had the courage to hope in. It took his life and left someone else's life in its place. It left someone who was numb and dead inside.

"Stop coming by here. What are you deaf?" he screeched as I dodged the chocolate jello pudding that he threw at my head.

"He didn't mean it sweetie, he's just having a bad day. Why don't you try back tomorrow," Nurse Collins said as she handed me a Kleenex for tears that began to fall as I stood outside his hospital room.

He was like that most days and it hurt. He tried to tell me so many times that he wasn't the person that saved me that day. That person was confident and sure of himself; ready to hold the world in his hands. He'd planned on a lot of things, but he never planned on what had taken place in his life. He tried to tell me in his own way that everything had changed for him and that he wasn't sure of anything anymore—not even me.

He had been dealt a heavy blow and I was determined to see him through it to the end. It wasn't much to think about. I was sure that he was going through a horrible phase of the worst kind of depression, but in time, it would pass. I wanted him to know that without a doubt I would be there for him, just like he was for me.

I needed him to know that I wasn't in love with him because of basket ball. I wanted him to know that his career never mattered to me at all. I wanted him to know that I fell in love with him because he was the only guy who ever opened a door for me. He was the only guy who ever asked me to be a part of what he was a part of. He was the only one that ever told me that I had a nice smile and that I should smile more often. I loved him because he noticed me.

I never even liked basketball. I forced myself to like it because he liked it. I knew that he hung all of his hopes and dreams on a vicious sport. A sport that only loved you for making it look good. It would never be there for you through the good times and the bad. But I had to be there for him, regardless. I had to support him no matter what. So many people loved Jim. He had lots of family and friends. That should have been enough for him, shouldn't it? He still had a great opportunity to go to college; and the prospects were endless because of his academics. But none of that seemed to move him. Without basketball, there would be no academics, because there would be no school.

It was one year after he completed his therapy and was released to come home. It took a while for him to adjust and to stop feeling sorry for himself. He called me one day and asked if I could come over to see him. First of all, Jim has never asked me to come over to see him for anything. I've always been the one to visit. And I've always invited myself.

I remember being anxious and apprehensive. It was pretty cold out that day, about seventeen degrees and I had just finish up washing my hair as I got out of the shower. "Where do you think you're going?" my mom asked in her usual concerned voice.

"Jim called. He wants to see me," I answered.

"Jim?" she snapped. "You're hair is wet. You're barely dried off, and you're goin' where looking like that?" she asked. "Nothing is that important, Michelle. You'll catch a death a' cold if you go out there like that," she spoke as she followed behind me raging in my ears as I reached for my coat.

"No it can't wait," I explained. "Look Ma! I have my hat, my gloves, two pair of tights, my ear muffs, and my scarf. I'll be warm, don't worry.

"Jim," she grunted. "Since when did he start calling you?" she asked smugly.

"Ma please," I begged. "Okay, I'm not gonna' say another word…not today," she promised.

She was right. Jim had never called me before. Why couldn't he just tell me what he wanted over the phone? What was the big mystery all about? Not knowing was killing me. I got there in about seven minutes and noticed that he was in a bizarre mood. I could barely get two sentences out of him on a good day. But this day was different. Instead of me talking, he did all the talking and I listened.

"I know you're wondering why I called you over here. I thought it was time that I thanked you properly for everything you've done for me in the last year and a half. I want you to know how much I appreciate your support and patience with me. It hasn't been easy for me," he said. My heart began to flutter and my knees became weak, what did it all mean?

I sat down slowly while keeping my eyes fixated on his dark, juicy, nectar sweet lips and how he formed his words when he spoke. "I appreciate your loyalty and the fact that you never gave up on me, even when I was being a complete jerk. I think taking all of that into consideration—we should get married," he said.

"What did you say?" I asked him to repeat himself because I knew he didn't say what I thought I heard him say.

"I said—we should get married. "Married?" I questioned.

"Yeah, married. Why not?" he asked. "You've proven to me that I can depend on you. I think you're worthy and I think we'll make a pretty good team. What do we have to lose?"

I sat there for a long minute and knew in my heart that I was looking for something a bit more extraordinary. It really wasn't the way I had imagined it to be at all. It was something about that proposal that sounded too much like a business proposition, and too little like a marriage proposal. I mean, I've never even heard him say he loved me—not once. He wanted to marry me not because he thought I was the greatest thing since fried chicken, or because I was all that he ever thought about or ever wanted.

He didn't speak about how he loved how I walked or how he loved how I said his name. He didn't disclose how he wanted to marry me because of how I made him feel all warm inside when he held me or kissed me, or how he never wanted to be away from me. No, that's not why he wanted to marry me. He wanted to marry me—because at that point, he wasn't sure of much of anything, as his life had become unrecognizable and I made him feel safe. He felt that his life had taken a turn for the worst and he felt I was the best that he could do; giving all that had transpired. His life was a mess. He wasn't able to have what he really wanted and so he was willing to settle. And just like that—I said yes to marriage at nineteen. I guess I wanted to have him any way that I could get him. My Mama—she was wiser than I ever was. She was right to worry. She knew best.

Chapter Six

||||||||||||||||||||||||||||||||||||||||||||||||||||||||||||||||||||||||||||||||||||||||||||||||||||||||||||||||||||||||||||||||||||

What Honeymoon

The wedding was short and sweet. It wasn't big or fancy. We spent our honeymoon in Jamaica, where Jim watched the sports channel for almost the entire time. We consummated our marriage during half time. I went out every evening alone. I'd find some lovely restaurant to experience and bring a plate back for Jim.

Four years had quickly gone by. Jim hadn't been happy with me for the last three. He touched me only when he was drunk, and that was most of the time. And I have three children to prove it. This year for my birthday, I hadn't received so much as a card. He began to stay out all night, mostly binge drinking. For the last year or so, it's been the same routine each night. He'd get home late, head straight for the ice box, pull him out a six pack, and park himself in front of the television. He never wanted to be bothered with his children or anything that interested them. He mostly wanted to be left alone with his beer and his television. I couldn't make head or tails out of what was going on.

Drinking became his past time. It became his wife, his children, and his best friend. Since he wasn't able to do the thing that he really wanted to do the most, which was play basketball; drinking seemed like the next best thing. Sometimes he'd stop at the gym after work to relieve some of his frustrations. I didn't mind much at all. Cause if he was at the gym taking out his frustrations on the bag, there was a great chance that when he came home he wouldn't have the strength to take it out on me. I can remember the first time I realized that my love for him would never be enough to ward off the self pity brut that raged war so deep inside him.

I had just gotten home from an emergency visit to the hospital. I was pretty sure that they were going to find something wrong with me this time. The headaches were coming more and more frequent. I had been suffering from migraines since I was a child, but lately, since I've been married, they've been coming more frequent and lasting longer. I'd go to the emergency room, the doctor's would run test and take x-rays, but could never find anything wrong with me. This one had come three days before my cycle had arrived and caused me to be bed ridden.

The pain was excruciating. My back, my head, my eyes, my legs, my breast, and my stomach; all had me calling out to the Lord for some relief. I came home and began to call Cadence. Even that proved to be a task as I could hardly make the numbers out on the phone, I was in so much pain. She'd seen me that way once or twice before and knew that I was suffering badly. She volunteered to pick my kids up from school and take them to her house for as long as I needed. I always kept a change of clothes for them at her house for these types of instances.

The light and the noise had caused the level of pain I was experiencing to escalate and become ten times greater in its intensity. Every nerve in my body was sensitive to it. I could barely stand without becoming nauseated. I cut the lights and the television off and closed the drapes before I lay down, only sleep would be able to help me now.

Jim had come home about an hour earlier than usual, reeking of alcohol and nicotine. "Michelle," he called out in his loud and demanding voice. "Michelle." I woke up in a scared and startled state; my head felt like it had just been shot with a nail gun and would soon explode. The migraine had temporarily blinded me in one eye, and it was difficult to see out of the other. My legs weren't responding properly to the commands of my brain. Everything was a fog. Dizziness struck me as I got my legs to move and began to stand quickly. Shaky and wobbly, I made it to the door. With both hands sliding across the walls of the hallway, I tried to keep my balance. I stumbled towards the sound of his voice.

"I'm right here," I cried out. "What is it?" I asked as I worked my way down the stairs with one eye opened and pain shooting through the other.

"What is it?" he repeated my words. "Where is my dinner?"

"I'm sorry Jim, I didn't get around to fixing dinner tonight. I spent most of my day in the ER. I'm bad off today, real bad."

"Well what am I supposed to eat?"

"There's leftovers in the frig."

"Leftovers, since when I start eatin' leftovers?"

"There's nothing wrong with that pot roast Jim. I just made it last night. Please, I can't do it today." I saw him look at me in a way that told me maybe I needed to desperately try and fix him something. But before I could make my way over to the cabinet, suddenly and without warning, he grabbed me by my neck and threw me over to where the stove and sink stood as he shouted, "Fix my food and then you can go back to being sick." My head, in all it's trauma, hit the kitchen cabinet door.

"All I want is a decent hot meal when I come home," he said angrily with clinched lips. "Is that too much to ask; for you to get up off your lazy ass and have my dinner ready when I get home? I'm tired of you using that migraine crap as an excuse," he continued. I reached up and felt my head, brought my hand back down to eye level, and cried at the sight of a significant amount of blood that was on it. I held my head up as long as I possibly could as I blacked out into a state of unconsciousness. Cadence said that she called me twice that night, but Jim told her that I was napping.

Jim had a couple more beers before I came to and had passed out on the sofa. I laid there on the floor almost until morning. I awoke to find that my migraine was no longer there. I found out a long time ago, there was only one way to do things in that house. It was Jim's way or no way at all. Believe me when I tell you. I've had to learn this the hard way; through a broken collar bone, a broken nose, a broken arm, fractured ribs twice over and a few blacked eyes on numerous occasions.

I would hate him except I felt sorry for him. I knew I was the only one that hadn't given up on him. I knew I couldn't fix what was broke inside of him, nobody but God himself could do that. His anger and bitterness ran so deep that he wanted everyone around him to experience a taste of what he was feeling.

Cadence liked most people, but she had a real bad taste in mouth when it came to Jim. And that's an understatement to say the least. She loathed him. She tolerated him for my sake. She would often say that there was nothing sadder than a man who was a coward and a bully. She stomached Jim for the most part because she was afraid for me and the children, and I knew that. Halstead was a lot of things but he wasn't a women beater, not from what I could see.

I don't know if it was true for his nature or whether he was just being smart in that capacity. I truly believe that if he could get away with it he would. He has put his hands on Cadence once or maybe even twice if I'm not mistaken, but Cadence was never afraid to hit back. And I guess he figured he'd better leave well enough alone for something bad happened.

I always thought of Cadence as being the lucky one, though she might beg to differ. Our situations were similar but different, seeing as though we were both caught up in a mess and didn't quite know how to get out of it. I wanted so much to confide in my mother, but I couldn't really open up to my family about it and neither could she. Cadence was the only one who I could reveal my complete soul. I knew in my heart that she really understood me and didn't look at me any differently for staying in my mess. She could relate to how hard it was for me to just up and leave, no matter how much I wanted to and how much I knew that I should. She knew first hand how difficult it was to just stop loving someone, even if you knew they weren't capable of ever loving you back.

In many ways I found comfort in knowing that I wasn't alone. Our bond was stronger than super glue as we drew our strengths from each other. We would always talk and we'd dream and we'd dream and we'd talk. We talked many times about just packing the kids up and jumping on the first train that was smoking. We'd be dreaming about starting over and running our own establishment. We planned to leave when the kids got old enough. They weren't really babies any more anyway and we were running out of excuses. My baby was eight and hers, nine. We'd plan to open our own Café'. I called it a coffee shop on numerous occasions, and Cadence would become irritated and explain that there was a distinct difference between a coffee shop and a Café. A Café was French and tasteful with many different blends and a variety of beans available. A Coffee Shop was limited in its selections.

Chapter Seven

||||||||||||||||||||||||||||||||||||||||||||||||||||||||||||||||||||||||||||||||||||||||||||||||||||||||||||||||||||||||||||||||||||||

Room 707

The very next day, after Cadence spoke to me about her plans to move, I waited for her to phone me like she did every morning. But I never received the call. She would usually call me by noon like clock work. But something strange happened that morning. Instead, I received a call from her sister Mindy. Mindy told me that Cadences daughter Angel had phoned her around ten that morning when she wasn't able to wake Cadence. The Paramedics were called out to the house and got there around ten fifteen and transported her University of Pennsylvania Hospital where it was ruled an attempted suicide.

When I heard the news I didn't know what to do or what to think. I mean, she was just over here explaining to me what was about to go down, and now this. "Awl man," I thought. Maybe she had second thoughts about it after all. Maybe she felt like she couldn't do it, and that it would prove to be just too much for her. Maybe she felt that she couldn't live with Halstead and she couldn't live without him. But what happened between the time she left my house and the time she went to bed? Oh Cadence, what happened? I was so confused. I knew that Cadence was a natural born fighter, this suicide thing wasn't like her at all. She wasn't the type to do harm to herself, she just wasn't the type. But then again—do we ever really know a person's depth? Who knows what another person's breaking point is until they've actually reached it? Maybe this divorce thing was hers.

I'll tell you this, I was terrified. I had gone up to the hospital for three consecutive days; and for three consecutive days they wouldn't allow me to see her. At this point I began to worry. I cried for each and every one of those days. I didn't know what was going on. I didn't know how bad it was. My mind began to imagine all sorts of things. I visualized her strapped in a straight jacket in a padded room, heavily drugged.

The nurse explained to me that she could only have visitors from her immediate family. But by the forth day, Mindy phoned me just as I was on my up to the hospital and told me that Cadence had asked for me personally. I was truly moved that she would think enough of me to want to see me during her time of crisis. She had always made me feel like I was somebody important in her life. Some people have to go through great measures to implement themselves into the families and lives of others. But fortunately, I've never had to do that. I was always welcomed in. And that meant more to me than words could express.

My heart began to race at the thought of seeing her. I was a bit nervous at first. Although I loved her like a sister, I still had reservations about seeing her under these circumstances. I was very uncomfortable because I didn't know how I would find her. I really didn't know what I could do or what I could even say to her. I only knew that I had to be there. I prayed that the words would come when the time was right.

Continual streams of sweat began to slide down my face as I approached her room. Ooh the unique smell of hospitals and all their disinfectants brought back memories of the last time I was there. It always gave me an uneasy feeling right in the pit of my stomach. The hall seemed to be an extension of an extension of a corridor, as Cadence was just around the bend. I drew near to room seven hundred and seven. I saw Mindy and Ms. Marie in the waiting area. We immediately hugged. "Is she woke?" I asked.

"Yeah," Ms Marie said. "The nurse is with her right now and you should be able to see her in a minute. She looks good, don't worry"

Just at that moment, the nurse came out. "This is Michelle," Ms. Marie said to the nurse.

"Oh you're Michelle," the nurse said in a friendly tone.

"She's been waiting for you. You can go in to see her now." She was in a secured area on the seventh floor, for those who were at a risk for harming themselves or others. I always thought that the seventh floor was for crazy people. After this, I don't think I want to refer to it in that manner anymore. I knew Cadence wasn't crazy, she wasn't no more crazier than I was.

She was a bit drowsy when I came in but she was awake, alert, and waiting for me. "Hey girl, how are you?" I tried to greet her with an up beat spirit.

"I'm good," she answered sluggishly.

"If you needed a vacation, all you had to do was say so. You didn't have to be so extra." I laughed and she chuckled. Great! I thought, the ice was broken.

"Yeah, I know girl, these people got me up in here treating me like, l don't know, like I'm fragile. They got me taking medication that I don't need. They said if I don't cooperate and take it, I won't be able to come home, Shell."

"Well you know what you need to do, don't you?" I asked. "Do what they say, so you can come home."

"I'm not you know," she said.

"You're not what?"

"Crazy. All I wanted was a good night sleep. That's all," she went on to explain. "I couldn't remember if I took the pills already or not. So I took two more. And here I am. I wasn't trying to do that to myself, it was just a mistake. You believe me don't you? I wouldn't do that to my kids."

"I knew it was something just like that," I assured her.

"I heard you were up here every day."

"You know I was."

"I love you girl. Thanks," she said.

"You don't ever need to thank me for anything, you know you're my sister. The main thing for you to concentrate on right now is getting home. Did they give you any idea as to when you might be leaving?"

"I don't know. They're constantly asking me questions about what happened, how often I use sleep aids, why do I use them, and where were the children when I took the pills. I keep telling them it was a mistake. It was an accident," Cadence became upset. "Have you seen Halstead?" she changed the subject.

"No," I responded. "He hasn't been up here has he?" I was afraid to answer. Cadence looked away.

"No. nobody's seen him," I responded. "Why does he even bother to come back and forth?" I began to show signs of irritability and frustration at the way he's been neglecting my best friend and his children.

"Cause I let him," she said softly.

"Excuse me, no this is not your fault girl," I tried to show her my support. I will not let you take the blame for his trifling ass.

"Yeah…it is," Cadence confessed.

"What, cause you love him?" I asked.

"No, cause I enable him," Cadence stated.

"Look CC, Halstead is addicted to that fast life, he always has been and he probably always will be."

"Exactly. And he's not going to change, not even for me. That's the problem. I've been looking and waiting for him to come to his senses, you know, and realize that the best thing that he could do would be to think of his family, just for once—do some things differently. Not just for me, but for himself, because it's the right thing to do. But why should he change? I'm still here allowing it. I could be dead right now Shell, dead. And where is he; with Gabby, maybe Denise?"

"Don't do this girl."

"No, I need to do this. He's never around when I need him. Loving him has been the hardest thing that I've done in my entire life, even harder than deciding to leave. It shouldn't be this hard. He does nothing for this family except hinder it. He cares only for himself and his own needs and desires and its always been that way, and to hell with everyone else."

"CC, we can talk about this when you're feeling better."

"I feel just fine. You know I don't profess to know everything, but I profess that none of this is right. I've carried this family while God has carried me. But I'm tired now Shelly. He uses our home as a pit stop. Our home is his home away from whatever he's chasing. He doesn't love me and he never has," she became emotional.

"What are you saying? You stop it now CC please, don't get yourself worked up, like this. You know that man loves you. He's ignorant yes. But he just doesn't know what he has is all. He doesn't know any better."

"At what stage in a grown man's life does he learn to know better, huh? No, um umm. I'm not gonna' do it this time, Michelle."

"Do what?"

"Make excuses for him. I've been doing that my whole life, and where has it gotten me? Where has it gotten my children? His behavior grows worse with each passing day and each passing year, and I can't do it anymore."

"You know, life was hard for my sisters, brothers and myself, not to mention my mom. But I decided that things would be different for me and mine once I had a family of my own. Steady could've made the same decision. He could've decided to be different and choose us. I can't pass this mess on to my children and I won't. Not this way. No child should have to carry their parents baggage. I wonder if he understands that we're failing our children and they don't deserve that."

"I don't want you worrying yourself about this right now. You and the kids will be fine. I know you'll make sure of that," I said. "But you rest now. You'll be coming home in a few days. And when you get home, you'll see, we're gonna' laugh about all of this girl. Can you receive phone calls yet?"

"No," she said. "Not as long as I'm in this unit."

"Well, I'll be back tomorrow, you need anything?" I asked. She became silent and shook her head no. I could see that she was tired in her spirit. "OK then, I'll see you tomorrow," I said as I brushed her hair out of her face so that I could see her eyes. There was no response. I repeated myself in hopes of a reply, "I'll see you tomorrow...I love you."

Chapter Eight

‖‖‖

They're Laughing at Me

Cadence had literally saved my life countless amounts of times. She would send the police to my house when Jim would come home in a rage. "What you all dressed up for, you going somewhere?" he asked.

"Jordan had a show at the school today remember?" I asked.

"Yeah, I remember. But what's that got to do with you dressing like that? Your goin' to our daughter's school looking like you just got off of a pole at the strip club. I'm busting my chops everyday selling cars at that God forsaken dealership with that ungrateful old man, who's on my back every minute of every day. You know how hard it's been for me. It's bad enough that you tricked me into marrying you while I was vulnerable and at the lowest point in life; saddling me with these kids; and to humiliate me even more, you're walking around town like you're available. What, I'm not good enough for you?"

At that moment, I knew that he was going through something so I began to try and change the subject. Although I saw nothing wrong with what I was wearing, I apologized for wearing it just the same, in hopes that it would calm him down. "You're right Jim, it's very inappropriate and I won't wear it again. I'm sorry. I'll go change right now." As I began to leave the room, he became even more infuriated.

"No, don't leave now. Did I say you could leave? How about showing me a little more respect," he yelped. "You know how hard it is for me to drag myself to work day in and day out, doing everything in my power to please everybody, and never getting so much as a thank you in return," he yelled. "No, I guess you wouldn't know about that. You wouldn't know the first thing about work. Have I ever asked you once to get a job, huh? Do you know that most of the men I know make their wives work, but not me; no, not me. All you have to do is sit up here all day looking like a pre-madonna, and what, watch the stories and flap your gums on the telephone all day long. Ain't that right?" I began to back up out of his way.

"You and my old man are sticking it to me real good at both ends. The both of you are in competition over which one will kill me first. Aren't you?" I stood there while he vented. "You're nothing but a hore and everybody around here knows it. Everybody in town is laughing at me, you know that, their laughing," he yelled as he slapped me with the back side of his hand upside my head. The only thing that seemed to calm him down was to unleash the fury that brewed inside him. He was never good at expressing himself verbally. The only thing he was good at was showing me how he felt with his hands. So he began to hit me as many times as it took to release the resentment that was bottled up inside him.

Jim would come home sometimes, and I could tell just by the way he closed the door behind him, what type of mood he was in and what kind of night it was going to be. There were times I'd make my way to the phone, call Cadence's house before things jumped off, and leave the line open. That way she would be able to listen in and hear when things started to turn bad. She'd send the police to my house right before Jim was able to seriously hurt me. Who would help me now? It was never Cadence that I was worried about. She wouldn't just be leaving Halstead. She would be leaving me too. For the first time in a long time, I would truly be alone.

Chapter Nine

||||||||||||||||||||||||||||||||||||||||||||||||||||||||||||||||||||||||||||||||||||||||||||||||||||||||||||||||||||||||||||||||||

Seventeen Years

Cadence was let go from the hospital about three days later. She and Halstead remained in the same house and shared the same bedroom for all intense and purposes but the sheets remained cold as ice. Seventeen years and five children later, oh how things were different for them than when they first began, or was it? Their lives became revolved around everything except each other. I had seen them go through periods in their relationship previously where it seemed they hadn't anything left in common. But as time went on, somehow they would always seem to find each other again.

This time it was definitely different. There was a peace about the whole thing that seemed so final. They weren't arguing and they weren't fighting. There were no spoken words. They were mummified. There was only stillness. They shared the same space but all ties and communication had ceased.

Their relationship had been rocky almost from the start. They would fight only to make up and regain themselves again. The fights and arguments had reached their peak around year fifteen. As Halstead came and went as he pleased, Cadence was practically made to single handedly run their household and maintain their bills, all the while, keeping her composure in securing a somewhat stable home for the children and herself. She knew how important normalcy was at this point.

Both Cadence and Halstead had been in many different places and many different phases throughout their seventeen year plus relationship; and even before their nuptials. They'd experienced a cold and sometimes distant relationship and endured through dejected times that periodically revisited them. But they had always managed to pull themselves and their lives miraculously back together for the sake of the quote unquote family, because after all, family is what mattered most, at least from Cadence's perspective.

Cadence knew with all her being, that this place was different. The stage, the props, and the settings were all so strange. Cadence compared her life to that of a theater where everything seemed to be a performance, playing itself out scene by scene and act by act. Their lives had always seemed to be so dramatized and exaggerated, but real none the less.

There seemed to be flashing lights and cameras that were always in place with a zoom lens aimed and directed at them. It highlighted all of their faults and all their indiscretions, criticizing them before the entire world for a horrible performance. There was always an assembly of spectators, onlookers, instigators in disguise; feeding off the dysfunction of it all. But from the beginning, nobody would ever suspect that they would ever have even lasted this long as the odds had always been against them.

Cadence sat, looked, and listened while CBS announced that, during an incident of domestic violence, the life of Marvin Gaye had just been taken by the hands of his very own father. The neighborhood was all a buzz about the incredible and unfortunate circumstances and events that surrounded this very real tragedy. Cadence was devastated. It was true that Marvin Gaye was a celebrity and didn't know one fan from another; and did he even care? But Cadence and I brought every record Marvin Gaye ever made, solo or duet. And although he didn't personally know us—we felt that we knew him better than anyone. The phones were ringing off the hook. We phoned everybody and everybody phoned us.

Cadence tried to call me first but was unable to get through. I forgot that I had signed a permission slip earlier that month, where I committed myself to help chaperone Jr. and some of the kids in his class on a trip to the Franklin Institute that day. Jr. was excited, and all he could talk about was walking through the inside of the enormous sized heart at the institute. But as soon as I got home, the phone was attached to my ear for the rest of the evening.

So when Cadence couldn't talk to me, she called Izzy. Izzy hung around the two of us quite a bit. I guess you could say she was in the click. "Hey, yeah girl did you hear?" Cadence asked.

"I'm just turning to it now," Izzy responded.

"His mother must be losing it by now."

"I know. I wouldn't wish that on my worst enemy," Izzy replied. "I just saw stead about twenty minutes ago," Izzy threw in.

"Oh yeah," Cadence responded as if she wasn't swayed one way or another.

"Yeah, I saw Judy get in the car with him and they took off," Izzy made it clear.

Girl, I don't know how you stay married to that man. If I ever caught my husband blatantly disrespecting me, out in the street, running around cheatin' on me wit' everybody, like Halstead do you, he would never be safe goin' to sleep in my house again, and he knows it. After my brothers got through wit' him, you wouldn't even be able to identify him. Yeah, Brian knows; he knows not to even go there wit' me like that."

"Ok, then," Cadence said while trying to change the subject. "Well, I'll talk to you tomorrow Iz. I just wanted to know whether you heard about Marvin or not."

"Oh yeah, Ok girl, yeah I can't believe he's gone, that's just crazy. Listen if I don't talk to you tomorrow, I'll definitely be around on Sunday.

Cadence got off the phone and sat there for a moment with a blank stare on her face. She looked up to the heavens with eyes that pleaded for mercy. Izzy was cool and Cadence knew that she really didn't mean to do any harm. She recounted how amusing it was that other women could seemingly suggest what they would do if they were in the shoes that she was wearing. But little did Izzy know, her husband Brian was on the down low. He'd been in the life for sometime now. Everybody knew it except Izzy. And who's place was it to tell her, not ours.

Cadence had appeared to be in a somewhat remotely familiar and less significant place in her life. Its measurement seemed to be exaggerated to a certain extent; so much that it forced her to see what she never could see before, up close and personal as it returned to her in reflected state.

Yeah, this time was most definitely different than all the times before it. She made a conscious decision to consider bringing in the New Year at a new church along side her children; and so she did. She thought about the course in which her life had taken, spiraling dangerously out of control. She questioned herself about what she could have possibly done differently to change the outcome and minimize the detrimental effect that the past seventeen years had placed on all their lives. Cadence thought about how desperate she was to find answers that would stop the treacherous cycle of poisonous relationships that have plagued her family for generations and was now trying to claim her life.

Cadence had attempted many times to break free from the deadly cycle, but was never able to do it. She drank heavily at times to silence the voices in her head and to conceal the shame she felt for failing to defeat it. But it was at every turn and every corner that she seemed to always run into a dead end. Aside from her children and a job that managed to barely meet her monthly financial obligations, nothing else in her life seemed to matter. All of her goals were rarely met. Her thoughts had begun to unravel as disappointment set in.

She pondered on everything that brought her pain and interrogated herself on everything that may have caused it. She began to grieve over the state of her pathetic life, the world, and all living things; causing her to sink deeper and deeper into a bottomless pit of hopelessness and depression.

One week prior, she unconsciously found herself purchasing some undesirable items from a drugstore store that would surely terminate her life as she knew it. Maybe she was suicidal. In her subconscious, the things that she purchased would somehow make all the evils in her life and in her world disappear forever. But they would also make her children disappear.

She had contemplated bringing on her demise on several different occasions. She tried to convince herself that her living was simply in vain and served no other purpose except to remind her of how meaningless and empty her life really was; what was the point of it all?

Bouts of depression decided for Cadence and she in turn decided for everyone else; that the whole process of life and all its mysteries and wonders would give the impression of a world without hope; a fruitless and impossible world, where joy and great peace could never be obtained. It fooled everyone into thinking that the more you tried the more you were bound to fail. The best anyone could ever have in this world was a temporary state of success. But just as soon as she thought about how much better off the world would be without her in it, something astonishing would always take place. She'd look into the buoyant and promising eyes of her children and take a glimpse into their hearts, and of the untiring and un-conditional love that they had for her.

How safe and protected they felt in her presence; trusting and depending on her. Instinctively they would come close to her, one would reach for her hand, another would wrap their arm around hers; giving a clear impression of their love for her as they felt her becoming distant. Because somehow they knew, even in their pre-adolescence lives, how difficult it was for her to smile through all of the monotony and discouragement; without displaying the discontentment with herself and disapproval of her faltering life. By some means, they knew her thoughts and wanted to assure her in an unsuspecting way that there was nothing further from the truth.

As she climbed her mountains and traveled through her valleys to escape the death that over shadowed her, alas! It was her faith and her efforts that would sustain her. Though the dark times that came to blind her and ultimately kill her, somehow she was able to see—and managed to survive it all. It would be those very same means that would bring her through time and time again. But what would it have in store for her this time? Would she manage to see clearly? Would it bring her through yet again?

Devine intervention would be her very last hope. She knew that if she was going to be successful at leaving Halstead and the dysfunctional life they shared, she knew that very night that she would have to lay everything right there on the altar with great expectations that God would do what he's known to do best; fix people's messes.

She laid down every ghastly thing that she'd turned a blind eye to since the very beginning. She knew that she had to crucify everything that tried to hinder her and put a charge against her. It was at that crucial moment that she would denounce them all; calling them out by name, as they no longer held her for a ransom that she could never pay. "Abandonment—I'm not alone, violence—be still, adultery—no more, suicide—I have worth, hatred—love will free me, abuse—I give you up to the grave, depression—the curse is broken."

She began to disown and reject those things that had been passed down to her from the very beginning; the lies, the betrayals, the treachery of it all. None of it would have a place in her life anymore. Discarding them would permit her to finally free herself and spare her offspring from a condemned life.

Cadence was absolutely sure about the urgency she felt in her spirit that led her to the service that night. She knew that it was in their best interest and definitely the safest place for all of them to be. She knew that the task that was before her was bigger than she was equipped to handle on her own.

Chapter Ten

||||||||||||||||||||||||||||||||||||||||||||||||||||||||||||||||||||||||||||||||||||||||||||||||||||||||||||||||||||||||||||||||||||||||||||||||||||||||||||||

Springtime

It was mid April, three months had gone past, and what started off as just an ordinary day, proved to be anything but that. Cadence searched the freezer for those microwavable pancakes and sausage that her kids loved, but her mother hated. Ms. Marie wasn't a big fan of the microwavable generation in which cancer would surely be the death of everyone.

Cadence packed everyone's lunch, and saw them off. The kids, they went to school. She would be on her way to work, and Halstead would be off to wherever it was that he went. She arrived at work and was having an alright day. It was fairly warm out and seemed like a decent day and so she decided to have lunch outside. Cadence purchased a Kielbasa, green pepper, onion, and mustard on and Italian roll and found herself a seat on a bench next to the nearest tree. She gently laid her hand upon her belly as she thought of the seven week life that was growing inside her. The birds were singing a melody all of their own, the sun was out, and a nice steady breeze lightly brushed against the side of her face. It was about seventy seven degrees out.

She reached into her bag to retrieve her favorite black head band and placed it on her head as the breeze forced every strand of hair on her head to wave erratically in an unacceptable direction. This had been her first seasonal sighting of an ice cream truck. The sun smiled down on her and warmed her face as she was almost instantly taken back to her childhood, reminiscing about the days when she, her brothers and sisters would hear the ice cream truck coming from blocks away as they played outside. They would quickly run down the street and up the steps into their home for money to purchase a

Mrs. Softee ice cream cone; frantically calling out to their Mother to hurry before the truck rode away.

The old familiar tune played as it made its way down each street at seven miles per hour. But now a days Mr. Softee had a little more competition as Rita's would be giving out free water ice later on that day and she couldn't wait to sink her lips into a mango/berry gelato. She knew she would first have to stop home for her children and then pick up me and my squad. She thought about the peace that she had experienced since New Years Eve and how nothing much bothered her anymore. But just as she began to think on it, her cell phone rang.

"Hello," Cadence Answered.

"Yes, is this Mrs. Griffin?" the voice on the other end of the phone asked. "Who's calling?" Cadence asked.

"This is Officer Gore from the Philadelphia Police Department. We have a Halstead Griffin down here who tells us you're his wife, is that correct ma'am," the officer asked.

"Yes it is, what's happened?"

"Well it seems that Mr. Griffin and a few of his friends have acquired lines of credit with the names of those who are no longer with us," he stated.

"I'm not following you officer."

"Ma'am they're obtaining credit by using the names of people who are deceased. That's fraud and identity theft and it's a federal offense ma'am," Officer Gore informed Cadence.

"If you come down to the station we can give you more information. We'll be holding him down here at the roundhouse until bail is set and a trial date posted.

"Oh God, not today Jesus", Cadence thought. Thank you officer, thank you."

"You're quite welcome ma'am, you enjoy the rest of your day now," Officer Gore replied.

"That's gonna' be impossible to do," she mumbled to herself.

Cadence phoned me almost immediately. "The police have Steady," she said in an unsurprising tone.

"Got him for what?" I asked.

"Identity theft and fraud."

"What! that negro really needs to stop. That's outrageous," I responded. "What are you going to do about it?"

"I have no idea. I have none at all. I depleted my savings the last time he got locked up. I don't have it Shell, and I don't even feel like tryin' to get it because I'm not going to be able to pay it back. I'm already in the hole. Steady took a check from my check book two weeks ago, for God knows what and set me back a couple hundred dollars. I just received a shut off notice from Peco and I don't even have grocery money this week. I can't do it, I'm sorry. Nope, and I'm not going to even try to."

"Girl, If you don't get that money and go down there and bail him out he's going to be mad as hell girl," I said.

"So what's new? I'm just gonna' have to call his mother and ask her to wire it. She'll send the money. Let her bail him out for once, I'm tired," she responded.

"You know how he feels about his mother knowing his business," I said.

"I know, but I don't have much of a choice, now do I?" Cadence insisted. "I don't have much of a choice at all."

Chapter Eleven

||||||||||||||||||||||||||||||||||||||||||||||||||||||||||||||||||||||||||||||||||||||||||||||||||||||||||||||||||||||||||||||||||||||||||

Out on Bail

Needless to say, Halstead was out one week later after his mom posted bail. He wasn't too happy about it either. "You could have talked to me before you called my Moms. My life and how I'm living is none of her concern," Halstead explained. "I don't need her worrying about what I'm doing. You should've talked to me first," he went on.

"Talked? It was way beyond being talked about," Cadence said in disbelief. "You could have talked to me before you decided to take those peoples' identity and steal all that money. Who did you talk to about that? What are you doing?" she asked in confusion.

"I'm out here breaking my neck working double shifts at the parlor, and you're out here making a career out of crime. So you're a common thief now, is that what you're telling me, I'm married to a thief?" Cadence asked.

"Number one, I ain't no thief. And number two, there ain't nothin' common about me, and don't you ever forget that. And if there is any mistake about what I'm telling you, I'll clarify that for you. Get off of my back. You don't question me about my business. I've done told you that. It's my business," his voice escalated. Mine.

"Well when I'm the one who constantly has to take money from this family, a family you obviously don't give a damn about, and bail your trifling behind out of jail for some nonsense, it becomes my business," Cadence retorted. "This isn't about you or your so called business," she exploded. "It's about the hardships that you continuously thrust upon this family. It's about the mess that you have such a knack of making; but always expect me to clean up. It's about you steppin' up to the damn plate and acting like you're the man of this house for once. I'm tired of wearing both hats. That's what this is about."

"Both hats? You're wearing both hats because that's what you choose to do. You wanted to be the man of the house so I let you. And you didn't bail me out this time did you?" Halstead rebutted.

"No, not this time, because everything we had, you've already taken," Cadence furiously exclaimed.

"Naw, Halstead continues, if you supported your man like a decent wife should, I wouldn't have to result to these things. I'm out here trying to make something happen the best way I know how, and all I get from you is diarrhea of the mouth," Halstead expressed.

"Oh, so that's what I do, run off at my mouth? So all of this is my fault, again? It's my fault that you're a liar and thief?" Cadence asked.

"If you weren't so busy stressing your man out about money and bills every day and how I should be like everybody else and find a nine to five job, I wouldn't feel pressured to make these types of decisions. I'm not you CC. Everybody can't do a nine to five like you. And that don't make you better than me you understand. You get your money your way, and I get my money my way."

"What is wrong with you? You're acting like we're enemies. We're supposed to be on the same side. We're supposed to be one. I'm tired Okay. I can't...," Cadence put her hands up and began to shake her head.

"You can't what?" Halstead sticks his head out as if he couldn't hear what Cadence said. "You can't do this anymore? How many times have I heard that? Let me hip you to something. You're not all of that CC. In fact, you're none of that. There are plenty of women out there who would love the chance to be with a guy like me. They wouldn't try and constantly change a brother. They would love to have me just the way I am. So you're not doing me any favors Okay." Cadence picked up the candle stick holder that was on the table and threw it at Halstead, nicking the side of his temple.

"You son of a bitch," she yelled as Halstead grabbed his jacket.

"If you wanna go, go...... It's a wrap," Halstead stated as he made his dramatic exit. Cadence went to Rite Aid the very next day and purchased a bottle of Castor Oil. She managed to force the entire bottle down her throat all the while gagging. Several hours had gone by before the cramping began. The pains became sharp and piercing as she heaved her trembling body into the bathroom, arranging her bottom onto the seat of the commode; with her head in her lap she painfully bear down as the clots began to escape her body.

She remained seated until the contractions ceased and the clots were extracted. In a weak state, she held on to the sink as she pulled herself up, while refusing to look behind her as she flushed the greatest proof of life. She made her way into the shower, washing away all signs of after birth. The days that followed were a blur. Overcome by guilt and sorrow; she took on symptoms that resembled a flu like bug. She grieved her loss and struggled with the concept of God's mercy and his forgiveness for what she had done. It had been seven days.

Chapter Twelve

||||||||||||||||||||||||||||||||||||||||||||||||||||||||||||||||||||||||||||||||||||||||||||||||||||||||||||||||||||||||

Butterfly

Metamorphosis right—Exactly! Cadence felt as though she was the personification of a caterpillar. As she slithered along on her belly with her body covered densely with yellow and orange, sometimes red or even black hairs, growing approximately two inches, not able to decipher anything that was above her, only beneath. She inhaled the very distinct scent of the earth as she trekked her way down the never ending path, moving at a pace most familiar to that of a tortoise; one of the only creatures who could sympathize with her plight.

As a Sparrow comes within reach of its prey—chaos drew near. It went by her and over her. Escaping her, due to her position and chameleon like affiliation with the body and branches of the tree which she explored; she was unable to be detected by dusk or dawn.

She settled into her cocoon of entrapment; years blinded by the darkness that held her captive. The silence that appeared to be golden would now be intruded upon by the muffled discord that began to pierce the sensitive shelter that protected her.

But while in captivity, she questioned how she arrived at that instant. What happened to her dreams? Where were the many ideas that she once possessed? Where did her imaginings escape to? Her world had become unreceptive and the face that stared back at her in the mirror had become a complete stranger.

Her eyes were blank and her soul unoccupied. Her journal was her only solace. It was the only place where she could express herself totally and completely without bias or judgment. It gave her the unadulterated consent and freedom to pour herself out like water onto emptiness; creating something out of nothingness. As she writes;

"I wish you could see me like I'm able to see you.
Darkness prevails, but a stream of light shines through....I feel a change coming on.
I was fractured and wounded just the other day.
Now I stand here broken before you... but I won't be allowed to stay....I feel a change
coming on.
My river is drying up, it's getting harder for me to cry.
Wings implementing colors, as caterpillars morph high. Tomorrow I'll be all brand new,
emerging into a sky that's blue... fly on butterfly—fly. My change has just stopped by."

Cadence was surrounded by disorder and more discord, but somehow conscious of the blessings around her; even when it was hard to see or believe in them. There were times when it was just too hard to be thankful; even when she knew she should. When she realized that getting over one hump would ultimately lead to an even bigger hump, she became dismayed. The difficult times and hardships made it virtually impossible for her to come to an understanding that she would eventually be better and stronger because of them in the end.

Cadence was unable to think that far a head. Three months later Halstead was MIA. And when he returned home after a week long rendezvous, he found that Cadence had packed the children up and gone; this time maybe for good. Right away, he phoned me to question me on the whereabouts of his family. "Hello," I answered.

"Where is she?" Halstead asked without even a greeting.

"Halstead?" I asked as though I couldn't place his voice. "Yeah, you know it's me. I'm not even gonna' ask you if you know where my wife is; the question is, where is she," he demanded?

"You know I can't tell you that," I responded.

"Oh you not gonna' tell me where she is? Well the next time you speak to her, you tell her for me, that wherever she is, she can just make herself good and comfortable there because I'm not looking for her to come back and I'm not goin' to wait for her to come home. I'm not goin' to do none of that this time. I'm finish playing these little cat chase mice games with her. You tell her that for me. You tell her.. as far as I'm concerned, she ain't never gotta' come back." And with that, he hung up.

He's tired of playing games with her? If that wasn't the pot calling the kettle black, I don't know what was. I did exactly what he told me to do though. I relayed the message to Cadence. She didn't take it well at all. A woman always wants her man to fight for her...even if she didn't want him back.

By this time Cadence wasn't doing very well at all. She stayed with her sister Mindy for about three months before she took a one bedroom apartment in an undesirable part of town; where the rent was cheap and a dollar could stretch. The break up began to take a toll on her mind and her body. She began to call out sick at least twice a week. She stopped answering her phone. Her nails and her hair became brittle. And she began to wear sweats everyday. That would be fine for some people, but if you knew Cadence, the only time she would have on sweats, is if she was on her way to the gym, coming back from the gym, or cleaning the house.

I received a call from her mom one Saturday morning, whom I called mom; at which time she expressed her concerns about the state of Cadences well being. We agreed to go over to Cadence's and not leave until we had seen and spoken to her. Mom picked me up and we were on our way.

Once there, mom began to knock on the door. "Cadence, open up sweetie it's me, Mommy. Open up." We stood in the hall for about fifteen minutes before it dawned on me that I had an extra key. She had given it to me when she first moved in. She said it was for emergency purposes only; and this was an emergency.

"Wait a minute mom, I've got a key." Mom paused.

"You mean to tell me we out here knocking this whole time and calling out, and you had a key to get in all the time? dear God," mom began to vent. "First of all, I'm her mother and I don't even have a key. Am I missing something?" she asked.

"No ma'am" I responded respectfully. "I was the first person to come to her mind I guess," as I tried to down play the accusation.

"I understand what you're saying," mom continued. "But what I'm saying is, I'm her mother, shouldn't my name had been the first name to come to her mind?" she asked.

"Yes ma'am," I responded as I quickly put the key into the lock and opened the door.

"Hi Aunt Shelly," Kote said as he ran to me. "Grandma," Kote and Zauria exclaimed at the same time when they saw Moms face.

"There's my babies," Mom said as she kissed and wrapped her arms around her grandchildren as if she hadn't seen them is years. "Why didn't y'all open this door for grandma, didn't you here me knocking and calling through the door?" she asked.

"Yes ma'am, momma said not to open the door for nobody, she don't care who it is," Zauria explained. "Good girl," Mom countered. "That's what you're supposed to do, listen to your mother.

"Speaking of your mother, where is she?" Mom asked.

"She's sleep," Kote answered.

"Well how long she been sleep?" Mom inquired.

"Since three days ago," Zauria answered.

"Three days ago, Oh my God," Mom cried out. Well didn't anybody wake her up or check on her? And where are the other children?" she asked as she rushed into her bedroom with Zauria, Kote, and myself following closely behind.

"She won't never stay woke for us grandma," Zauria explained. "She wake up for a little while, then she fall back to sleep.

"Well where is Angel, Cameron, and Zina; and why didn't somebody call me?" Mom raised her voice. She stopped for a moment when she saw the terrified looks on her grand-children's faces. "Grandma didn't mean to holler, it's not your fault."

"CC baby," Mom called out, as she sat on the side of her bed and pulled the covers down. "CC wake up." Mom began to look around the disheveled room as she noticed the two empty bottles of Rum and some beer cans on her night stand along with some sleeping pills. "Wake up baby come on," she said as she got a cold compress and placed it on her forehead.

"What's wrong with my mom, grandma?" Kote questioned.

"Nothing baby, your mom is just fine."

"Well why she sleep all the time now?"

"She just a little tired than usually, precious. She's gonna' be just fine," Mom played it off. "Why don't you and Zauria go into the other room and finish watching television?" Mom immediately turned back to CC. "CC mama's here, wake up now, come on. Wake it up"

"Nooooo," CC groggishly started to come to and oppose. "Go away." Mom looked up to heaven.

"Oh give me strength Father. I won't go away," Mom argued. "Shelly baby, open the blinds and the windows and let some sunlight and fresh air in here. It's so dark." As I opened the blinds, Cadence squealed. "Nooooo, leave me alone, please leave me alone," she began to cry. We all stood by and waited for Mom's next instructions.

"Shelly, go into the bathroom and turn the shower on, while I go put on a pot of soup." Mom came back and found a place on the bureau for the soup to cool off. Like the delicate skin on a ripe Mango, we peeled Cadence from her over used bed, undressed her and placed her in the shower, bathed her and washed her hair.

She was too weak to even put up a fight, although she tried with limp, semi fraying arms, and occasional out bursts. Mom and I changed the dingy linen that scoured the bed. We dressed her in fresh pajamas. I brushed her hair and placed it in a bun. Zauria, Kote, and me, mopped the grit covered floors, wiped and polished the juiced stained tables, washed at least two weeks worth of dishes that muddled the kitchen, and tidied the apartment that was over taken by clutter and disarray.

I listened as mom tried to spoon feed Cadence, but she wasn't that successful. "This is what you're gonna' do," Mom continued to speak to Cadence. "You're gonna' get you're strength back. And first thing Monday morning, I'm gonna' take you to see my doctor and maybe he can help you find your way out of this. I'm gonna' call down to that job of yours and let them know that you fell on hard times, but you will be back to work next week. You stronger than this thing Cadence. You can beat it."

"It hurts mama," Cadence said. It hurt so bad," Cadence sobbed.

"I know, baby. I know," Mom said. "You think you the only one that's gone through these pains. Thousands of women before you have been hurt by love and they survived. And you might not believe it now, but you will too, because of what you're made of. You think it was easy for me? You know what I went through. You know how hard is was for me. It's never easy. I stood by and watched your grandmother succeed in drinking herself to death over your grandfather. I tried to follow right in her footsteps and almost killed myself drinking. Now I come in here and see you like this. I refuse to sit by and watch you go down that road." She picked up an empty bottle. "You see these bottles, they're empty. And that's how they will leave you feeling inside, empty. Liquor is not, nor will it ever be your friend. It's meant to do just what it does—mask things and cover them up. It's like puttin' a band aid on a leaking faucet; It's just a temporary fix. It's an illusion. And once it gets a hold of you, it won't wanna let you go. If you gonna' be dependent on something, be dependent on God. With him there is no aftermath.

You are strong women CC, and you need to remember that you come from strong genes. You've always been a fighter and this time ain't goin' to be no different. You understand?" Mom spoke to Cadence with conviction and love.

"Yes mama," she answered in a frail trembling voice.

"You're not alone. Don't you ever think that. You're my daughter and I'm not going anywhere. I'll be right here as long as you need me."

Mom and I were over at Cadence's house everyday for about a month. Cadence stopped calling out from work and signed up for a support group to help her talk and deal with some of the things that she was experiencing. They met once a week and she always seemed to look forward to the meetings. She couldn't afford to go to the hairdressers like she used to, so I began to do her hair and her nails every two weeks.

I saw the agony that my best friend was in and I felt like there was nothing that I could do to help her. She thanked me so many times for just being there. I guess that was enough for her. But I came to the conclusion that, I would've never been able to undergo what she went through.

Chapter Thirteen

‖‖

The Formula

In all honesty, Cadence knew that ending her marriage wouldn't be easy, not by far. But she didn't expect the hardship to be quite so complex. But in VII, she had been literally broken and destitute in all her ordeals. At times she would lose track of the days and the hours.

Cadences' near ending, proposed a newness and some what of a rejuvenation of life, if only she could accept it. She felt a breakthrough coming on, but it demanded complete honesty and frankness. She could no longer lie to herself about any of it. She had compromised herself until she had lost herself amongst all the other atrophy that had conveniently set up shop—deep down in her bosom where love still lived. It made a comfortable home there as it lay amongst the falsehoods, and perpetrations.

She didn't know exactly where all the false hoods were hiding, but she had a pretty good idea. Just as sure as the sun rose and set, they were there. She began to draw them out. She started with the person that stared back at her in the mirror. She saw them masquerading, as they hid themselves behind the haze and murkiness. Like a cancer that plants itself amongst the healthy cells, choking and killing them off one by one, overpowering them as they multiplied. It anonymously waited patiently and systematically, never intending to reveal itself until death was almost imminent. Cadence was blind to the cancer in her relationship. Most times it was easier to accept the deception, rather than to face the scrutiny of truth.

The pretext of the trickery awaited. It waited for the perfect opportunity to gloat with satisfaction at the distress and suffering, as it took pride in its work. It labored long and hard at deceiving and dismantling that which had been built up, just to witness its destruction.

Yes, it was evident. Silently, there was sadness and weeping at its obliteration by the entire universe.

Cadence had to decide whether she would settle for a marriage or an arrangement of convenience. She wasn't in the position to understand that there was a distinct difference between the two. Why didn't she see it? A big part of her wanted nothing more than to see the truth as it stood before her, staring her straight in the eye, daring her to come boldly before it and face it. But a smaller yet premeditated part of her, knew that she intentionally kept away from the light; understanding that the light was the truth and would lead her to a revelation that she feared would, in due course, be more than she could possibly bear.

The day had come where she could no longer run from the light, as it shone brighter and brighter; forcing her to face her worst fears ever. She had to confront the beast that chased and shadowed her. Cadence knew that she was engaged in anything but a marriage. She recognized that she didn't even have a roommate, because even roommates share in the expenses.

> *"A bond so strong, a union great, nonentity should impede, nor a soul could break,*
> *down—or inter between two for all,*
> *'cause a house divided will surely fall."*

Halstead's and Cadences' house was indeed divided, and thus could not remain standing. She remembered the day that she knowingly and willing stood before God and took her vows; the mutual agreement that she so lovingly entered into. She knew that the formula for a flourishing relationship consisted of the prominent three **C's; (Compromise, Commitment, and Consideration).** To **compromise** means that you give up what you want sometimes, even when its difficult. And at times you take some, but you give indiscriminately. It is a settlement of differences, where both sides make concessions. **Commitment** means that you have entered into an agreement, whereby you choose to fulfill the act of loving another completely, putting your mate before all others; yes, even before family members. And then there's consideration. **Consideration** means that you have thoughtfulness in contemplating much care in paying attention to the needs and details surrounding your mate, whom you are committed, and with whom you compromise. Anything else is a mere form of insolence. Keeping in mind, you are now connected as one, and should regard your mate with high esteem and admiration. When putting the three C's together, and carry them over **respect** (the state of regarding with honor and esteem); this formula will allow you to achieve something that's not easy to achieve nowadays, a loving and flourishing, not perfect, relationship. $\mathbf{M} = \dfrac{3 \times C}{R}$

Chapter Fourteen

Overdrawn

I t had been ages since Cadences checking account was over drawn. She was very particular about paying her bills in full and on time. But it had gotten to the point where her bills had surpassed her income. It had been almost a year since she had seen a dime from Halstead, but did she really expect anything less?

Cadence had heard dreaded stories of fathers who would move from state to state, quitting their jobs in order to evade their child support obligations. And she'd heard stories of a court system that wouldn't enforce the child support laws. But as Cadence began to live it; she found she had a child support story of her very own that became a nightmare.

Halstead never had any intention of paying support for the children. He knew that Cadence wouldn't pursue him in court because previous separations had proven this to be true. Any attempts that were made on his part to do right by his children were dismissed by the demon addictions that ruled and controlled all of who he was.

Cadence had been beaten down by the tediousness of it all. By now, Halstead had become involved in a pretty serious relationship which had resulted in the birth of a child; and there were rumors of a proposal. But Cadence decided to call upon him against her better judgment, out of a need for her children.

"Hey Stead, how is everything?" she politely greeted him.

"Everything is everything," he commented. "How you been?" he asked cordially.

"I've been good," she responded. "Look, the reason I'm calling is to ask if it was any way possible for you to make a payment this month, you know a child support payment. I haven't received a payment in about eight months now. My hours just got cut, and my bills are getting' crazy," she came clean.

"Un huh," he began. "Well, right now, everything that I have is tied up in something. Uh,..I don't know what to tell you. Um, that's kinda impossible right now. I don't think I'm goin' be able to do that for you," he finished.

"You're not going to be able to help me out at all?" Cadence responded as she felt impatience festering deep inside her. "Naw," I don't um..I don't, I don't have it," he stuttered.

"It's been nine months Halstead," Cadence came back strong. "I've never asked you for anything. And if I didn't need it, I wouldn't be asking you now. Don't you care anything about your children? Is there anything decent in you at all? It's obvious that you don't care if we're making it or not," Cadence was clearly running out of patience.

"Wait just a second. Don't call me tryin' to guilt me about this thing," he huffed at Cadence. You're the one who wanted this. You left me. You wanted to be on your own remember?" he began to raise his voice. I got other responsibilities now and Andrea is not going to allow me to take money from this household and give it to"… he tried to finish.

"Give?" Cadence jumped in. "Excuse me, Andrea?" Cadence interrupted. Don't you dare bring that woman's name into a conversation that I'm having with you about the needs of our children, when you haven't given me a damn dime since last year. The only reason I haven't taken you to court, is because I tried to give you the benefit of the doubt. And let me explain something to you," she exploded with anger. "I'm not concerned about the fact that you're shacked up with a women who is morally, ethically, and decently disabled—nor am I concerned about your so called obligations to her. The only obligations that I'm concerned with, are the ones that you have over here with me. And you can tell Andrea, that it's not about what she will or will not allow, that's not even an issue here. Let me make it clear so you can understand. You will be held accountable for your children. You will not negate your responsibilities to them. I don't care what kind of a relationship you're in. Mine come first. You will pay for them now or you'll pay for them later—it makes no difference to me. Now you have a blessed day. And I'll see you in court." And with that she hung up the phone.

After that episode with Halstead, I knew Cadence was back. The pain she felt subsided just enough for her to find the strength she needed to confront him. She could never comprehend why anyone should have to stand before any Judge and petition the courts to arbitrarily interfere in such a very private matter, as to force the law of custody and child support onto anyone. It was hurtful, shameful, and a down right disgrace in her eyes. Why should she have even wasted her time? She knew about the statistics. But she would have never imagined that her family would be part of them.

Chapter Fifteen

||||||||||||||||||||||||||||||||||||||||||||||||||||||||||||||||||||||||||||||||||||||||||||||||||||||||||||||||||||||||||||||||||||||||

Child Support

I rony had played a very cruel and malicious joke on her, but nobody was laughing. Her eyes were wide opened. The situation had intensified the anxiety and apprehension that she was already experiencing because it was all surreal. "Oh God," she prayed, save me from these feelings of despair," she cried out.

Cadence dragged herself to work on a wing and a prayer, forgetting many times what day it was or even how she got to work. There weren't many clear days for her as she continued to live in a fog. She had taken on a second job and barely saw her children. The long and crazy hours she worked kept her tired but sleepless. She found it difficult to keep with what was true.

Cadence was now concerned with the fact that the children were getting older and growing quickly. She wondered if Halstead would ever come to a realization about that. Time had a tendency not to wait for any of us to grow up and be straight up. His opportunities to be a positive and significant force in the lives of his children as they emerged from childhood and slowly into adult hood was becoming less and less. God had kept his word just as he always had. Cadence was meeting all of her financial needs and therefore didn't trouble herself with the child support payments that she was not receiving from Halstead. And although Cadence would rather have not made Halstead's non-support of the children an issue, the court's enforcement unit and circumstances beyond her control would continue to pursue him.

But even if she could relieve him of his obligations and responsibilities as a father without the courts intervention, did she have the right to do so? Should she have even considered it? It was never about the money, but rather about Halstead's character as a man.

As Cadence sat in court room #7, along with so many other dissatisfied mothers and bitter fathers, labeling the mothers of their children—gold diggers; she became sick to her stomach with disgust and repulsion. She found it hard to believe that it had all come to this.

Her eyes scoped the room as she questioned the entire process of the child protection laws, services, custody, and support. She wished for the opportunity to survey every man and every woman in that room for an account of what brought them there to court room #7 that day. And for most of the men, she would question the whereabouts of their dignity and their manhood as she began to journal:

"Is it between your legs? The conceivable juices that profoundly explode from your love maker? Oh! I know you player—and the different ring tones of your pager.

You'll always come on, to turn them on, make them hot, their heads are light and dizzy while you sweep them off their feet. You make them wet, so they'll forget just who you really are; building them up, to let them down, now you don't come around anymore. Shut! my door.

You left your seed, with no water, their weeds. But with God's graces they'll still grow, but they'll grow slow, and what hurts them most is they'll never know, about your strength, your power, and your agility.

All the gifts that you were endowed, but they only see … you once in a while. The streets and your ego have a strong hold on you. The women and your demons have full control, they do. So you forfeit your inheritance and you trade in your legacy; for treasures stored upon this earth, don't you know it's only temporary?

Rewind, if you would. Do it over like you know you should. Treasures stored in heaven, will defy vice attempts upon your life. You better think twice, you never seemed to put up a fight, for what you know is truly right; I say—where is your manhood?"

Chapter Sixteen

Signs

Cadence rose early that November morning, by the day's defiance of the approaching winter months and the previous summer months. Its deep ruby colors accented every bush, as the reds and golds cloaked the autumn trees. Awakened by the reoccurrence of a proverbial lucid dream; she lay motionless, paralyzed by the signs and indications that Halstead had never been worthy of the endless love that she maintained for him.

The dreams that were memories taunted her constantly. They reminded her of a deteriorating and loveless marriage that held her bound. They were always triggered by real live hurtful events that had taken place prior to; but were never settled—never resolved, so they lived and breathed just as she did. They sneered at her and mocked her for not adhering to the signs that were all about her.

A sign…That particular day began with a routine weekly visit to Gillespie's Cleaners. Cadence dropped off a few pairs of slacks for Halstead and a couple of dresses for herself. It was discount Tuesday, all shirts were seventy nine cents for clean and starch, and slacks and dresses were half off.

Mr. Gillespie was getting up in age since working in Gillespie's from a youth of seven—some seventy years ago. His father left Ireland in eighteen seventy nine, at the age of twenty three due to the economic depression and great famine. He and his family was just one third of the hundred million people who gained passage to America by way of Ellis Island.

Upon arriving in America, Coilin Gillespie and his family, like most immigrants arrived in America with little money. He found trouble communicating for jobs and housing, as he could not read. He moved his family into a tenement that was over crowded, diseased, and infested. Health care and nutrition was almost unheard of or limited as first monies went towards paying rent. Most tenements proved to be fire traps. Fire escapes to the buildings were often used as extra rooms, especially in the extreme warm summer months.

Coilin Gillespie found pretty steady work at Seaman's Press, while his wife, Kaitlin, worked as a maid. Mr. Seaman had taken ill and his wife, Iona Seaman, asked Coilin if he would be interested in taking over the business, until she found a buyer; since Coilin was a close and trust worthy friend of her husbands.

There were many offers to buy Seaman's, but none proved good enough for Mrs. Seaman. Coilin ran Seaman's for seven years. He managed to save a great deal of money, at which time he came to Iona with an offer to buy the cleaners. It was as if that was what she was waiting for all along. She made it clear to Coilin that she never wanted to sell to strangers and would be grateful if Coilin took it off her hands.

Iona Seaman took Coilin's offer to buy the place as is, all equipment included. Iona made it clear that it was just as her husband would have wanted it to be. The Seaman's had occupied the upstairs as a living quarter for their family, raising two sons and a daughter atop the cleaners. Once Iona made arrangements to move out West with her daughter and her family, Coilin moved his family atop the now renamed Gillespie's cleaners, where the Gillespie's began their new lives.

Forty four years had passed and so did Coilin Gillespie. His son Coilin Gillespie Jr., Mr. "G", was prepared to take over. And here we all are today. Mr. G's wife had been gone for a few years now, and so he was left alone to fend for himself and to run the shop. And he would be retiring in just a little under a year. With no one to leave the cleaners too, as his children had chosen other professions and did not want to inherit the cleaners; Mr. Gillespie would be forced to sell to strangers.

He slowed down quite a bit in his frail state and the damaging effects of osteoporosis and bone disease was evident in his posture. His glasses were thick and he shuffled all the day long back and forth across the floor without lifting his feet, wearing his striped shirts and suspended pants with cuffs.

He slowed down but his work was still quality. The shirts where cleaned and starched and the pants would always have a crisp press about them. You could leave your clothing there for two, sometimes three years, come back to retrieve them without a ticket and they would still be there.

He would sometimes let you get your stuff even if you didn't have the money to pay for them. He'd tell you to pay him when you had it. Nobody could beat his prices or his service.

Just as Cadence was about to leave, Mr. Gillespie stopped her. "Excuse me sugar lumps, I found several receipts in the pockets of your garments here. I didn't want to throw them away because they may be of importance to you", he said as he handed them over to Cadence.

"Oh thank you Mr. G," Cadence said. "Thank you very much". She took the receipts and continued out the door. "See you next week," she said.

"I'll be right here, God willing," he responded.

She threw the clothes in the trunk and returned to her car. She began to slowly look through the receipts. She came across a receipt for the End of The Dove's Inn one week after her birthday. She thought long and hard but she couldn't ever remember going there, and why would she be there a week after her birthday. Come to think of it, Steady hadn't taken her anywhere for some time now; maybe two years or so. But this receipt was dated for August; just a few months back. She became preoccupied, and as she attempted to move forward, out of the parking space she was in, she accidentally put the car in reverse instead of drive, causing her to tap the car behind her. Luckily it was just a tap and nothing serious.

Chapter Seventeen

||||||||||||||||||||||||||||||||||||||||||||||||||||||||||||||||||||||||||||||||||||||||||||||||||||||||||||||||||||||||||||

Cinnamon

After she returned home, I came over for a visit and noticed that Cadence was very distant. She had almost finished a bottle of Merlot and seven cigarette buds were in the ash tray. Cadence cleaned her ash trays every night before going to bed. So it was safe to say, that all of the cigarettes buds in the ash tray were placed there that day. I went on to tell her about the little girl that my son James Jr. was accused of touching inappropriately and was given two days suspension.

I went on for about thirty minutes before I realized that Cadence was not listening. "You haven't heard a word I've been saying, have you? What's wrong?"

"I don't know," she said as she reached into her purse that was on the table and pulled out the receipts. "Mr. G found these in a pair of Steady's pants this morning when I picked them up from the cleaners.

"OK," I paused. "What are they?"

"Receipts," Cadence hesitated.

"Receipts for what?" I inquired.

"The End of the Dove," she said.

"The End of the Dove?" I repeated as I waited for a response from Cadence. "When did Steady take you to the End of the Dove?"

"He didn't."

I saw how upset Cadence was over this. Although it was very typical of him, I still couldn't believe the audacity that man had. I stood by and watched how Halstead literally sucked the life out of Cadence. And all I could do was be there for her—just as she's been for me so many times. You wouldn't think there was anything more that he could do to hurt her. But the heart is a very unique organ. It has the capability to be broken a million times over.

"Where are your credit card statements?" I asked as I took control over a situation that Cadence was clearly not able to handle.

"Credit card statements?" she repeated.

"Yes," I said. "Your credit card statements, where are they?"

"Why?" she asked.

"Because you want to find out how he's been spending your money and on who, don't you?" I asked her. "Now where are they?"

"They're in his office in the file cabinet."

We found the statements and it was obvious that Cadence never took the time to examine them. "What, you never review these, you just pay them?" I asked. She just looked at me and never even bothered to answer. All the credit cards were in her name, yet she never bothered to even read the statements. I found that odd for a person as smart as she was. I'm really one to talk.

"Look at this one girl," I said. "What did Steady get you for Christmas?" I questioned. "Didn't he get you that Forman Grill or something like that?" I asked.

"Yeah, he got me a grill."

"Well this receipt is showing that he purchased a bracelet that cost seventeen hundred dollars, from Zales the week of December twenty first. I mean, has he ever brought you anything that cost that much recently? He just recently ordered something from Victoria Secrets last month. Did he give you anything from Victoria Secrets last month?" I asked aggressively. Cadence stood there looking dumb founded. "This is crazy, this fool is running up your credit card bill, purchasing all kinds of stuff for somebody, and that somebody ain't you; and the kicker is, you're paying for all of it."

It was obvious by the look on her face, that what just took place, and with all I said, made her only sink deeper into herself, as she was swallowed up by the humiliation of it all. And so with that, I decided to try and lift her up to her original state of mind. "Look, there was no way you could've known. These things never crossed your mind, and he knew that they wouldn't. You would have never ever thought that he could do something this despicable. And he knows that about you. And that's the reason he's so bold with his game; because he feels you will never catch on to it. But guess what we need to do right now? We need to call these numbers and find out if any of the things he purchased were delivered, especially these flowers that were ordered at the beginning of the month. And if there is an address, we need to pay it a visit ASAP." She shook her head in agreement. She was clearly distraught.

As fate would have it we found an address. I had my cousin Sophie, who works at a flower shop, deliver some roses to the infamous address, while Cadence and I parked behind some bushes. We had the card signed, "Halstead." When Sophie showed up with the flowers, the women who answered the door in a lacy negligee, looked to be no more than about seventeen.

She read the card and became as giddy as a school girl. "Oh my God, I've got the best man ever. It's not even my birthday," she said.

"Wow, Yes you do," Sophie commented. "I wish I had a man like yours," Sophie made small talk. "How long you been hooked up, if you don't mind me asking, and what's your name?" Sophie didn't hesitate to ask.

"Oh my name is Cinnamon," she replied. "And we've been together for about two years now."

"You're lucky to have such an attentive man. You know good men are hard to find now a days. Where did you meet him? I met him at a networking party. He lives in New York City, but he does a lot of business here in Philly. I see him a few times a week. He's looking for us a place in New York. I should be moving out there with him in about a month. We plan on getting married next year," she said.

"Married? You look awfully young to be married," Sophie responded.

"I know, that's what everybody says. I turned twenty-one in December," she said. "I'm legal."

"Well, that's good to know. I guess you better hold on tight to that man of yours then," Sophie replied.

"Oh I will. He is not going anywhere trust me."

"Well good luck on that marriage thing," Sophie said. And you have a nice day."

"I will and you do the same," Cinnamon said as she closed the door.

Sophie looked around and then came over to where Cadence and I sat outside of Cinnamon's house in Cadence's car, underneath a tree and beside some bushes. "Naw," Sophie said. "She ain't even worth doing nothin' to."

"What?" I said.

"Yeah, I get the impression that, that trick doesn't have a clue that he's married. She thinks he's some business man from New York," Sophie informed us.

"Well guess what CC, you're going to knock on her door and let her know that her man is your man—and he is very much married with five children, and that she is to keep the hell away from him," I told her.

"What would be the point?" Cadence responded.

"What would be the point?" I repeated.

"Am I missing something? The point would be… to let your presence be known, and to let her know that he's already got a wife."

"She's just one of many," Cadence said as she held her head down. "She's a victim just like I am. They all are. I wouldn't get any justice by approaching this woman or doing anything to her for his sake. He's lying to them like he's lying to me."

"Yeah, well that's all fine and good. Slapping the taste out of her mouth right about now would be justice enough for me. I know you don't feel up to it, and you don't have to do a thing—just let me."

"No Shelly, I'm tired of fighting. I can't keep fighting these women over him, I'm past all of that. I can't keep letting him belittling me like this. He's played us all. So let's just go home."

"What about miss thing, you're really not gonna' say anything to her?" "No, she'll find him out sooner or later."

Needless to say, we left and went back to her house; pulled out the Newports and Zinfandel. I found it strangely odd and ironic, that I could always be strong when it came to her and she was definitely strong when it came to me. But we had no strength for ourselves when it came to our very own situations.

Cadence was characterized as one of the strongest women in our community. She was always in the Alderman's office or down at City Council addressing issues about the elderly, the unemployed, and women's rights. She was responsible for the new playground and recreation center in our neighborhood. She was always passing around a petition for one thing or another. And I was always right there beside her. I always wanted to be a part of what she was apart of it because it always seemed to be greater than our circumstances and made me feel like I was a part of something good. But it was obvious that our strengths were limited when it came to the men in our lives. With them we felt powerless, feeble minded, and weak. I saw the tiredness in Cadences' eyes that day. It was almost as if she was ready to give up at any moment, and I could never let that happen.

I fed off her strengths. And if someone like her could be conquered and defeated; surrendering to her Achilles' heel; than what kind of hope was there for me? See my fate was determined and subsequently based upon the outcome of hers—in that my admiration for her was what enabled me.

Chapter Eighteen

‖‖

The Gift

As time went on, Cadences days all seemed to resemble the one that preceded it. It was an unusually warm and uncomfortable morning; one that broke a record for that time of year. She prepared for a long day at work. Her job at the morgue was not a glamorous job to say the least, but it paid well and she took pride in it.

She constantly reminded herself, that though her client's spirits were no longer present, the bodies that encased them were still bequeathed from God and should be treated with dignity and respect. It was for this reason that Cadence took her job serious and earnestly. She would be the last to touch them before their families laid eyes on them for a final time, and she felt privileged to do so and she did not take that privilege lightly. Her work spoke for itself. From their heads to their toes, all of her clients looked as is if they had just stepped out of a magazine.

One client's sister pulled Cadence aside and asked to speak candidly with her about her concerns and reservations she had about Kearsy's. Cadence was always willing to oblige them with a kind word and reassurance. "Hi, my name is Cadence and I'm here to answer any questions that you may have at this time," she began.

"Yes," the client's sister responded, "Given the trauma that my brother sustained, how sure are you that you will be able to make him look as natural and intact as possible?" she asked nervously.

"Let me just say," Cadence spoke softly and sincerely, "I don't like to brag about my work, but I've been told by many who have passed through these doors and used our services, that my hands perform works of art. And I'd like to think of myself as an artist, if I could. It's not just important that you and your family be satisfied with my work, but it's important to me personally to be satisfied in knowing, that if my clients could speak to me, they would express their satisfaction as well. I'm aware that his presentation will be a very significant and lasting imprint on many hearts. And I promise that you and your family will not be disappointed."

"Thank you ma'am," she responded with gratitude. "Thank you."

There were so many professions that were dehumanizing and routine, but hers remained fresh and anew. She would cut and do her clients hair. She would do their makeup, manicure, and paint their nails. And when she finished their faces, they were a sight to behold. Their families were always astonished and grateful for choosing Kearsy's Mortuary for the preparation of their loved ones final curtain call.

Most people in that profession didn't allow themselves to associate or think of their client deceased as anything but a shell. Some say that to disconnect themselves would only allow them to do the job that they were paid to do; as a corpse could no longer see, hear, or feel.

But for Cadence it was just the opposite. She felt that she could only do her best work by connecting to that person's spirit. With pictures of the deceased that she requested from family members, she was able to capture a glimpse of who they used to be prior to their departure. She would talk to them about what they would be wearing and would ask how they felt about certain colors and styles of the clothing chosen for that big day, promising them that they would look better on that day then they had every looked alive.

God would often show Cadence pieces of her client's lives and sometimes even the situation surrounding their deaths. That would be confidential information that she was unable to disclose. Because of the sensitive nature of the matter, Cadence was unable to discuss her ability with anyone. The first time she experienced it at Kearsey's, was her seventh day on the job. Everyone had gone home for the day but she wanted to stay longer because she wasn't quite satisfied with her work. Some might call her a perfectionist.

Her client—a seventeen year old female victim of a suspicious death, was found in a borough underneath the seventh street subway station at Market East. She had two broken legs and a small hole at the nape of her neck. She was petite, maybe about a size three, five feet two inches, bust size of about thirty two B, size six and a half shoe, long brunette hair with hazel eyes and of Mexican descent. She did not have any identification on her person when she was found, but was identified twenty four hours later.

As Cadence commenced to brushing and styling Jane Doe's lifeless and insensible hair, her psyche began to reveal to her bits and pieces of Jane's life. Cadence was terrified at the start of the revelation. She saw the young girl begging and pleading with a young man. He seemed to be threatening her or at least demanding that she stop doing a certain thing. Was he her killer?

They were in a room filled with stuffed animals, a vanity covered with makeup and pretty barrettes of all sorts. The comforter set and curtains were splashed with colors of assorted pinks. There were pictures of Jennifer Lopez, Selena, Penelope Cruz, and a host of other Latino celebrities taped to walls of the room.

The young man seemed to be enraged about something he'd seen. Cadence fast forwarded to the night before when everyone was asleep in the house. Jane Doe was asleep in the room with the stuffed animals, pretty bedding, and superstar posters, when she heard a tapping noise at her window. Jane Doe approached the window and opened it. In climbed a young girl who seemed to be around the same age as Jane. She had neck length hair with blonde highlights, pale skin, heavy eyeliner, dark mascara, gothic attire, biker boots, and black nail polish, and skeleton jewelry. She looked to be the total opposite of Jane.

Jane Doe began to cry as the blonde haired girl consoled her. They remained in a long lasting embrace as they began to fondle and kiss. The blonde haired girl proceeded to open Jane Doe's shirt and began to gently kiss her neck. She moved downward to her breast, as she placed her mouth on Jane Doe's aroused pink nipples. They retreated to the twin sized bed to engage in night full of forbidden obsession.

Cadence then saw a moment when Jane Doe is confronted by a group of five girls as she waits the next train. In an instant, Jane turns and runs as she is then pursued by the girls who chased her into the tunnels of the underground subway. She is caught and beaten.

One of the girls saw a rusty tire iron that lay near the tracks and reached for it. She picked it up and commenced to hitting Jane about her legs—breaking one leg and then two. The train approached and muffled the loud and painful cries of Jane. Four of the five girls decided that Jane Doe had been beaten enough, they stopped and retreated. The fifth girl decided that the beating wasn't enough and pulled out an ice pick and poked her once in the back of the head. Jane's resistance came to an end. She was still and silent. The girl then searched through Jane's pockets and found a letter and threw it toward Jane Doe's body.

Tears began to stream down Cadences face as she peeked into the letter:

I saw Jose yesterday. And by the way that he treated me —I think he knows. I know that it is supposed to be wrong to feel what I feel for you, but it is out of my control. It hurts to be away from you. It hurts not being able to tell anyone how overjoyed I am to have someone like you love me. I don't know how much longer I can keep my love for you a secret. Our families and our friends will never understand. Run away with me. Meet me at the Eleventh Street Subway tomorrow at seven.

I love you, Bridgette.

Before Bridgette had a chance to take the letter to school and place it in Jane Doe's locker; her brother, Tiger, snooped through her book bag the night before and found the letter. He copied the letter, placed it back in her book bag, and circulated the letter in school the very next day. He assumed that the letter was written to some guy that she had a crush on and had no idea that the letter was written to Jane.

One of the five girls got a hold of a copy of the letter that had confirmed what they had suspected all along, since there were rumors of their relationship. The girls arrived at the train stop before Bridgette. Bridgette showed up and waited two hours before she gave up on Jane Doe. She went home and later heard on the news of the tragic incident. Bridgette was questioned the next day by Detectives in regards to the letter that they found at the crime scene and the extent of their relationship.

Chapter Nineteen

||||||||||||||||||||||||||||||||||||||||||||||||||||||||||||||||||||||||||||||||||||||||||||||||||||||||||||||||||||||||||||||||||||||

Visions

Cadence could recall how frightened she was by her first visions early on. She became very secretive and almost protective of her capability and came to realize that she had it in her power to somehow help the powerless through her spiritual connection with them. She believed that it was God's decisive purpose for her gift. In the process of assisting her clients, she would often find herself in unfamiliar areas of the city, making anonymous phone calls from different phone booths to the crime tips hotline. There she would disguise her voice and give out bits and pieces of information that would help those assigned to the cases—solve them.

She was not only able to connect with the dead, but somehow the living as well. My first awareness of this, came on a semi- cold day in December. Cadence and I had gone to the Shoprite off of Passyunk and Oregon Avenue in South Philly a couple of years back. We needed some things for the annual Christmas Party that we always gave together, Halstead, Cadence, Jim, and me. Every year we took turns having it at each other's homes.

There was a female bagging groceries at register seven. The name on her tag read Gloria. She seemed to be a very nice, pleasant, and polite person. You could tell she was just common folk, like Cadence and me. She stood out because she had on a smock that looked like it hadn't been washed in weeks. Her hair was short and slicked back and looked quite greasy. She suffered with bad acne as you could see it protruding from underneath the heavy makeup she was wearing. Her nails were covered with thick and unshaped, press ons.

She continued to bag our groceries while we paid the bill, and then we were on our way. Upon exiting the store, Cadence showed signs of anxiety; she became real anxious to get home for some odd reason. I couldn't put my finger on the change in her demeanor. Usually she drops me off first. But this time she stopped at her house first.

Jim and I had one car in our family and Jim mostly used it for work. So Cadence would usually pick me up and then we'd go shopping and run errands. So when we got to her house, she told me that we would only be there for a few minutes. She threw her keys on the table and ran up stairs just as soon as we came in the house. I'm thinking to myself, "What is so urgent?" She came back down with her check book and an envelope in hand. "I thought you mailed your bills off earlier this week?" I asked.

"I did, this is something else," she responded. I saw her make the check out to somebody named, Gloria Getsky.

"Gloria Getsky?" I asked. "Who in the heck is Gloria Getsky?"

"You don't know her, she was the lady who bagged our groceries," Cadence told me. I was baffled.

"Okay," I said, trying to understand what that just meant. "How do you know her?" I asked. "I just do okay," she said.

"Well why you writing her a check though, that's what I'm not understanding? You can't possibly know her like that," I continued in a confused state.

"No, you're right, I really don't if you wanna be technical about it," she said.

"Yeah, I do," I said with my full attention. "Let's be technical."

"I just have a feeling bout her," Cadence tried to explain. "OK, that's not technical enough for me. A feeling, I questioned. A feeling, are you kidding me? What kind of feelings do you have that would merit you writing this woman a check?" I continued to push.

"Look," she said, I don't know how to begin to say this and it might sound a bit strange, so don't look at me funny. But as she was handing me the grocery bags, I saw something."

"What are you talking about girl?" I said as she began to lose me.

"I saw something about her life," she began to shake her head while trying to make me understand. "It was like a flash, like a quick preview of a movie, where my mind opened up to let me see into her life."

"What in God's name are you rambling on about Cadence? I don't know what you're saying."

"All I can tell you is that I saw a bit of what her life is like, and it's not really good. She has no electricity, only candle lit rooms. Her children are at home most of the time alone, while she's working. I don't see a man at all. And there's not much in their refrigerator. I just want to help," she finished.

"I comprehend what you're saying. But I gotta tell you, it sounds off the chart. Whew." I blew through my mouth as I picked up a pamphlet from off the table and began to fan myself. "And you got all of that from that woman handing you a bag of groceries? What does that mean CC? You trying to tell me you can read minds or something? You, you, you're psychic?" I stuttered.

"I'm trying to say that I see things some times," she tried to make me understand. "Please don't make this a big deal Shelly. I need you not to make this a big deal," she begged.

"She wants me not to make this a big deal," I muttered under my breath aloud, as I scratched my head and cupped my mouth.

"Look, they're just feelings okay," Cadence rebutted. "That's all…feelings."

"So you never met this woman before, so where are you mailing the check to? You don't even know where this woman lives," I said as I looked her into her eyes. "Let me guess, you saw that too?" I asked. There was no response.

I began to overheat. I took a deep breath, closed my eyes, and unconsciously began biting down on my lip, something I do when I get nervous. I felt with the left side of my face with my left hand, my legs came from under me as I collapsed into the chair that was behind me. Oh Jesus, I said as I shook my head in disbelief. I began to think…and then it came to me.

"These visions or feelings that you have, whatever they are; do you ever have them about me?" I was almost afraid to ask. There was silence for a moment. "Do you? Does God allow you to see into my life?" I had to know.

"Sometimes," she said.

"Well what do you see?" I asked in curiosity. She was reluctant to say. "What CC?"

"I just see that you shouldn't be with Jim. You need to leave him Shelly," she said. "I've told you, you just need to leave."

I was speechless. I thought about our first day together in the cafeteria when she handed me a piece of her sandwich. The look she had on her face when she touched my hand. It was like she knew something that I didn't. It was strange how she gravitated to me. She didn't even know me. Why did she want to be my friend? What did she see?

Cadence was right about a lot of things and I was sure she was probably right about this too. I knew what she said was true and it didn't take a crystal ball to figure it out. I just didn't know how to make it happen. Before I could make any movements towards that, I had to see my way out of it first.

For the next week, Cadence and I spent hours talking, as she shared her different visions with me, telling me unbelievable stories and legends about witches back in the eighteen century, and how they were shunned or even murdered because their gifts were misunderstood and associated with evil.

She made me understand why it was important that people could never know her secret. She recognized that if people found out that she was clairvoyant, things might never be the same for her. She knew that people were cruel and judgmental, and that knowledge of her gift could have a detrimental effect on the relationships she's formed with people and the lives of her children.

She understood that what people have a hard time understanding, they become afraid of. And that would definitely be more than she was capable of handling at this point in her life. But the more and more that we talked, Cadence revealed to me that she wasn't the first person in her family to have the gift.

Chapter Twenty

Snow

Mom has always been aware of Cadences abilities, because Mom's mother, Cadences grandmother, Snow, also had the gift. Cadences grandma was born on the snowiest day of the year; a blizzard that shut the city down. And so it was only befitting that she be named Snow. Mom was explicit in describing the treatment that Cadences grandma Snow received as a consequence of her abilities. People had always gravitated to Snow; just as people gravitate to Cadence. But Snow made the mistake of revealing to one of the women in her Sunday school class, something that she regretted for the rest of her life.

When Sunday school let out, Snow went to Miss Mabel, a member of the congregation. "Mabel," she said. "If I could take just a minute of your time, I know you have to get back to the house, and I'm not goin' to keep you."

"Sure Snow, what's on your mind?"

"Well Miss Mabel," Snow started. "I've been having the same dream for about a week now.

"A dream?" Miss Mabel began to listen.

"Yes Ma'am, a dream," Snow confirmed.

"Un huh, go on," Miss Mabel paid close attention.

"Um, well about this dream of mine, in it I see lots of smoke and fire coming from your property."

"My property?" Mabel repeated.

"Yes Ma'am."

"Well Snow, it's just a dream. You can't possible take it seriously."

"I know Ma'am, but…it seemed so real, and like I said, I've dreamed it more than once, if you know what I mean."

"Well I thank you for being so concerned," Mabel said sincerely. "It's sweet of you. But I don't think you have anything to worry about. I wouldn't lose any sleep over it. How's Malachi and the children?" she changed the subject.

"They're just fine, everybody's just fine. Thanks for askin'."

"Well I guess I'll see you next week in Sunday school," Mabel said as she departed.

"Yes Ma'am," Snow replied.

Seventy two hours later, there was a fierce fire down on Hackingwood Rd. You could smell the smoke from miles away. Snow was inside her home preparing supper for her family. She dropped what she was doing and ran out to the road. She came back inside. "Malachi," she called. He came in from the back. What the hell you screaming about woman?" he asked. "It's the Coopers. I think their farm is on fire. We have to do something."

"I don't have to do nothin' but mind my business, and that's what you should be doing. Did you wash my work pants? I don't see them out on the line," he asked.

Snow ignored what Malachi said and rounded up her two eldest boys, and took them down to where Mabel Cooper and her family lived. It was so much smoke you could barely see. The shrieks and squeals of the live stock burning to death filled their ears. She ripped her apron into three pieces, dipped them into a watering hole. She tied one around her nose and mouth, and tied the other two, to the noses and mouths of her sons. "MJ," Snow cried out over all the commotion. Take your brother, help fill those buckets and pass them up to the front line. I'm goin' around back to see if I can help back there."

Snow came back around to the side of the house, where she was relieved to see that everyone had gotten out safely. She saw Miss Mabel laid out near the shed and ran over to her and knelt down. "Oh thank God," Snow said. "Thank God you're alright." Miss Mabel, coughing and choking on the smoke and soot that had over taken her lungs; looked up at Snow and said, "You did this."

"What?" Snow asked.

"Yooouuu did thisss," Mabel shouted.

Snow got up in disbelief. "No ma'am. No," she said as she stood up. I was just trying to help.

"How could you know this would happen? How could you know?"

"I told you ma'am, it was a dream," Snow said as she backed away.

"Witch," Mabel began to scream. "Wiiitch!"

"Get away from my wife," Mr. Cooper ran over yelling. "Get off of my land."

"Wiiiitch," Miss Mabel continued. Snow ran to M.J. and Isaac.

"What's wrong Mama, what happened?" Isaac asked.

"Nothing," she said. "Just come on. These people are just over come by their woes is all. We need to go now.

From that day on, Snow and her children were shunned by all the town's people. They were labeled witches and were made outcast. Malachi left Snow and the children about six months later and moved over to Goblintown where his long time mistress, Caroline lived with her two daughters. One of which was said to be fathered by Malachi. Malachi was a weak man who would always run tail and hide at the first sign of trouble. He left that day never to return. The children were no longer safe in school as they were mocked, teased, and frequently chased home and beaten.

Most of the town's people were afraid of Snow and what they believed about her. But some were curious about her abilities. People began to call her or show up unannounced to her home many times after dark; asking if she could reveal anything to them regarding their lives, their health, and loved ones, living or dead—but she refused. They would offer to pay her for whatever she could tell or do for them. She was very reluctant at first. But as time went on, and with no food or money, she re-thought the propositions. Mom vividly recalls people coming to their house so Snow could read for them. It was mostly in the evenings because her clients didn't want anyone in the town to know that they believed in Snows gift. She made quite a modest living for herself and her family as her business picked up and her clientele began to grow.

Chapter Twenty-One

||||||||||||||||||||||||||||||||||||||||||||||||||||||||||||||||||||||||||||||||||||||||||||||||||||||||||||||||||||||||||||||||

Affliction

Unfortunately, Cadences' Grandma Snow died when Cadence was just a young girl. She met her once or twice and can remember her face as clear as day. Although she really didn't know her that long, it was apparent that there was a very strong connection between them. Cadence loved her grandma, and for that, she would forever pay a tribute to her. She embraced the gift that God had given her as she wore it as a badge of honor. And so with every opportunity that she's had to help her clients, their grieving families, and those lives that she has so graciously been allowed to peek into through her psyche, no matter how painful or frightening it may have been, she was grateful.

While Cadence was able to see into the lives of perfect strangers, the one thing that her telepathy would not permit her to do, was see into her own life; dangers seen and unseen. And for that she seemed sorry. She was constantly looking for an opened window in her mind that would authorize her to steal just one look into her own life to see what her future held for her. She desperately wanted to know how her life was going to turn out; and if she could do anything to assure herself of a positive outcome.

The year so far had been pretty gruesome for the city of Philadelphia. The city had suffered great losses of life and there were many allegations of political treachery that surfaced that year. With each passing year, crime and corruption had grown like an infectious disease. A murky gloom caused a thick eclipse to lie over the city of brotherly love like a toxic sheath; or maybe it just saw fit to lay over Cadence. She was extremely sapped of all energy or vigor for days on end. She tried meticulously not to confuse her present condition of lowness with that of her contentious weak spirit.

Although very thankful and managing pretty well, Cadence still experienced bouts of depression where she continued to be overcome with extreme sorrow for over almost everything. She was saddened by the inexcusable state of life and humanity. It was enough that her life was snowballing off a cliff fast and at an alarming velocity, but her gift allowed her to feel the suffering of those she prepared and those she'd never even known. Their lives and their circumstances was at times, more than she could bear. Why would God allow her to see their lives but not her own?

She was aware that her life's tragedies and misfortunes were merely a snippet of discontent, compared to those whose lives had suffered a more substantial lost than even she could imagine. So her joys and her pains were always clouded by the tears of affliction concentrated by that of the world and all those who were in it. She felt so afflicted by everyone else's bewilderment, not to mention that of her own. She felt that we were all afflicted to some degree by each other. We were all morally and eternally connected as she continued her writings:

"Didn't you know that the money you stole when you pick pocketed that lady that day caused a series of ill-fated events to take place? Didn't you know that? It caused my aunt not to be able to pay her rent. As a result, she and her children were evicted from their home. With no immediate family around and with no place to go, she and her children found refuge at a near by shelter. Didn't you know that? During her short stay, the youngest of her seven children contracted meningitis and was near death, she had to be hospitalized. Child Services and the Health Department were notified because the child and her family didn't have a permanent residential address. Yes, they were homeless. Child services were forced to take temporary custody of her children, who were then placed into foster care until my aunt was able to raise enough money to provide a decent place for her children to live.

But unfortunately, that day never came. Her state of affairs and state of mind led her to drink heavily and snort a couple of lines of the white horse everyday, as she attempted to numb the pain of being homeless and separated from her children. Losing her job to her addiction eventually robbed her of the opportunity of ever winning back custody of her children. The children, now in foster care and wards of the state, depend on taxpayers support for food shelter and clothing. Didn't you know that statistics show that many of the children in foster care will remain in foster care until they are emancipated or turn eighteen years of age? And for most of them, their futures remain bleak. The high school drop out rate for children in the system is astounding, leading them to lives of poverty, crime, and transgressions. You didn't know that?"

"Yes you afflict me with your schemes and your scams, with all of your plots and plans, your falsehoods and shim shams. You afflict me. I remember you. I saw you quite a few times. I thought that you were cute. I went out with you once or twice—and once we got together, I thought that it was nice.

But you began to fade away and I knew that it wasn't real. The lies grew longer, the rights became wronger and my heart grew cold as steal. But did I afflict you like you afflicted me? You fooled everyone we knew, with your deluding and mendacities. No, I've never ever known you, I've only known a heart that bleeds, I have died to myself... but only to renew myself... and now I've been set free. You used to afflict me."

In *seven,* Cadence was faced with the difficult task of having to get to know herself for herself. She became disturbed that she barely recognized her own hands anymore. As difficult as it was, she had to accept the fact that she and Halstead would never grow old together. It was evident that the years were not kind to them. They were two strong forces opposing one another; a positive and a negative force, always canceling each other out. Was it just fate or coincidence that their marriage and everything as Cadence knew would come to a head in *seven? Would* it have anything to do with her life before Halstead or his life before her; or would that have even played a part in the demise of their marriage at all?

"It's definitely an infraction," Cadence thought. Love, the nature thereof, and how our society perceives it. Today it means; short term, conditional, and contingent upon, and all of which demeans the authentic meaning of its original counter part. It is not moldable, and it cannot be twisted and shaped which ever way we would like to have it.

She cried out, "Rescue me and liberate me now. How much longer will I suffer?" There were so many things that she wasn't sure of, and so many things that she needed to learn and re-learn. But one thing that had been proven time and time again, was that every time a storm had come upon her life, something in her life was about to drastically change.

During the times in her life when there had been the most turbulence and unrest; when her life had been turned inside out and flipped upside down, that was when she knew that there had been an appointment by God himself. In order to get her attention, and to cause her to look at what he wanted her to see, he would bring her down; causing her to be able to look upward, into the next phase of her life. It was never unproblematic or comfortable. It never went off without a hitch. Nothing that would amount to anything in her life ever did.

God would then began to remove people and their circumstances from out of her life. He removed those things in her life which she perceived to be good, that which only came to destroy and devour her. He had taken away, only to add that which would suit her better. There were times when she couldn't understand this concept, because of the pain that accompanied it. It somehow felt like retribution to her; had she done something so awful that she would now be punished forever?

Cadence knew she had to make her way from underneath that mountain, and let those people and things go for her own life's sake. But she would not take away her love and concern for those things; but to distance herself from them in order to become new and improved.

This had been her third time trying to change the destructive course of her life and end a caustic relationship. Cadence knew that God's hand had been on her life from a young girl. He'd been there all along, but she just couldn't see him because her visions had been clouded and obscured. He had made his presence known to her time and time again. But this time she would know once and for all, that nothing was coincident or happened by chance.

Her life spoke for itself. It was madness in every sense of the word. But in the past, she would depend on her own problem solving techniques. She always thought that she would be able to fix it on her own. She would turn to her own false comforts. She would purchase her new outfits for the evening. She would buy her Newports, and her burgundy wine, and the party would be on. And everyday she would awaken to the same ole' same ole'. Leading herself to her own understanding was not going to be an option this time because clearly she didn't understand.

Cadence identified with the wave of destruction that came with the winds and the tides, determined to annihilate any possibility of a real life. She swam against the currents time and time again and witnessed others that had surrendered to them. She knew that if she had any chance of surviving at all, she would have to learn how to go with the current instead of against it. She would have to learn to ride it out. She was unsure of how far the terrain would take her. How long would she last? *Ten minus three* was full of uncertainties that left her hesitant and vague and there weren't anymore options; she was completely out.

She believed that she had been long suffering in running a race she wasn't quite sure she would ever be able to finish. She didn't always have this attitude about it, and who could? But she had a goal. She wanted to be a constructive and affirmative force in her children's lives that would forever remind them of the power of God and how everything and every entity revolved around him.

She wanted them to know the importance of decisions and the results thereof. Cadence had difficulty balancing their lives. She knew how the life of a young adult could spiral into chaos because of poor judgment, bad decision making and lack of knowledge. She wanted to be very careful not to allow her influences and the spillage from her past to shape and defect them.

Their ability to adapt and adjust to a new set of circumstances was remarkable. She reflected back on the closing stages of her parent's marriage and could vaguely remember how she modified her life as a result. With tears in her eyes, she felt it strange that she still sensed the affects of her own parents divorce, some twenty years later.

Somehow she didn't detect any break downs in her children's personalities. Their characters seemed intact and they were managing just fine; almost better than they did before, if that's even possible. Cadence on the other hand suffered from sense of guilt. She understood that there was nothing in her power that she could have done to change the outcome of that relationship, none that she knew of; even so, there was an overwhelming feeling of responsibility.

She felt almost an urgency to do whatever she had to, to make their lives better. It was her responsibility. They were her vice. How could she deprive them of a complete family? But had she really? She realized that in order for something to have been broken, it would have had to been whole to begin with. It would have had to been inclusive in its totality. But it had always been a patch job, full of holes and clearly insufficient.

Cadence was sure that that the angels encamped around her children, and for that she was grateful. She couldn't change what happened, but she was determined to make sure that it would not end in vain. In her analytical state, she pretty much came to terms with who she was and from wince she came, but to make sense of it all, once again she glanced back into her past, piecing together and configuring the basic fundamental elements that helped to make up her life.

Chapter Twenty-Two

‖‖

Jessup

The truth was—it had never really been easy for Cadence. From the time she emerged from her mother's womb, making her grand entrance into the world, life had always been a brazen challenge, filled with calamity and tragedy.

Most people didn't like to be reminded of their past because the past would in most times, be equivalent to that of pain. Cadence knew that there were things in everyone's past that should never again be looked upon or brought back to life, and her past would prove to be no different.

But should she let the golden rule of letting the past stay in the past hold true for her? No, Cadence knew that in order for her to embrace herself and love herself precisely the way she needed to, it required that she be reacquainted with herself; the good, the bad, and the fateful.

Who was she really and from wince did she come? What kind of stuff was she really made of and what were the circumstances surrounding her existence? Why did she fight so hard not to have those circumstances define who she was or the decisions that she chose to make?

She loved the times that she spent with her Uncle Jamison and her Aunt April. She would learn about her paternal legacy from the perspective of her father's brother and sister. They would tell of their history and the struggles of previous generations. Cadence realized some time ago that others in their family were reluctant to ask or speak about certain things, because there were visible stains upon the family that could never be washed away. Cadence would learn things about her father's life that were too agonizing even for him to speak on and she respected that. But she still had a need to know—for her sake and for the sake of her children.

Her father periodically divulged to Cadence and her siblings, bits and pieces, of their great inheritance; always leaving holes like an old antiquated, tattered blanket at the end of its life span. She identified with the fact that an inheritance didn't always pertain to money or wealth. An inheritance would be that thing which was either passed down or given to you as a birthright.

Cadence knew that her father, Thomas, wasn't one who preferred looking back, and so she and her siblings never pressed him on those issues for fear it would do more harm than good. As a consequence, Cadence would anxiously and patiently wait for Uncle Jamison or Aunt April to disclose more information on their family's yesteryears; but it would be in their own time.

"CC" was forever inquisitive, always asking questions and listening attentively. She found the saga of legacy, while hurtful and insensitive, to be powerful and explosive. One of her first attempts at piecing together her family's history was difficult, as she struggled to piece it all together in relationship to their family lineage.

She came across a genealogy form that she found in the family's bible that came with the set encyclopedia's that were purchased by Thomas from a traveling salesman many years ago. In her research, Cadence was only able to locate paternal information dating as far back as three generations, before she came to an abrupt halt.

Cadence became dismayed at how little she really knew about her family's history. She felt almost shameful. Now she wanted to know more than ever about her history and all that it entailed. It really didn't matter what her history revealed, because it was going to be exactly what it was intended to be. She wanted to experience the joys and the sorrows for herself. She wanted to experience the blessings and misfortunes, the privileges and the hardships alike. She wanted to know all about them. She wanted more than anything to understand the course that her life had taken.

Her siblings purposely chose only to be concerned with where they were right at that moment and where they were headed—as oppose to where they derived from. Cadence had spent a life time trying to figure out why so many things had even taken place in their lives and why did chaos always seem to be a central point of it all?

Why did everything have to be so difficult for her and was there anything particular that she could have done to change history? As she began to think back over her days, she realized that most of the things that happened during the span of her life thus far hadn't happened by chance. She never felt like she was ever quite aligned with the universe or the purpose of her life. The stars were never in sync. The sun never quite shined bright enough and the moon always hung just a little too low.

She thought of Thomas and how he managed to support and provide for his family, better than most despite his story. He'd always provided for the family financially, but like most people, he was far from perfection. He gave as much of himself as he could, no more and no less. He wasn't consciously able to think much about others, their feelings, or their needs; because those emotions were systematically cut off from the most important organ in his human body…his heart. Emotions were just a state of mind as far as he was concerned; you controlled them and you never let them control you. He was always defensive, proud, and never apologetic.

His refusal to accept that anyone was better than him or his family was pompous and a part of his everyday living practices. You knew that he loved you, but that it was very difficult for him to express it in a way that let you truly know the extent of it. He once informed Cadence, that in his youth, it was rare for anyone to see an African American adult express love openly to their children in the South. "Well how did you know that they loved you?" Cadence asked.

His response was, "Because you just knew. Every body was aware that we lived in serious times. Our parents and guardians showed us that their main concern was to keep us as safe as possible and alive. There were no hugs or kisses for children in those days. We lived in a time when children and adults would often go missing; turning up dead or never turning up at all.

During those days, the adults were rigid and firm with their children as it was a matter of life and death. The adults sacrificed open and outward love as a precaution because deep down inside they were afraid for them. We were constantly reminded to be on our very best behavior at all times, as our lives would literally depend upon it.

The more white folks knew you loved something or somebody, the more determined they were to take it away from you forever. You did what needed to be done in order to keep your life and to keep your family alive. It was always yes sir, no sir, yes ma'am, and no ma'am; always looking down, never to be caught looking them straight in the eye. If they couldn't see the fear in you, then you in turn became a threat; and in their minds, all threats had to be extinguished."

Uncle Jamison was often reminded of the time when his best friend Jessup got into trouble in the center of town. He accidentally bumped into a little white girl named Abigail; causing her to spill her strawberry ice-cream on her dress that was recently purchased from Ms. Sally's dress shop, just seven days prior. Jessup apologized over and over again, but Mr. Taylor, Abigail's father wanted more than an apology.

"I'm sorry Mr. Taylor sir, I'm very, very sorry sir," Jessup continued.

"I bet you are boy," Mr. Taylor responded. "But sorry is not gonna' pay for my Abby's dress now will it? You got money to pay for this here dress boy?" Mr. Taylor asked.

"Money sir? No sir," Jessup said.

"Well how you reckon this dress goin' get paid for? Uh…uh," Jessup began to panic and stutter. "Get in the car boy," Mr. Taylor commanded. "Let's go ask your pappy if he's got the money," Mr. Taylor insisted as he opened his car door. Jessup climbed into the back seat of

Mr. Taylor's car while Uncle Jamison looked on. Uncle Jamison remembers that Jessup was scared as a turkey on Thanksgiving Day as they drove up the road to his house.

Jessup's father and his brother Jr. were out in the yard tilling and raising a bed of soil when Mr. Taylor drove up with Jessup in the back seat. At a glimpse, Jessup's father could see the fear in his son's eyes and was a bit troubled at the thought of what was about to take place. He slowly dropped his tools and walked towards the car as it drove up.

"Hey there Jackson," Mr. Taylor said as he exited the vehicle.

"Mr. Taylor," Jackson took off his hat and nodded. "Is there sumpin' I can do for you today sir?" he asked. Jessup found his way out of Mr. Taylor's car and immediately walked towards his father.

"That's what I came to ask you Jackson," he stated. "It seems your boy here, done ruined my Abigail's brand new dress, while rough housing with that Heshard boy," Mr. Taylor explained.

"Is that right Jessup?" his father looked to him for an answer.

"Yes sir, it was just an accident, and I apologized."

"I'm sure my boy didn't mean no harm, Mr. Taylor sir, isn't that right Jessup?" he asked.

"Yes sir," Jessup responded.

"Well, all that might be well and true. But the question still remains, who's gonna' pay for the dress? I paid a pretty penny for that dress and it means the world to my Abby. I wouldn't be making such a fuss about this if it weren't for the dress being so pricey and all. I'm sure a man like yourself understands that. So what I need to know is; how you spect to pay for it?"

"Pay for it sir?" Jackson responded as Abigail stood outside the vehicle still and silent with her strawberry stained dress as she studied Jessup's features.

"Yes, pay for it," Mr. Taylor said.

"Well sir," replied Mr. Jackson. "How much would that be exactly?"

"Seven dollars, and we can call it even," said Mr. Taylor. "Seven," Mr. Jackson answered. "That would be about two days pay for me sir. I'm afraid I don't have that kinda money all at once. But I could get it to you though a little at a time," Mr. Jackson affirmed; maybe two dollars a week."

"I would love to do that for you Jackson, but at that rate, it would take almost a month to pay it off."

"Tell you what I'm prepared to do," Mr. Taylor explained. "I'd be more than happy to take Jessup up to the house for a week or so; that way he could work off his debt," Mr. Taylor explained.

"A week or so?" Mr. Jackson repeated in disbelief. "That's right," Mr. Taylor said. "That would make us even."

"Well how you figure that sir?" Jackson paused, "a couple of weeks of work seem to amount to more than a seven dollar dress that's only worth two days work. I need Jessup around here to help me meet my responsibilities Mr. Taylor. Surely you can 'preciate a man in my position?"

"I understand perfectly," Mr. Taylor replied.

"But you can't pay me for two days Jackson, isn't that right?" Jackson didn't respond. He stared at Mr. Taylor with hateful eyes that could burn a hole through steal. "It's either that, or I'm gonna have to put a claim in with the courts which would force the banks to put a lien on this here piece of land of yours. And that wouldn't be good Jackson," Mr. Taylor continued.

"I don't think that'll be necessary," Jackson responded. Jackson knew that Mr. Taylor would work Jessup hard from sun up to sun down, nearly breaking his back. But he had no choice but to go along with it, he couldn't risk losing his land over seven dollars.

Jackson had seen colored folk lose their property over less then that; even after paying what white folks said they owed. The banks would find a way to tack on all kinds of fees and processing charges, and interest, making it impossible for them to pay. "We'll be going inside now to tell Jessups mama, and get a couple of his belongings. We'll be right out sir," Mr. Jackson said. And just like that, Jessup was up on Mr. Taylor's farm slaving for not one, not two, but for three weeks.

Chapter Twenty-Three

||||||||||||||||||||||||||||||||||||||||||||||||||||||||||||||||||||||||||||||||||||||||||||||||||||||||||||||||||||||||||||||||||||

Lorna Mae

Thomas came from an era where childhood virtually didn't exist. You were taught early on your responsibilities and there were no exceptions. The girls, as young as seven, would learn to cook, clean, do hair, and assist with the younger children. Seven was the age that Thomas first learned to drive a tractor trailer. He wasn't totally denied his education flat out, in the manner in which slaves were previously denied; but Thomas couldn't tell the difference between being a slave and being a share cropper's grandson.

Thomas' father, Alpheus Heshard was killed in an unfortunate roofing accident that left his mother widowed with seven young children. At least that was the story that Lorna Mae would stand by if anybody questioned it. Alpheus took his name from his mother's side of the family. His first name came from his grandfather on his mother's side, Alpheus Donkor who was part Greek and part Ashanti. Alpheus, which means successor in Hebrew and Donkor, meaning "humble one," derived from Ghana.

Thomas was the fourth of seven children born to Alpheus and Lorna Mae Heshard. With no recourse, his mother Lorna gave a distress call to her parents, Bartholomew and Giamara Anderson– better known as Blue and Gama for help. With no man, Lorna was having a difficult time to say the least, providing for herself and her children—with no money, it would be impossible for her to manage the children alone.

She was an only child who married four days past her thirteenth birthday. Gama was heart broken when she married Alpheus, left Greensville, and set out to start a family of her own. So when Gama got the call, she was eager to come to the aid of her only child, whom she missed and loved. Lorna was without hope and overwhelmed with grief over the passing of her husband.

Blue was suspicious and reluctant in his heart about the nature and the state of affairs surrounding his daughter and grandchildren, but kept his suspicions to himself. When he saw his daughter for the first time in two years; it was clear that she wasn't the little girl that he remembered. She was much older about the face than a twenty year old should be; as the stress and the worries of life grabbed hold of her in an unkind way.

Her beautiful and lustrous mane of hair had become like hay and all of its brilliance had left it. Her once lively and vigorous steps were now replaced with hesitant and cautious footing. Her eyes no longer sparkled and her nose no longer twitched when her cheeks pressed upward towards her eyes as she smiled with radiance to reveal the gleam of the straightest and whitest of teeth you've ever seen.

Blue hardly recognized Lorna Mae, and for that he was sad. Gama and Blue were sharecroppers. They, along with a few other families, sharecropped the land of Mr. Calloway in exchange for a percentage of the profits and a place to stay. Their earnings were just a fraction of what they actually took in. They had become dependant upon borrowing their own money from Mr. Calloway, who demanded repayment compounded with interest. This kept them forever indebted to him; which seemed to be the whole point of it all.

There were goals to be met on the farm. And that meant that nobody was afforded the opportunity of a real education. They needed every field hand, every man, women, and child's contribution to meet the needs of the land and of the crops. If there was a word for it, hell would be the only way to best describe it. The winters were rough. The Anderson's and the Heshards had only the old coal burning stove to count on to heat their modest home.

On nights when the temperatures were frigid, they would take turns bathing in a large tin tub, filled with hot water that had been boiled as it sat in a small room directly across from the stove in the kitchen. It was separated from the rest of the house by a curtained partition. They would all dry off and put on clean clothing that was fit for the out doors; layered with under pants, long johns, sweaters, coats, hats, and gloves. They were tucked in with blankets that were hand made by Gama.

After settling in, several months had gone by as spring was approaching, when Lorna Mae began to experience muscle spasms from her hips to her calves. She managed to keep it under wraps for sometime. But as it became more and more difficult for her to get out of bed some mornings, it was impossible for her to continue on with her secret. As she tried to rise, she would stiffen something fierce and would often cry out in pain.

"What's wrong with my mama, Gama?" Thomas would ask, as he witnessed his mother beginning to struggle with her legs and her feet.

"Nothings the matter baby," Gama would say. "Sometimes the weather does crazy things to our bodies. It's a mystery and only God knows. But your mama is gonna be just fine, don't you fret none—worrying is for grown folk, you hear?" she said in a way that only Gama could say.

Gama would begin to routinely message Lorna's legs and feet. She would rub her down every morning with a special tonic made of herbs from her garden and WD-40 oil that she got from Mr. Lees junction store, about two miles up from their house on Route # seventy.

Gama applied the tonic before Lorna Mae would rise and again in the evenings before she went to sleep. The tonic began to work wonders and Lorna Mae began to feel seventy five percent better. Lorna found the tonic to be soothing and refreshing, making her dying legs feel alive and vigorous again. She exclaimed that it relaxed her muscles, easing the pain and making it easier for her get around. Her symptoms had practically disappeared. But two months later, the pain came back and this time it brought along its friend—agony.

It became almost unbearable for Lorna to stand let alone walk as she became bed ridden. Worry began to set in as Gama and Blue couldn't make heads or tails of what was ailing Lorna or how to fix her. They admitted to one another that they needed to get her to some outside help. They decided to pack up the red pickup with Lorna and drive the seventy seven miles to Greensville Memorial Hospital to have her looked at by a real Doctor.

The Doctors at Greensville Memorial did all kinds of test on Lorna. They poked and probed her for two day. And finally, it was discovered, that Lorna was suffering from a disease that doctors didn't know much about. All they knew was this peculiar disease was attacking Lorna's immune system. That seemed to be the job of the disease. The doctor was unable to give many details about the mysterious disease because there was no cure.

He explained that he had seen only a few cases in his entire career, and that those patients survived the disease no longer than five years after being diagnosed. He also explained that there were several trial medicines available through research and planning, and that there was a good chance that Lorna would be eligible for the clinical trials.

Gama and Blue were distraught but hopeful. They were instructed to continue to do what they had been doing all along, in addition to the medication that he would prescribe to Lorna. He encouraged them to remain as normal as possible in their daily routine, so as not to alarm Lorna or her children. He prescribed pain killers and muscle relaxants in order to help Lorna cope with the difficulty of walking.

The medication slowed the disease down and gave everyone a chance to familiarize themselves with it. It helped Lorna show signs of improvement. But after a third set back and a painful effort on everyone's part, Lorna succumbed three years later. Gama and Blue were devastated. They had never known anguish and sorrow, like they came to know it, the day their Lorna departed this world.

Chapter Twenty-Four

Blue

Blue, a quiet man, was very much reserved and was always deep in thought. He never showed too much emotion, even as a child, while his parents were raising a house of eight boys, one of which died after developing diphtheria. His father P-man cooper, Coop for short, was a great disciplinary who never believed in sparing the rod. Coop had a temper and a firm hand with a tolerance level of zero. Out of the seven boys, Blue and his oldest brother Gus, unfortunately adopted their father's temperament. Blue was never known to lay a hand on Lorna, but instead, occasionally exhibited such ill-behavior that seem to be set aside especially for Gama.

Thomas, his three sisters and three brothers were to now be raised by Gama and Blue. Life on the farm was gruesome and tedious. Thomas really had a hard time with it since Blue developed a disliking toward him after Lorna died. Thomas was a carbon copy of Alpheus, who stood as a constant reminder to Blue, that it was because of Alpheus, that his life was so different now and that he would die with the burden of raising his grandchildren.

Blue some how managed to blame Alpheus for the death of his Lorna. He had convinced himself that Lorna's illness was a direct result of a broken heart caused by abandonment. Blue had a festering anger inside of him because of his beliefs, and little Thomas would suffer by his hands because of it.

Over time, Blue's anger turned into down right resentment, for the fact that he had been saddled, near that latter part of his life, with seven extra mouths to feed, and had been left with a laborious and sorrowful memory of his lovely daughter. Blue didn't love anybody the way he loved Lorna. He regretted the fact that he never really got the chance to tell her how much he loved her. It was with that very bitterness that Blue would pour his wrath out on Thomas every possible chance he got.

Cadence's great-grandfather Blue, had handled her father Thomas with a severity and hatred that only a child of six would etch in his heart for all days. It wasn't enough that white folks hated him for the color of his skin; but to be despised by your very own flesh and blood—by someone you should have been able to feel safe with, and protected by would be enough to scar any child for life.

Thomas' description of his grandfather and the tales that he told of him were nothing short of terror. Thomas recalled his grandfather and his frightening unpredictable mannerism on a hot August day. Blue liked nothing more than that to sit on the back porch in his rocker, sippin' sweet tea, and spittin' snuff. There was a can that stood about three feet away from the house, where Blue would practice his spittin'. He often bragged on being one who could spit far and accurate, when it came to his dip.

"Thomas," grandpa Blue called out in his husky voice."

"Yes sir," Thomas answered, as he came running.

"I need you to go to the general store and pick me up a pack of chew," he said. He reached into his pocked to retrieve two dimes, when he looked down at Thomas' feet and realized that his shoes were untied. Blue had an obsession when it came to Thomas. Everything about him had to be perfect. Blue would study him from head to toe, always looking for imperfections and deficiencies in him. Blue had a calmness about him that was creepy and unsettling, making it virtually impossible for anyone to determine his demeanor.

"First go in the house and get me a glass of sweet tea," he told Thomas.

"Yes sir." Thomas replied. Thomas returned with a frosted glass he retrieved from the ice box, filled to the rim with sweet tea. Thomas stood there waiting for his next set of instructions. He waited while Blue, in one gulp, drank the sweet tea down to the very last drop. Blue's adams apple was huge. It was like watching a marble move up and down in his throat. It almost didn't look real. When Blue finished, he placed the glass on the small wooden table that was flanked by the two chairs that were on the porch.

Thomas began to feel fearful as Blue proceeded to reach down slowly and picked up a wooden paddle with a worn leather band on the end of it that he kept beside one of the chairs. Blue stood to the left of Thomas. To the right of Thomas there stood a banister that came to about the height of his neck. Thomas had a gut wrenching feeling about what was going to follow. But he couldn't for the life of him, figure out what he had done wrong. He looked around for an escape. He thought about running, but he knew that if he ran, it would be so much worst for him later, once Blue finally caught up to him.

"Now, a boy yo' age," Blue started in his slow and distinct twang. "Should have sense enough to tie his own shoes, and keepem' tied. You think that's too much to ask?" he posed the question cynically to Thomas.

"No sir, it's not too much to ask sir. I tie them all the time but they won't stay," Thomas explained.

"Well maybe if I gave you a little centive, you might figure a way to tie em and keepem' tied, what you think bout that, he asked? Go on," he waited. "Tie em," Blue said.

"Right now?" Thomas asked as he swallowed the frog that was lodged in his throat.

"We ain't got all day and tomorrow's not promised," he said. Thomas knew how shifty his grandpa was. He didn't trust him as far as he could see him.

Thomas began to bend down slowly, cautiously keeping his eyes upon his grandfather's and watching his hands. At the very moment that his fingers touched the strings to his brown shoes, whose soles were run over with open mouths in front; Blue drew his hand from his side, carried his right hand way above and behind the back of his head and came down with his might upon Thomas' backside. With that thrash, Thomas let out a scream as Blue had him trapped in the corner. Wham! Blue struck again and again. The two scurried back and forth in the tight confined area as the pounding continued. Finally, Thomas saw an escaped through an opening between Blues legs, as he leaped over the porches' banister, came crashing to the ground, and ran straight out into the woods. Two hours had gone by when Jamison and April appeared. Jamison was fifteen and April was sixteen years of age.

"Tommy, April called out. Where are you? Tommy," Jamison called. "It's me Jamie. You out here?" Just then, April heard a whimpering sound coming for the Southwest end of the Heally's place. She ran toward the sound. It's April and Jamie. She observed a piece of metal moving about the leaves. Thomas had hid himself under an old piece of tin near the well. April rushed over and uncovered him.

"You alright?" she frantically asked as she pulled him close to her and held him on her lap.

"Un huh," Thomas moaned.

"Where does it hurt Tommy?" Jamison asked. April pulled up his shirt and saw that he was black and blue all over.

"Gama sent us to get you," April said.

"Why doesn't God protect me from the dragon April?" Thomas sniffled. April paused before she answered.

"He does squirt, she said, you still alive ain't you? Now come on, let's get you back to the house. Gama is worried sick."

Blue beat Thomas with such severity that Thomas could barely walk the next day. He told Gama that it even hurt to swallow. Gama rubbed him down and apologized, like she always did. Thomas could see that Gama was holding back her tears and was sorry for Blue's treatment of him. But Thomas didn't blame her. She wore scars of her own with Blue's name on it and she never stopped smiling. "Everything's goin' to be alright," she said. "You'll see. This will all be a distant memory for you one day soon. Nothing last forever," she assured him.

Blue took away Thomas' shoes the next day and made him go bare feet for a week. It had been at least one hundred degrees out, and the ground was as hot as the blazing sun. The bottom of Thomas' feet had blistered and burned until it hurt to step down on them. Thomas was twelve years of age.

Chapter Twenty-Five

||||||||||||||||||||||||||||||||||||||||||||||||||||||||||||||||||||||||||||||||||||||||||||||||||||||||||||||||

The Monster

Thomas remembered so much of his early childhood because he had been battered for the most part of it. Thomas found it challenging to love his grandfather through the hate and contempt that he let loose on him in a moments notice. He wanted Blue to forgive him for reminding him so much of his father and the hurt and pain that he felt over his mama's passing. But Thomas knew that he couldn't change his face or bring his mama back from the heavens. So he spent most of his days dreaming about the day when he would leave Greensville forever. It was all he could do to keep from giving his grand father back a dose of his own medicine that he'd been giving him.

Thomas was convinced that Blue was the biggest man that he'd ever seen in all of his twelve years of life. He believed that Blue was a giant amongst all giants. He stood about ten feet tall with thick and matted hair. He was as dark as molasses and as bitter as wormwood. He held a black tobacco smoking pipe made of the finest briar with an acrylic mouth piece tightly clinched between his teeth and had a brown patch that covered his left eye that had been taken by a group of crude mouthed white boys who stoned him and his younger brother Jeremiah for entertainment purposes. His feet were as big as the Sasquatch and the skin on his hands were so dry and coarse that he could cut you with just a touch.

The entire house would shake when he walked. His right eye was bugged and blood shot red and he breathed smoke through his nose like a fire breathing dragon. Upon entering the room on any evening, he would swing the door wide open, as an enormous gust of wind would follow and smother every lantern's light throughout the entire dwelling, causing darkness to fall upon it. His shadow would reflect from the moon's light as he swooped down on Thomas like a vulture, savagely ripping the flesh from his bones.

That was how Thomas saw his grandfather. That was a reality for Thomas. But the truth of matter is; Blue was no more than about five feet seven inches tall with a stocky build. He wore an eleven and a half shoe that was average for a man of his stature. He was as fit as any man twenty years his junior. He would rise every morning, hitting the floor with a hundred push ups for starters. His eyes were mediocre and beady, his nose thick, and his lips were hidden beneath an overgrown mustache that housed food particles and was in need of a serious trim.

Thomas, now fourteen, recalled one blustery, turbulent evening when he came home a little past curfew. On the very tips of his toes in a pair of shoes that Jamison, who had moved up North less than a year ago, sent him recently. Thomas chose his steps carefully seeking to confirm that Blue was fast sleep. Their home was moderately small and made of wood and sap.

Winter was preparing for spring and would present its evidence—as the ice began to melt on the patched up roof that leaked on the back porch and in the sitting room. The back door was barley hanging on to its hinges and would slam against the side of the house on most windy days and nights with no latch to secure it. The stairs were old, creaky, with a few missing.

Thomas often used the back door to come in, as it led to the kitchen where the fireplace burned. It was Blue's favorite place in the whole house. Thomas was as apprehensive this night as he was any other night; afraid that he had done something, or not done anything at all that would ultimately cost him a thrashing. But even in his fear, Thomas had become defiant despite the horrible beatings, and did what was on his mind to do, as was evident by the lumps, bruises and contusions that were all about his body. He came in that night and walked ever so lightly, his feet barely touching the floor. Nobody ever wanted to disturb Blue while he was asleep, awake, or other wise; cause if you did, you wouldn't be able to sit down for days to come.

Thomas practically floated across the kitchen floor that night. Blue, completely inebriated, slept in his favorite wooden rocking chair with its shabby floral print cushion, softening its seat, in front of the coal burning stove,

Three hours had gone by and Thomas would have passed his grandfather a half a dozen times or so, never awakening him. Blue sat with one shoe on and one shoe off; revealing a medium sized whole in his wool grey work sock, where his big toe would be exposed. His feet reeked of stale corn chips and onions, an odor that encircling his feet and filled the room with an ungodly stench that would clear a house.

Blue had a dermatomycosis based fungal infection of the toe nails; a tinea fungus that grows and spreads out in a circle on your skin, hair or toes, in a ring worm like manner. Tinea is usually called ringworm although there really isn't a worm under the skin. The skin is lifted up at the edges and is red and scaly. Gama would usually soak Blues feet and powder them down with baking soda before he came to bed; a job that only a wife could perform.

Every morning when they woke, they would see white foot prints traveling through the house. Usually, wherever Blue fell asleep, is where he would remain until morning. Gama came out to wake him on this particular evening, so that he could go out to the shed for more coal, since the fire was beginning to die out as a chill came back over the house. She would realize at that moment that Blue was not snoring. He was silent.

"Wake up Blue," Gama said in a frenzy. "Wake up." Blue would not wake. Blue was dead. Blue was fifty-three years old.

Upon that discovery, the entire house was stunned. Its first initial shock was bewilderment, as they all assumed that Blue would live forever. Shock set in, and then all at once.. joy came. Thomas had never known such feelings of joy in his life. There was a sense of relief and a sense of emancipation. He'd never known the meaning of liberation until that very moment. Great feelings of ecstasy had overcome him. Gamma was right, "Nothing last forever."

Thomas would no longer be tormented and blamed for the face that he wore. The Heshard children ran into the streets, rejoicing and proclaiming that their grandfather was dead. They partied until day light. Everyone was happy; everyone except for Gama. Even though the occasional beatings that Blue would give her would be a thing of the past, she would be alone now.

Chapter Twenty-Six

||||||||||||||||||||||||||||||||||||||||||||||||||||||||||||||||||||||||||||||||||||||||||||||||||||||||||||||||||||||||||||||||||||||||||||||||||||

Marie

Two and a half years had passed now, and Thomas was coming of age. Although Blue wasn't around anymore, he still wanted nothing more than to leave Greensville, never to return again. He would spend hours reading old beat up pamphlets from one of Uncle Sam's recruiting office. He decided that the only way he could escape Greensville, like so many others, was to join Uncle Sam's Armed Forces. And that's exactly what he did. At sixteen years of age, Thomas enlisted in the United States of America's Air Force and became a candidate for jump school.

Becoming the third African American Air Man to become a part of a selected group called, "Tiger Company" was more than an honor. "Tiger Company" was a special ELITE group designed for counter terrorism during a time when African Americans weren't recognized for contributing anything significant to their country. Thomas enlisted shortly before Chapter nineteen, A New Era Begins, in nineteen fifty-four, under which the Secretary of Defense announced the last racially segregated unit in the Armed Forces be abolished. It came one year after the Supreme Courts decision to desegregate the schools came into effect.

Chapter nineteen laws made little headway in the first decade of integration. So Thomas had a chance to witness and experience the nations historical contrast Pf Am era of black awakening. Much of the country went about business as usual, but Thomas wore his stripes proud and boldly. Aware of the racial discord that left him incensed, Thomas used his fury as an advantage in fighting a war where African American's assistance was misplaced and omitted from American history books.

Contrary to popular belief, Thomas chose against adopting sentiments of resentment and despondency; that which so precisely defined the African American mood during that time. But Thomas had bigger and better plans. So he stood tall and fought hard and for a country that had no respect for him. It would be a means to get him to the next phase in his life.

After his four year enlistment was over, Thomas came up to Philadelphia where most of his family had now migrated. Thomas would visit his Aunt Becky, sometimes two or three times a week. And just a few doors away was where he met Cadence's mother, Marie.

Now twenty years of age; Thomas possessed a confident and persuasive personality, with many young women wanting to sip out of his cup. He was very calculating, knowing just the right things to say and do concerning the ladies. And that would be true of Marie Atwater.

Marie often frequented Philadelphia. She came up North from Virginia to visit her older brother, Christopher and his wife Gail. Marie was the youngest of nine children and the last to leave home. She was poised and quaint. She had evenly spaced eyes of amber with a cappuccino shade of skin tone, and an hour glass silhouette that was equally defining in its circumference. She was country and cute. She was a tad bashful in her confining ways; wide eyed with hopes and expectations. On her seventh trip to Philadelphia she met Thomas Heshard.

"Let me get that for you," Thomas said to Marie, as he helped her with the door. "I'll take those bags if you don't mind," he said.

"No thanks," Marie responded as she came out of her brother's house with bags in hand.

"Have we met before?" he asked.

"No," Marie replied. "Do you live here?" he inquired.

"No," she replied.

"Well are you going to be staying here long?" he asked.

"No," she responded.

"Is that all you can say is no?" Thomas asked.

"Yes," Marie said with a smile.

"Oh! She smiles," Thomas responded sarcastically with a smile. "So you're fine and you're feisty huh?" Thomas asked with his usual charm. "Seriously though, who's house is this?" Thomas questioned.

"It's my brother and sister in-law's house. I'm here visiting for the while, if you must know," she said.

"Oh! yes, I must," he responded. "Can I ask for how long."

"I'll be here until next week this time."

"Well that's just grand. That's just enough time for me to show you around town, maybe let me take you out for some custard," he said with his flawlessly shaped head and a striking smile that stretched from ear to ear.

His shoulders were broad and his back was strong. "Maybe I will," Marie responded.

"What are you doing later?" Thomas persisted.

"What are you doing later?" answering his question with a question.

"I'm picking you up around six," he said.

"Then I'll be ready," she responded. And with that she walked away in one direction and he parted in confidence in the opposite direction, down the street to his Aunt's house.

"Aw, somebody's got a hot date tonight," Gail said to Marie as she watched her sister in-law curl her hair and make up her face. "Who is he?" she asked.

"Some guy I met earlier."

"Does he have a name?" Gail asked.

"Yes he does. His name is Thomas," she said proudly.

"Where did you meet him?"

"I met him on the block today as I was going out to work."

"You say his name is Thomas?" Gail questioned.

"Yeah," Marie answered. "Is he about, six feet tall, with beautiful teeth, dancing eyes, and has an answer for everything," she asked.

"That sounds like him, yeah, you know him?" Marie asked. "Yeah, I know of him," Gail responded.

"So, what do you think of him?"

"All I know is that he's dated most off the girls on this side of town," Gail responded. "He never takes them home to meet his family. He gets what he wants from them, in all of about two weeks; and then with a subtleness, he severs all intimate ties. And even in his ability to use and displace them, he manages to have a somewhat bizarre lasting friendship with all his ex's."

"Well what do you think he wants from me?" Marie inquired.

"What he's gotten from all the rest of the girls he's dated, your jewels," Gail spoke candidly.

"My jewels?" Marie asked unknowingly.

"That's what he does girl," Gail elaborated, "He has a thing for virgins. Every one of the girls he's ever had was a virgin until they met him. It's like he has a particular appetite for them. As he extracts their virginity, they become weaker and he becomes stronger. They become clingy, attaching themselves to him, at which point he dumps them."

"Don't you think you're being a little over dramatic? You act like the man is after my soul or something," Marie said.

"He just might be. I've been living around here long enough to know that he's up to no good. He's a gigolo Marie—he conquers things. You'll just be one more thing that he conquers. I just want you to watch yourself. Be careful that you don't end up like all the rest."

"Well I'm sorry. I don't see the person that you just described. That's not the impression that I got from him at all."

"I don't care what you got from him," Gail stated softly. But I can tell you what you gonna' get from him if you travel down that road; and that's a broken heart. Don't let them eyes and that smile fool you." Gail finished as she left the room, giving Marie something to think about.

The next few weeks Thomas showered Marie with a lot of sweet nothings and sex appeal. He enticed her with his smooth and polishing ways; cascading her with chocolates and mixed tulips and iris' every chance that he got. He was very attentive, complementing her always on what she was wearing, how pretty and how exceptional she was. Marie never felt so special in her life, nor had she ever been this much in love in all of her sixteen years. Thomas and Marie were going at hot and heavy pace. They were basically inseparable. Every where Marie went Thomas wasn't too far behind, often showing up uninvited. Marie had no doubt that it was an indication of how committed he was to her and how much he loved her.

Chapter Twenty-Seven

Welcome To The Family

Two months had gone by when Thomas unexpectedly proposed to Marie. She was shaken with surprise. "Marie think about this," Gail pleaded. "You barely know him. It's only been two months."

"Well how long exactly do you need to fall in love with someone? You and Chris have this great thing between you. It's obvious how much you two love each other. All I want is a chance to have the same thing. Is that too much to ask? Can't you just be happy for me?"

"Out of all the girls he's been with, you don't think it strange that after only two months, he professes his undying love for you. I know you're a great girl, and you're special, but I just question his motives."

"I know him enough to know that he loves me." Marie insisted.

"Oh really, I've known guys like him my whole life, and I know that he may like you, but he only loves what you will symbolize in his life," Gail said.

"What does that mean?"

"I mean you'd make a real good wife, and a good mother for his children, and a great house keeper. You're straight from the country. You don't know nothin' about city life. He's marrying you for your ignorance," Gail maintained.

"Why are you saying these things to me? You think I'm stupid? Why is it so hard for you to believe that someone like him could find me interesting enough or even attractive enough to marry?"

"I'm just saying that I love you, and that maybe he assumes …. he won't have to change much about his life as it is if he marries you, because you won't demand that he does," Gail explains.

"Well you're wrong. I thank you for your concern, but I'm not as fragile as everyone seems to think—so there's no need to worry. I can take care of myself and I'll be just fine. You'll see. I'll be just fine," Marie stated as though she was trying to convince herself.

The big day had arrived and it had been two weeks since Thomas proposed to Marie. Thomas and Marie wed in Aunt Becky's house. Aunt Becky was the only living sister of Thomas' assumed to be late father, Alpheus. She was like a second mother to him. The day was long and the vows had come and gone as the matrimonial evening was nearing its end. Although Thomas made a modest wage as a roofer, a trade he took after his father, the thought of a honeymoon was never to be entertained. It was common for people back then who were of African American decent, to sidestep a honeymoon for obvious reasons—money.

Marie's dress was white and plain with a tint of pink. It was simple but chic. It was Aunt Becky's gift to her as she spent hours making it. Aunt Becky could make anything without a pattern. She was naturally gifted in that way. "You're a good girl Marie," Aunt Becky said, "And I like you. This family could use a breath of clean fresh air. I think you're just what we need." Marie didn't have a clue as to what Aunt Becky meant by that. All she really knew was that she had been welcomed into Thomas' family with open arms; and for that she was thankful.

On the day of their nuptials, there was a lot to see. She noticed that almost all of Thomas' family members were drinkers. They had so many boxes of liquor donated to them, and they were practically all out. She'd never seen Thomas drink until that very day. Marie felt that it was a celebration befitting a drink or two. Thomas had been drinking since mid-day to commemorate the new life he was about to embark upon with Marie. Marie, who was not fond of drinking herself, because of her own family's history with dreaded drink, so she sat back, listened, and witnessed as the drama unfolded.

"Flo, where you goin' with all that food? Some of us haven't even eaten yet. That don't make no sense now, leave some for somebody else," Cousin Lucille stated.

"What are you talking about?" Flo responded.

"You do this at every function; packing up enough for you and your tribe to eat on for a month, while the rest of us have to starve."

"This ain't none of your business Lucille, move out my way," she insisted. "Stay outta other folks business, that's what you need to do."

"This is my business," Lucille thrashed back. "And Everybody up in here who brought something."

"You come in here empty handed and you leave with everything cept the kitchen sink. If you wasn't' so ignant and trifling…" Lucille tried to finish.

"Trifling? you must be a joke'," Flo snapped. When's the last time you bathed or combed that rug on your head? Those cruddy feet of yours haven't seen water since the flood, you ole bat. You should know all about trifling, you eat dog food, not because you have to, but because you like it."

"I will slap your ass into next week, you keep talking," Lucille promised.

"You'll get your ass whooped trying," Flo responded as she threw the plate of food that was in her hand in Lucille's face. With rage, Lucille took the pocket book from off her shoulder, wrapped the strap around Flo's neck, and commenced to choking the living hell out of her.

As the tables fell and the food became airborne, Thomas, Jamison, and Cousin Richard, interceded as they jumped in to break the two women up—the two women were very strong. Cousin Richard threw his back out and suffered a concussion during the break up. As he was pushed up against the breakfront, and Aunt Becky's cast iron casserole dish fell atop his bald head and knocked him out for a few minutes.

Everything was completely destroyed. The cake was ruined and the children screaming in distress. Marie was in tears. Christopher and Gail took Marie outside to comfort her as the women were separated and made to depart from the premises anxious and livid. "This don't make no sense," Aunt Becky screamed. "Yall ought to be shame of yourselves. I don't want either one of you to ever set foot in my house again, not now, not ever." Aunt Becky said with conviction. She and a few others helped to start getting the place cleaned up as everyone began to exit the home with food and drink soiled clothing.

After Thomas finally got Marie to calm down and assured her that, what happened was no big deal. All that he cared about was that they were married and together. His words were slurring together and he was unable to sit up without falling over. It was the end of the night and in spite of the evening's disruptions, all Marie could think about was how she so wanted to be a good wife to Thomas and a good mother to their unborn children.

She wanted all of her in-laws to accept her and like her. She wanted nothing more than to be received as part of her new family, notwithstanding the fact that her reception was a total disaster; she was determined to be everything that Thomas needed.

It was approximately 12:00am, the cleanup was complete and the last person had gone; even Aunt Becky was gone. She would spend the night at her niece's home, not far from where she lived. She knew how important it was that Thomas and Marie be left alone on this their wedding night. Marie helped Thomas up stairs and to their bridal suite, as Aunt Becky had prepared her bedroom for the matrimonial occasion.

Marie left Thomas lying on the bed as she excused herself. In a girlish manner she proceeded to the bathroom to freshen up. She wanted to make herself as desirable as she had seen the women on the cover of the magazines down at Joe's newsstand. Joe would let Marie read some of the articles in the magazines without paying for them, because he loved to watch her face light up as she flipped through the pages in awe. She sprayed a new fragrance she'd purchased from the drug store with the aroma of lilac with a hint of vanilla; brushing behind the earlobes, across her upper breast, and lightly on the inside of her thighs.

She'd been given a two piece red negligee, trimmed in black as a wedding present from a lady named Ms. Martha, who owned a little boutique down on South St. Marie didn't know her personally, but she would often observe Marie admiring the boutiques specialty garments.

She particularly observed her admiring the two piece tantalizing number every time she'd come into the shop. "How soon you think you'll be able to buy it?" Ms. Martha asked.

"Not soon enough. I'm getting married tomorrow," Marie mumbled.

"Say what child?" Ms. Martha questioned as she came from around the counter.

"I said," she paused. "I'm getting married tomorrow."

"Married?" Ms. Martha repeated in disbelief. "How old are you child?"

"Sixteen," Marie answered.

"Why you just a baby. Why you wanna marry so young? You gottcha whole life in fronta you."

"I love him."

"Well," said Ms. Martha, you go on and take that little number there," she paused. "Take it as a wedding gift from me."

"Oh my God, really?" Marie rejoiced.

"I sho hope he's worth it."

"Oh he is," Marie established as she hugged Ms. Martha. "He is. Thanks Ms Martha," she shouted as she ran out the store. "Thank you so much."

Marie counted the lady and her gift as a blessing. She could never get pass the striking resemblance the lady bare to her very own mother whom she missed and longed to see. It had been a year since she left Dacatur. As she held the negligee up to her small curvy frame, and caramel tone, she gazed into the mirror and thought, "Oh how I wish mama were here with me now. I know she'd be so happy for me.

She was taken back to Dacatur for a moment; a small town in the South from wince she came. Marie was a long way from home and at times felt the absence of her mother deeply. Oh how she ached inside. She came up North for the same reason most people did, in hopes for a better life and a new start. The North had been known to be kinder to people of color in comparison to the South.

It was in early 1958 and Marie's sixteenth birthday had passed. She was the last of nine children to leave Decatur. Her two oldest brothers, Boston and Frayer stayed behind and made lives for themselves. Her oldest sister Louise, didn't live far from her brother Christopher and his wife Gail. Jason and Todd moved out West and Stella and Mitch were no longer among the living.

Shortly after Marie arrived in Philadelphia she found a job picking peaches on a farm about ten miles outside city limits. She worked twelve, sometimes thirteen hour days at a rate of fifty cents a basket. At the end of her work day she would catch the bus back into the city and walk about a half mile before she would reach the block in which she lived.

She returned from her past thoughts to resume her wedding night. She proceeded out of the bathroom, her stomach in a bunch of knots, nervous about how the rest of the evening was going to turn out. This would be her first time ever with a man. She wondered if Thomas would delight in how she looked? Would he be enchanted with how she smelled? Would he be pleased with how she tasted?

She exited the bathroom and entered the bedroom where Thomas was. She noticed that the lights had been turned completely off. She knew that Thomas was anticipating a night full of erotica and romance, just as she was. But she couldn't see a thing. "Thomas," she softly called out. But nobody answered her back. Maybe he had gone down to the kitchen to get them both a snack for afterwards.

As she began to make her way to the door, her arms extended out as she tried to feel her way through the darkness. Just at that moment, Thomas mysteriously appeared. Marie was startled "Oh my God, you scared me. Where were you, I was just about to go downstairs to see if you were in the kitchen?" Thomas blocked out everything that she just said, grabbed her forcefully by her hair and pulled her in close to him and whispered in her ear. "You look beautiful," he said. He clinched his fist and in a second he began pounding her face, one vicious punch after another. After the shock set in a few seconds later, Marie began to beg him to stop. Suddenly he stopped.

With sincerity in his words, he said to her, "I love you so much. I need you to believe that." Marie, in a daze, not able to comprehend anything of what just took place, laid there sobbing as Thomas began to have his way with her.

First thing the next morning, Thomas got up and left out for his regular coffee and breakfast; grits, toast, and eggs—sunny side up. He ate breakfast out every morning. Marie was found in a battered mess a few hours later by Aunt Becky and her niece, Matty. "Oh Lord, Jesus," Aunt Becky said as she clutched her heart, upon laying eyes on Marie. "I'm so sorry."

"Why?" Marie asked, barely able to open her black ringed eyes. "Why would he do such a thing?" she sobbed.

"I don't know child," answered Aunt Becky. "Ghost have a way of haunting people," she stated as she began to clean Marie up. "Hurry up Matty with those rags. I know its no excuse," she went on. "But some of the men folk in this family have a hard time holding their liquor and keeping their hands to themselves. I was praying that Thomas wouldn't be one of em'. Maybe I didn't pray hard enough."

Aunt Becky and Matty were disgusted at Thomas' actions towards Marie. They were clearly upset. They stayed and comforted Marie the best way they could. They cleaned her up, fed her, and allowed her to continue to rest. They watched as Thomas came in later that evening with flowers and candy, apologizing for his dreadful attack on his new bride. Marie forgave him and they never spoke of the incident again.

Thomas did show remorse. He refused to look on the beautiful face that he had pulverized in his drunkenness. He would not put his hands on Marie or drink while under Aunt Becky's roof. Seven months later a trip to the doctor's office revealed Marie was pregnant with their first child. Thomas took the money that he saved and found them their first home. The drinking slowly but surely returned, and so did the ghastly beatings. He'd apologize and she'd forgive. Their marriage existed in the same manner for the next twenty years.

Chapter Twenty-Eight

The Great Sacrifice

Cadence had always been bothered by the turns of events in her life stemming from the very first night her parents became man and wife. She thought of how different everything could have been if Marie would have just disappeared that night, never to lay eyes on Thomas again. As Cadence approached adult hood, she mustard up the courage to ask her mother what she had been longing to know her whole life; why?

"Why didn't you leave that very night, after he had fallen into a drunken stupor; or even the next day, nobody would have blamed you? You were only sixteen. You had your whole life ahead of you. There were no children at that point to be concerned with. How could you ever consider staying with someone who beat you on your wedding night?" A dead silence fell upon the room. Marie looked somber at Cadence and said, "I thought I could make him love me enough to change", she said. I was too ashamed to admit that I had made a horrible mistake and I didn't know how to take it back. I couldn't bring myself to tell anyone. What would they say? It was a selfish act and I know that now", Marie confessed.

As the years went by and Cadence and her brothers and sisters witnessed Thomas' indiscretions, his relationships with his mistresses, his comings and goings, the children he fathered outside of his marriage to her mother, and his wrath that he spewed upon their family; they grew closer to their mother and farther away from him. The more Thomas drank the more Cadence and her siblings were afraid for their mother. They would lay awake many nights in shear terror. Each beating came with a different accusation.

Thomas would accuse Marie of all the things that he himself indulged in. Their family was ordinary by day, but by night they were something different. Cadence had heard about praying and although she had been to church a lot of Sundays, she really hadn't witnessed anything extraordinary as a result of it. Was she doing it right? She began to be less formal and more casual; talking to God as a friend. She prayed that he would remove Thomas from their lives forever so that their mother would be safe and somehow find happiness.

She and her brothers and sisters, three girls and two boys, began to despise Thomas as each year passed. They loved him sometimes for being their father, but hated him more times than not, for being their mother's husband and oppressor. He provided very well for his family, but the everyday stresses that came along with being part of his family overshadowed every morsel of food, every piece of clothing, every dollar and every cent. Cadence tried to overlook the disturbing and unsettling things that were taking place in her home on a day to day basis. She tried to overlook Thomas' inability to be human and Maries' inability to come from under the shadow of darkness aka Thomas, and emerge into her own beautiful light.

Marie possessed a force within her that was evident since the day she graced this world with her presence. Like Thomas, she had to forfeit her education to stay at home and work on the family farm. She remembered hiding behind the sycamore tree that was near the road at the end of their property, wiping the tears from her eyes as she watched the more fortunate children board the bus to school.

It became more and more difficult for her with each passing day being married to Thomas. Marie tried desperately to hang on to what was left of her dignity and her sanity; with each pregnancy and each birth; loosing herself and purposely trying to forget about herself as Thomas handed down to Marie the same portion of hatred and revulsion that his grandfather handed down to him.

Cadence knew that we were automatically given certain parts of our character upon conception; but then there were things, bits and pieces of our characteristics, and the environment, that become a part of us as we grew and developed outside of mother's womb.

Marie knew that all the good stuff in Thomas, the candy, the flowers, the charm, and the determination to provide the best for his family; that was all him. But all the bad stuff, the violence, the mood swings, the disrespect; that was bits and pieces of the ugly things in his life that somehow merged with his good qualities and turned him against himself. That was Blue.

But where was Marie? What happened to her? She'd always been able to stand her ground even as a child of twelve. She would come to the rescue of her older brother Christopher and occasionally fight the battles that would prove difficult for him to win. Marie had a tendency for standing up for those she loved but fell short when it came to standing up for herself.

Although Thomas and Marie came from two different towns, they didn't grow up that far away from one another. Both of Cadence's parents came from a time where assignments were a part of their everyday lives. They were assigned everything from chores, right down to the sections of meat that they were given at supper time. From the chicken, Thomas was assigned the neck. No matter when they were served fried chicken, this would always be his assigned piece. The piece with the least amount of meat on it.

Chapter Twenty-Nine

Business Before Family

As children, Cadence and her siblings couldn't relate or recall a time such as when they were rationed food. She and her brothers and sisters were blessed that they were privileged to eat whatever piece of chicken they wanted. Thomas only demanded one thing, and that was that they were not to be wasteful. "Make sure you eat whatever you put on your plate," Thomas would say and that was exactly what Thomas meant. Cadence was made to spend many evenings left at the table until bedtime if her plate was not cleaned.

Thomas Heshard made sure that his family didn't want for anything financially. He made sure that he and his family would never be cold or go hungry. He did whatever he had to in order to guarantee that never happen. Thomas never did well working for others. After working on the farm and later on, an assembly line, and a roofer; Thomas went to welding school and got his license and began to save his money. He started his own business with money he saved from hustling card games. Thomas was born to hustle and he was good at it. He was one of the biggest hustlers and well known business men on the North side of Philadelphia.

As his business began to prosper, he purchased three of the local bars within a five mile radius of where his Company Shop was located. With each new establishment that Thomas opened, his family saw him less and less. The money began to pour in. Cadence and her siblings would spend their afternoons and weekends counting money and bagging change.

There was no room for friends, as the Heshard children were not allowed to have anyone in the house during business hours. Marie was responsible for closing and locking up one of the three bars that Thomas owned. She would do this every night without incident. She would often glance at the women that she suspected of being very fond of Thomas; as he began to distance himself from Marie and the children.

The police were constantly raiding the shop and the bars, and even their home; hoping to find something that would help to incriminate him and put him away for a long time. It was hard for the police to come to terms with the fact that Thomas owned so many establishments without some assistance from an illegal activity. They were convinced that he was a bookie or a drug dealer. They would ransack his establishments and take any and all monies they could find for their trouble. Marie was taken into custody a number of times only to be home in time to start dinner.

As a youth, Cadence and the other children were victimized as they were illegally searched. They were taken into a room in their home without the presence of either parent and asked to disrobe. A flash light would be shone in private parts of their bodies, as they searched for evidence that was suspected of being hidden. Life as a Heshard child was no walk on the beach or in the park. They became accustomed to the money, but all the turns of events came with a price. For Thomas it was all about eat or be eaten. He refused to let any of those things, which he referred to as, "minor set backs," deter him from getting what he believed belonged to him; the almighty dollar.

The Heshard children began to grow and come into their own. Cadence recalls going around to Sam's convenient store everyday to get her daily supply of penny candy. Sam and his family were clearly not from around there. They were of Polish decent and a bit on the short side. Their demeanor was pleasant and funny. Their business temperament was professional and everyone in the neighborhood respected them.

Cadence took off for Sam's store about noon, as she always did on a hot summer day. It felt like a hundred and seven degrees out. It was muggy and very moist, and the humidity was high. There were fire hydrants being open up all over the neighborhood. Every time the po-po came to shut one down; the kids around the way would open it back up minutes later.

Cadence did her best to avoid walking pass the hydrants because she never wanted to get wet or get her hair messed up. She couldn't avoid the hydrant on Harold St. though because it was right across the street from Sam's. She was awfully careful to walk outside the perimeter of the length of the water. But just as she was passing this particular day; the terrors of the neighborhood, twins Buddy and Bobby came up behind her without any warning, grabbed her and dragged her to the hydrant. Cadence terrified, began kicking, screaming and pleading, as everyone on the block laughed as they watched them soak her.

Cadence returned home soak and wet about seventeen minutes later; drenched in water and in her tears. She attempted to make it up the stairs to her room before anyone would notice her. Denton, the oldest of the five, who was about fourteen years of age at the time, asked Cadence, then ten, what happened. Cadence hesitated as she continued towards the stairs. She knew that the twins and Denton didn't care much for one another. She also knew that with Denton's temper, nothing good would come of it, so she remained quiet. "Cadence, did you hear me, I asked you what happened?" Denton spoke louder.

"Nothin'," Cadence said agitated. "Nothing ok, I'm fine."

"I didn't ask you how you were." Denton began to display frustration in his sarcasm. "I asked you what happened." Denton knew that Cadence wasn't about to give him the information he wanted; he grabbed her forcefully by the hand and pulled her down the stairs, out the door, and back around the corner.

Denton saw a number of neighborhood kids coolin' off in the hydrant, but there were two faces that stood out in the crowd. It was Buddy and Bobby Clark. Denton walked Cadence over to the group of kids and asked Cadence in front of them, "Who did it Cadence? Huh, who did it Cadence?" He walked closer to Buddy and asked, "You know who wet my sista?" He turned to Cadence and asked, "Which one of them did it?"

"I did it, why? What's up, you want some?" Buddy asked boldly. And what did he ask that for?

"Yeah! I want some," Denton said with eagerness, and it was on.

Denton walked and lunged into Buddy with both fist following one after the other. Denton had been practicing at Joe Frazier's Gym and you could tell. He was throwing all kinds of combinations and flurries. Buddy's face started to become bloody as he began to bleed profusely from the nose; when his brother Bobby, came from behind. Cadence yelled out to Denton, as he turned in response, Bobby smashed the bat across his shoulders. Cadence picked up a stick and began hitting Bobby with all her might. Bobby turned from Denton to focus his attention on Cadence. Denton suddenly retreated from plummeting Buddy when he saw Bobby grabbing Cadence and pulling her toward the hydrant once again. Denton ran for Bobby and Buddy ran for Denton.

The twins were a couple of years older than Denton and bigger too. The two began to over power Denton and Cadence. Bobby and Buddy had Denton in a head lock. They managed to force Denton's head under the water. Cadence fought hard for her brother, and she too was over powered. Both their heads were forced under the water and the power of the hydrant. The water beat against their faces, pounding and hammering against them while cutting off their oxygen. Mr. Frank, an older man who lived in the neighbor hood, tried to persuade the twins with his cane to let Denton and Cadence go. "Let em' go," Mr. Frank yelled as he swung. "Somebody call the police." With all the commotion, Denton and Cadence eventually broke free. Denton vowed to have his revenge. The twins could never beat Denton one on one, so they always had to jump him. But Denton didn't care.

Drenched and sopping with water, Denton and Cadence began walking home. "You alright?" Denton asked.

"Yeah," Cadence responded as she looked away. They walked the rest of the way home in complete silence. Denton didn't know it, but he was Cadence's hero. She was so proud to have him as her brother. See, it didn't matter to her that they were almost drowned. But what did matter, was that Denton was brave enough to stand up to the Clark Brothers when nobody else would.

Many were afraid of them. But Cadence could honestly say and know without a shadow of a doubt, Denton wasn't. And because he wasn't, she wasn't. They returned home, explained everything to Thomas; dried off, changed into clean clothing, ate dinner, and went to bed. Cadence saw the disappointment in Denton's eyes; and as she left the room, she said, "I love you Denton and I'm glad that you're my brother," he smiled and she was gone.

Chapter Thirty

||||||||||||||||||||||||||||||||||||||||||||||||||||||||||||||||||||||||||||||||||||||||||||||||||||||||||||||||||||||||||||||||||||||||

The Promise

Now 16 years of age, Denton had to fight almost every day on his way home from school. He was surrounded by gang wars and initiation rituals, and he knew that it was only a matter of time before he would have to choose which gang he would belong to. Thomas intervened in many of the fights that Denton encountered. But he continued to fight tirelessly as they kept coming; one after another, sometimes three or four at a time. They were determined to break his will and his strength of mind. The gang members from Sergeant St. was relentless in trying to recruit him. But he decided against them and pledged to Cool World Valley, 2-1 and Montgomery Ave.

The initiation took place at the Lippincott St. playground and proved to be very trying. He managed to fight his way through the line of twenty and come out with minimal damage. Thomas enrolled Denton and Cadence's oldest sister by two years, Forrester, in Tai Kwan self defense classes. They both had become rather good fighters, winning all their competitions and earning a new belt with each defeat. Denton became so good that he no longer needed Thomas to intervene in anything. He went on to build an impressionable reputation for himself. He was determined to let every tough guy or gang leader know that he could hold his own and that he wasn't afraid to die.

Denton became less and less interested in school. He'd always had a hard time accepting the fact that education was the key to success. He believed he didn't need education to be successful. Eventually he dropped out of school and began to hang out with friends that he'd known his whole life, friends outside of the gang. They formed their own gang. Denton stood up to anybody and he fought anyone who wanted to take him on. If he couldn't beat you with his fist, needless to say, he'd get you with that gat. Either way, you would get got.

Denton made such a reputation for himself that he was barely recognized in his spirit. He always had the type of personality that everyone loved, and that never changed. It was his disposition that became uncompromised. He couldn't see pass the streets and the violence. He began to fight just for the sake of fighting. He had to make sure that there was no doubt in anyone's mind as to what he would do to them if they tried him.

Now seventeen years of age, Denton knew the street game rather well. What he didn't learn from Thomas he learned from the streets. He began to distribute small amounts of marijuana, purchasing his packages from a close friend of the family at an unbeatable price. Denton, like Thomas, kept late hours. They would often run into each other from time to time, and because of the nature of things, Denton began to feel uncomfortable and to a certain extent, awkward, when running into his father and his mistresses when he was out and about taking care of business.

Denton started to notice that feelings of remorse and shame begin to set in. He was torn between the loyalty he had for a father who put himself before everyone; and the love and trust that he felt for his mother. Denton would never condone his father's actions, but he didn't feel like it was his place to question or judge him.

So why did he feel so bad about what he saw and what he knew? He had gone home many nights to find that he would be the only one who was able to console his mother after a round with Thomas. He did love his father, but he hated his ways. He knew that Thomas would never appreciate or love his mother the way she deserved to be loved. As a result of the children growing older, Marie did suffer less beatings, but a leopard would never change his spots.

It hurt Denton to know that his father had a weakness for women. But it hurt him even more to know that his mother was alone because of it. Every time Denton looked into Marie's eyes he could see that she felt alone. He had seen how Thomas treated the women he ran with in the street, given them much respect, compared to how he treated his mother, with contempt.

As time went on Denton became restless and edgy. Marie would confide in him about her suspicions of his father's careless ways, and Denton knew that he could confirm those suspicions as he knew them to be true. He felt compelled to confess to Marie everything he knew about his father's activities and apologize for them. He told her everything that he knew, he gave up names, places, and dates.

Marie realized that Denton was becoming a man right before her very eyes. She expressed her concerns about his safety and how he was living his life. "Yesterday, you were just a baby," she said. "Today I see you as a man. Every decision that you make right now will determine the rest of your life. Be wise in your decisions and think them through thoroughly. Your father's ways are his ways. My ways are mine. You think and do what's best for you. You,

Forrester and Cadence, all of you are so much smarter than me and your father could ever be. Stop competing with him. You don't need his approval to be happy. You're heart has always been bigger. You can succeed at whatever it is you put your mind to. You don't have to be a statistic. I want you to promise me, that you'll stop doing whatever it is you're doing out there in them streets. There's nothing out there for your but death or a one way trip to the penitentiary, and I refuse to bury you. Please Denton," she begged.

"Alright ma," Denton looked away from his mother's tearful eyes. "Alright."

"You promise me right now."

"Alright, I promise."

Chapter Thirty-One

||||||||||||||||||||||||||||||||||||||||||||||||||||||||||||||||||||||||||||||||||||||||||||||||||||||||||||||||||||||||||||||||||||||||||||||||||||||||||||

Loyalty vs. Love

Thomas felt a change in Denton and his attitude towards him. A year had gone by and Denton continued his street activities despite his promise to Marie. By this time, he and Thomas' relationship had become strained. It showed as Denton began to talk to Thomas with anger and resentment. Something subtle but fierce began to stir within him. He commenced to wage a war against his own flesh and blood.

Every evening Denton and his crew were out and about, seeing what they could see. Always looking out and keeping tabs on Thomas. Aside from being very much the ladies man, Thomas was known to be a very liberal and generous man with the people he knew. On the contrary, his family knew a different Thomas. He was a man who always put business and pleasure ahead of family.

The Thomas the immediate family knew, never respected the sacred institute of marriage and didn't even pretend to; not even from the very beginning. The Thomas the family knew, used his family to work and help build his empire, but insisted that the empire that was built, was his and his alone. He hid his profits in various safes that where built into the walls of their home, securing it from his wife and children.

Marie had to literally beg him for practically every dime she needed or wanted. She always had to give an account as to why and what she wanted it for. Whatever Thomas needed her to do Marie was willing and able; realizing that it was important that she be there for Thomas, as a wife and as the mother of his children.

In the beginning, Thomas was seemingly gracious. He was cordial and respectable. He was always generous to Marie and the children. But as time went on things began to change.

Although he still remained liberal to some degree with the children, giving them what they asked for and needed; he became nit picky with Marie.

She started to show signs of growing weary of the daily monotony. Exhaustion began to set in. She began to tire of Thomas' late hours and late night calls. The scent of his garments were often heavily saturated with perfume that was unfamiliar to her. Thomas rented many of the properties to single mothers. He spent a great deal of time at those properties doing maintenance work. But Marie found it to be questionable, especially when there were calls in the middle of the night that a pipe had busted or bulb needed to be changed.

Thomas instilled in Marie the belief that a woman had no right to question a man about his business. She should only be concerned with the run of the house and the children. He worked everyday and provided for his family and you were never to question him or his motives. He would become infuriated with Marie if she stepped outside of her place and questioned him about anything he did pertaining to business. With each inquisition there came a response, and with each response there came more violence.

Denton, a man now, found it more difficult to ignore his mother's late night muffled cries. He could no longer stand to see the bruises that where visibly on her face the morning after. More and more he felt disgusted over the abuse and felt compelled to do something about it. He went over it in his mind many times. He loved Thomas, but he knew that Thomas' perception of love was quite different than most. Although Thomas had lots of faults, the one thing that he taught Denton and the other children was to stand up for what they believed in.

He said, "you always had to let the world know that no matter what their color, size, or how much more fortunate they thought they were over you; it would never mean that they were better. You would always have to stand your ground, be counted for, and let it be known that you will not make it easy for any of them to mistreat you".

He felt that, as long as you did that, you would always win out in the end and they could never beat you. And so with this, Denton understood that he had to stand up to Thomas for Marie's sake; for all of their sakes, just because it was the right thing to do.

The Heshard home had become a war zone. Just yesteryear, Denton, his sisters, and baby brother, were too young to have a voice that could be heard. But now that they were teenagers and young adults; there was no mistake about it. The fear of how all of this could play out was daunting. They could no longer remain silent or neutral. Marie needed them. Thomas had managed to kill every spirit in that house with his hatred, but Denton couldn't allow Thomas to kill his mother along with it. He knew something had to be done about it. He felt that only he could stop Thomas before it was too late. One hit too many; one push too hard, and it would be all over for Marie and Denton would never be able to live with it or himself.

Thomas had come home reeking of alcohol and perfume as usual. He came in, sat and stared out to nothingness for a moment and then started up with Marie. "Next time you plan on stoppin' pass the shop, call first."

"I had no idea you weren't gonna' be there," Marie explained.

"That's why you should call first. When you saw I wasn't there, why didn't you just go home?" he asked.

"Bill said that you would be back shortly. I came all the way down there; I didn't want it to be for nothing."

"You sure that's all it was? You sure you came to see me?" he insinuated. Marie knew where this line of questioning was headed. She started to clean up the living room, ignoring the last question that Thomas had posed to her.

"Oh, you not gonna' respond to that? So it must be true."

"No I won't respond to such foolishness," she retorted. Thomas stood and walked towards her as she continued on with what she was doing without showing fear as he tried to intimidate her.

"You think you slick don't you?" You were gone the entire day, doing what?"

"I went to Links before I came to the shop, and picked up a few steaks for dinner. And before that, I stopped past the post office to purchase a book of stamps."

"Well what time did you finish at Links?" he asked.

"I don't know what the exact time was. I didn't bother to look at the clock. But it was right before I got to the shop. It was before two," she answered.

"Why did you stop having Links deliver?" Thomas began to press.

"Thomas, it was a nice day. I like to go walking sometimes," she clarified.

"Why couldn't you wait until the children came home and took them with you?" he asked.

"The children have homework to do. Why would I wait all the way to the end of the day to run errands? That don't make sense."

"So what I say is stupid?"

"You twistin' my words Thomas."

"No, you think you smarter than me don't you?"

"Thomas, no, I didn't say that," Marie responded.

"The reason you didn't take the kids was cause you was out shaking your ass."

"Thomas why are you turning this into something crazy." She said.

"Oh it's crazy, is it? Let me tell you something. You won't ever be smarter than me. I'm always goin' to be one step ahead of you. You understand," he yelled as he smacked Marie's glasses from her face and punched her in the stomach.

Thomas insisted that Marie had a bunch of friends that only he knew about. He would often accuse her of running around with various men in the neighborhood. And it wasn't clear to Marie, whether he really believed what he was saying, or if he was clearly delusional. But either way, it almost always meant that he would hurt her because of it. Thomas had convinced himself that Marie was out doing to him, what he in actuality had been doing to her since their wedding night.

Marie recognized that Thomas' drinking and his guilty conscious were a deadly combination and they were getting the best of him that evening. She began to try to reason and persuade him to change his mind about the deceiving and untrue thoughts that were over taking him. She pleaded with him, trying to assure him that she had never been with anyone else in her entire life except him. But once Thomas was stuck on something, there was nothing that anyone could do to turn his thinking around. After she had been called every slut and every hoe in the book, the blows would follow like the force against nature that they were.

Marie took her normal defensive stance, trying to cover her head and her face. She had so many previous black eyes that the dark bruising around them seemed to be permanent. She would always use makeup to conceal the discoloration that had formed. The blows had become so many that Marie lost count.

Denton woke from his sleep as did Cadence and the others. They heard the one sided dispute clear up to the third floor. Then Cadence, Mindy, and Forrester began to cry out in fear as they stood in the doorways of their rooms, too afraid to come out. Denton attempted to make his way down to the living room where the attack was taking place. Thomas heard his footsteps coming fast as Denton called out for his mother in a concerning voice. "Mom," Denton called.

Thomas yelled back, "Don't you come down here. You a man now huh, is that it?" He warned Denton to stay where he was. Denton continued on in hopes of somehow aiding Marie. Thomas immediately turned his attention from Marie and quickly went to the liquor cabinet to retrieved two colleagues of his, Smith & Wesson. He warned Denton a final time that if he attempted to continue down the stairs, that he had a bullet waiting for him with his and Marie's name on it.

With a bloody nose, a bloody lip, and a contusion on her forehead, Marie called out in desperation, "Its ok Denton, I'm, alright. You hear me Denton," Marie crying frantically, "I'm ok, I'm ok, I'm ok. Just don't…come…down here." Cadence wanted to make sure Denton heard Marie as she too cried out afraid for his life, "She says she's ok Denton." All became silent.

Denton stopped, and began to turn around when he heard shear distress in the voices of his mother and sisters. It took everything he had in him to turn back around and not to continue on to defend his mother, as he listened for the assurance that she was ok. "Go head now. You'd better listen to your mother and go on," Thomas advised. But Denton couldn't go back upstairs. It was two thirty in the morning and all Denton could think about was getting as far away from Thomas as possible.

He could still hear the blows and strikes ringing in his head, the fear in his mother's voice, and the intimidation that held his family in bondage. He wanted so much to help free Marie. He wanted to rescue her from her oppressor. Thomas heard the front door slam. He wasn't sure where Denton had gone or when he'd be back. After about a half hour or so, Thomas settled down and had fallen off to sleep. Marie stayed up worrying about Denton's whereabouts. Denton found himself at a friend's house replaying the events of the early morning and beating himself up about not doing something about it.

"He was gonna' shoot me," he told his friend Oscar. He was really gonna' shoot me, I know he was."

"Yo' man, that's crazy," Oscar responded. "You know whatever you wanna do, I'm here for you." As hurtful as it was, Denton had come to the realization of that night. He knew that the thoughts of harming his own father to save his mother had crossed his mind. But he also knew that those feelings were not normal. But then again, there was nothing normal about any of it.

All he knew was that something had to change. And he knew that once he actually took steps towards protecting his mother, there would be no turning back. The first step was to move out of the house. He knew that Thomas didn't trust him and he didn't trust Thomas either. He worried about Marie, but somehow he knew she would be okay. He wouldn't be far from home and only a phone call away. He made sure that Cadence and Forrester knew how to get in contact with him in case they needed him.

Chapter Thirty-Two

The Confrontation

Denton set in motion his reign of terror. His rampage was only just beginning. He watched Thomas carefully from afar. He and his crew began to visit Thomas' establishments; ransacking, terrorizing, and robbing Thomas' places of business in hopes of sending a message to Thomas. The message was; as long you continue to terrorize and hurt my mother, I will terrorize and hurt you where you live; in your pocket. This went on for a period of three months. Marie and the children began to really get worried. Nobody was sleeping in the Heshard Home.

Thomas began to beat Marie just for breathing. He didn't know the whereabouts of Denton, because Denton never stayed in one place long enough for anyone to get a handle on him. Marie felt the tension building in her chest with each day that passed. She knew what Denton was trying to accomplish and decided that she couldn't allow him to make such a sacrifice on her behalf. She was tired of the beatings. She was fed up with the terror her children were living in. She was tired of being afraid. She finally made a conscious decision to fight back.

Marie instructed Forrester and Cadence to hide Thomas' gun. She disclosed that she had never really been afraid of Thomas; it was the gun that she was terrified of. She told them that the very next time Thomas raised his hand to her, he would know that he had been in a fight. She told them to call the 911 if it looked like Thomas was getting the best of her. Forrester was completely disabled. Cadence's nerves were frazzled. Nobody bothered to tell Mindy what Marie was planning, because she was very sensitive to those matters. They thought it best to try and spare her the extra worry. Marshall was just a baby and didn't have a clue as to what was going on. Cadence cried and worried for three long days. She wasn't so much afraid of not having a father, as she was of not having a mother. She prayed more than she ever had before.

It had been seven days since Thomas had beaten Marie. Thomas came home that evening, madder than they'd ever seen him. Denton and his crew had gone to the shop after closing the night before, and destroyed practically all of Thomas' brand new store equipment. They turned over and destroyed desks, broke windows, turned on all the water and flooded the place.

Thomas began to question Marie about where Denton lived and how he could find him. Marie saw the fire in Thomas' eyes and could smell his blood boiling. She was truly afraid for her son's life. But she didn't know where Denton was, and if she did, she would never divulge that information to him any way. She continued to try and convince Thomas that she never knew where Denton lived because he made it a point not to tell her. Denton stopped past the house periodically when he knew that Thomas was not there. He stayed in many different places and therefore didn't have a permanent place of residence.

Thomas was furious. "You're not gonna' tell me where he is, is that what you're trying to tell me? You're not gonna tell me?" He picked Marie up out of her seat by her throat, as she sat in the kitchen snapping string beans for dinner. At that moment, Marie grabbed a hold of the glass bowl that the snapped beans were in, and broke it over Thomas' head. Cadence, Forrester, and Mindy heard the crash and came running downstairs when Thomas cried out. They saw their mother like they had never seen her before; enraged and fighting back. At this point, the children were no longer afraid for their mother. Thomas smacked Marie to the floor. She picked herself up, and challenged him.

"If beatin' on me is what makes you feel like a man, Then I'm looking forward to how I'm gonna' feel after tonight. "Come on", she called out." Come on. She wanted her life back and she fought that day as if her life depended on it. There were chairs being thrown and dishes being broken; blood every where. Thomas gave Marie jolt after jolt, and Marie gave it all back, blow after blow.

"You crazy," Thomas said, as he realized that Marie was not going to quit. "Have you lost your mind?" Marie had been liberated. She had some bumps and bruises, but it was nothing that she wasn't used to. What she wasn't used to, was seeing Thomas beat up.

Thomas saw a look in Marie's eyes that day that he would never forget. Something in him told him that she was willing to die that day if that's what she had to do. And he knew that she was willing to kill him to get that very point across. Thomas saw the determination in her eyes and the resolve in her expression as he suddenly stepped away.

It became apparent to him at that instance, that had they continued on in that manner, there would surely have been a crime scene to investigate at that location. He paused for a moment to take in what was happening. Out of breath, he wiped the blood from his face, picked up all the things that had fallen out of his pant pockets, and he left. He just left. The violence had ceased that day and forever. Thomas and Marie stayed together for only a short time there after.

Chapter Thirty-Three

The Cycle

As Thomas and Marie's relationship came to an end, Cadence and Halstead's was just beginning. Ironically, Cadence fell hard for a, handsome, intelligent, and charming, young man, full of potential, and who remotely resembled Thomas in his traits. Halstead had ways that were so very different than Thomas', but yet they were almost the same. They both had a passion for the streets, almost a respect for it. They both loved to bet the horses, and play dice. And they both had a past that they couldn't get away from.

Halstead was intrigued with anything that was associated with fast money and the night life. He played the numbers and the numbers played him. They always took more from him than he could afford to give. He frequented the casinos and knew of people that could count cards; the risks that went along with that wasn't really worth his time, especially when he was just trying to have fun. Month after month he would gamble every dime that he had, as he constantly chased something that very few people ever caught.

His appetite for his drug of choice grew with every loss and with every defeat, and so would his appetite for women. They would for all intents and purposes compliment one another. He was confident in knowing that no matter how bad he messed up with Cadence, he could always find someone else, somewhere, just waiting to stroke much more than his ego. The women he was accustomed to, were obliged to kiss it and make it all better. The guilt he felt for his inadequacies, would diminish quickly—stroke, after stroke… after stroke.

Cadence acknowledged and took responsibility for the fact that she had always pacified Halstead. She always believed that he would come around one day, and be the responsible man she always thought he could be. She knew that he possessed everything he needed within him to grow into something better, something bigger, and something greater. She had been with him too long to give up now. And so she waited…and waited. She thought it sometimes simpler to blame him for all that had transpired. But that would be too easy. The truth of the matter is, that the women of her generation and those that preceded it, had made almost a ritual of choosing the wrong men. They made it a tradition to dismiss their heads and lead with their hearts.

They would blame the men that they chose to be in their lives, for lack of poor judgment, and bad decisions. They would blame them for the unmistakably regretful choices that they made. How could they not consider the finale when the tale signs were there all along? There were always signs all around. But they only saw what they chose to see, because they wanted what they saw, and love really had nothing to do with their determination.

From the very beginning, they set themselves up for failure. Her grandmother …she did it. And her mother did it too. But damn it….Cadence couldn't do it. But if it was good enough for them; why wasn't it good enough for her?

Cadence made it a habit to always look into a person's eyes. She'd read their eyes like a Jet Magazine; peering into the eyes of the women in her family lineage who were marked for life. And at first glance, she saw a cascade of emotions and despair. She saw loneliness and injury. She saw wretchedness, sacrifice, resentment, and grief. They all remembered a place in their heart were it used to be so warm and so loving; but had now grown so cold and bile.

Cadence was afraid that her life had began to look and sound just like theirs. It was so proverbial and familiar. Her eyes began to resemble that of her mother's, once full of determination and sparkling with fortitude. She became infatuated with eyes, because they truly were the windows to the soul. She studied the eyes of different women as they passed her on the street; hoping not to draw attention to herself or make or give the impression that she was precariously starring; although it was obvious that it was the case.

Their eyes told a story that was universal. A great number of them miraculously had more in common than they would ever know had they known each other. They too had suffered the consequences of loving those who were not capable of loving them back; yet they lived through it.

They managed to live through the contempt and the insolence. They lived through the disgrace, the dishonor, the lost dreams and the days of their youth gone by; just as all those before them had done. The difference would be that their techniques of endurance would differ considerably. They each prevailed in their own way. They coped on their own terms.

Some went on through it, never skipping a beat. They would decide it best if no one ever knew. There were those who made their suffering public knowledge to their family and friends, hoping that someone would say or do something that could somehow help to rescue them from their dilemma. And then there were some who decided to act as if it were happening to someone else in a far away place.

Some retreated and withdrew from life, beaten down like dogs, afraid to leave their masters. Some had indiscretions of their own, trying to give their husbands a little taste of their own discontentment. But it never meant the same to them, because the reasoning behind it was different to begin with.

Others fought back by having to leave in order to remain sane. They anticipated hopes of a new beginning and a new life. Cadence debated between the two. She would sit and wonder about which women was the stronger of the two; the one who decided to stay or the one who decided to leave?

She cried and prayed and she prayed and cried; until she realized that she could never be the type of woman who stayed. She couldn't bring herself to pass down such a disturbing practice of sorts to her daughters. She could never look into their eyes and be responsible for what she saw in them. It would never be passed down to them as it was passed down to her.… as she writes:

> *"With this gift, I give to you, the storms of life that will pass you by. I give to you a lake of lies, an ocean of disgrace and a sea of sighs.*

> *Taste my bitterness, eat my guilt, lick my falsehood, swallow my shame. Take in my anger, absorb my misery, clothe yourself with all of my blame.*

> *Now grab my hand and hold on tight, come with me to a different time. Where things are not as they used to be. There's been a mighty shift in the Paradigm.*

> *Now the storms of life that I gave to you, you now can overcome. With no reason to be afraid or even have doubts. You won't be chased because there's nothing to run from.*

> *I give you a temperament that's meek & mild. I give you hope and reason to smile. I give you joy, where there used to be pain, and its truth that shelters you from the rain.*

> *You now have a future to look forward to. I give back your dreams, now your nightmares are through. I give you a reason to recover what you lost, to claim what was taken, and the charge is no cost.*

> *I give this to you, what I didn't receive, an opportunity at love and a chance to be free. I passed on negative things through my flesh and my woes; when I was lost and confused and had no where to go.*

> *But as time went on, I was re-shaped and restored, from all that I was, because it was you I adored. My eyes have been opened, my spirit renewed, now I can pass on this gift, THE GIFT of LIFE to you.*

Cadence would never blame the women in her life for the choices they made. And if it weren't for all the sacrifices that they all made, she probably would have never considered leaving. With all that life had given her, she knew that she couldn't allow her children's lives to even remotely, look anything like her own. She made sure that they knew who they were, and that they were thankful for everyday of their lives, never taking any one thing for granted.

She had a brassiness about her, a black and whiteness about her. She was firm in her beliefs and stern in her ways. She was indeed an intricate and complex individual whose tongue would cut deep and spurned harshness at times; but her love was truly genuine and it was always and forever. Her back was straight and her stride was upright, as she always prayed:

"Lord take this sharpness from my tongue, the base out of my voice, the vibe out of my words, movement from my neck, and the pain out of my core. I know loving me will never be sweet as honey is to a bee, but just as satisfying. It's difficult to love what you can't identify with. This legacy that was passed down to me, twas' my birth right; it belonged to me. My mother, she inherited it. My nanna, embraced it through and through. My father he was also given his and that's all he ever knew. So I don't apologize for where I come from, or even for who I am; But I do apologize to whom ever I've wounded along the way.

p.s., hot buttered biscuits and jam."

Chapter Thirty-Four

A New Club

Oh! How she loved the aroma and taste of freshly made hot buttered milk biscuits right from the oven, ever so gently opened and filled with the creamiest butter and the grapest jam. Since a young girl, Cadence found that whatever was bothering her, she could remedy, if she had a biscuit or two, or maybe even three. She would relax as its soft middle would melt on her tongue, comforting her as it took its time making its way down her inviting throat.

In a time where it is almost the norm for fathers to abandon their children and pick up and start new families, avoiding the remembrance of that which was original by supplementation. Most adopted the out of sight out of mind policy. Cadence began to take notice of all the single and divorced women whom she'd run across as they broadcast their ex-husbands extra curriculum activities and the roles they didn't play in their children's lives.

One forth of their ex's paid child support and aided their children's mothers in the upbringing of their offspring without court intervention. Cadence thought to herself, "Wow." She knew in her heart that this was the type of responsibility that a man and a woman should share in equally. She felt a source of delight when she had the opportunity to meet a man who prided himself on the fact that he was genuinely interested in his children's progress in life and played a positive role in it, and there was never a price tag attached to it.

But now single herself, Cadence had a new respect for single mothers. She realized the degree of challenge that was before them; over looking the money aspect of it all. The time that it takes to instill values, to inspire morals, to persuade decency; was all so time consuming.

It was a job that would never end. The endless phone calls at work, having to be at three places at once. She knew that she wasn't able to do it alone and so she was carried by grace.

She recognized why there was such a bond between single mothers. Not only were they resilient, but they were multi-taskers, organizers, and planners. They knew how to take a little of nothing and make a lot of something. They were great at taking something small and making it into something considerable. They knew how to survive. This is what they had in common.

Cadence found herself belonging to a new club; Club Single. For a person who had been on both sides of the fence, she felt it wasn't a bad club to belong to at all. It was fulfilling and more gratifying than previously thought. She knew that it would be what she made of it, and she intended to make her singleness count for something great. She finally established that defining herself did not include her marital status. Nobody would define her, but her and her alone. Her existence would never be dictated or determined by anyone. She began to recite the single mother's proclamation:

"We've been tested and we've been tried.
We've been damaged and we've almost died. Like trees, we stand and sometimes we
bend. We help our sisters, we borrow and lend. We'll work two jobs plus overtime, this
is our pledge, our sacred bond. We are conquerors, that's what we are…
We are conquerors.

Cadence couldn't see the forest for the bills; quick hand her a pill and a glass of water. She couldn't sleep, her mind was racing, it was four o'clock in the morning, and she had to be to work by eight. Give her peace so she can rest through all this mess. As a vision interrupted her sleep.

It was a dark and foggy night. Cadence came to a bend in the road. Her sight was cloudy, but she proceeded without caution. She knew that she really couldn't see but she continued on anyway.

Carefully she stepped off of what felt like a curb. She began to cross the road in darkness with her hands out stretched in front of her. Without warning, she heard a car that was approaching fast. Within inches, the car stopped just before the two collided. There were loud sounds of horns blowing and bright lights flashing. Cadence was overcome by her blindness and her fear.

She was able to see only shadows, but still she advanced on—deciding to go further and take the risk. She had a set mind that convinced her that no matter what it looked like, or didn't look like, because her vision had been altered; that she was able to see what she needed to see. The object before her was obscured and camouflaged to look like something other than what it really was. With her mental eye, she transformed that thing that was; into what she thought it could be.

She saw drab, faded, and dowdy colors. Discernibly, she began to add her own tints of whites, yellows, and oranges, to the black and reds which were already present. The colors ran into one another and began to turn into shades of brown and gray. the radiance began to vanish. The vivacity was gone. What a sometimes perilous task we take on with the addition or subtraction, from and or to an original thing, enhancing or destroying it.

Seven spoke out to Cadence. You know me, we've established a long term relationship. The time up until now has been rather difficult, but you continued to wait for me. You've released me from all my debts. I've been let go from any future liabilities or responsibilities to the one whom it was granted. You were designed for my benefit. I can't and won't look back.... ever again. I've grieved long enough.

Chapter Thirty-Five

‖‖

The Family Virus

Cadence was her own worst critic. She witnessed the world evolve into a matrix of outlets, where everyone was plugged into a system and not into each other. Cadence felt the disconnection more and more each day. Although she was always a complicated individual of strong will, her perception of herself was slightly different. She was really a simple person in her own right with ideas that were simple.

She wanted to re-establish herself and make herself over again. She had insights that would take almost a miracle to come to pass. But somewhere in 6 + 1, she started to believe in miracles. She had a burden for the unfortunate, and a hankering for educating the youth. She often asked herself, "what gives me the right to have these visions and to dream these dreams?" Who do I think I am? She sensed that the visions she had only made sense to her, and the outside world could never grasp her ideas. Her faith allowed her to think bigger and broader.

In order for her to become a better extension of herself, she knew that it was significant to her transformation that she look at every aspect of who she was, and not just those things that would be so obvious. She was quite troubled about the new me society. She was disturbed with a culture that had become totally self absorbent in all of its ways. She saw that society was dangerously learning to put self first. She believed that it was the beginning stages of the breakdown of the family, and at last, country.

"Who do I think I am, defining myself, to never have to deny myself, trying to recreate myself in a generation entangled in a cyclone of texting. Entwined in emailing, derailed in a blackmailing tradition. Swallowing it whole, ultimately destroying it, by replacing it, and never restoring it again?"

Cadence remembered back to a time when money was harder to come by, but life was a lot simpler. The more that we have and are able to do, the less we care to do for each other. The division is unmistakable. We come and go at different times, and nobody really has time to even eat together anymore. Our lives have become unattached and we no longer take responsibility for one another anymore. Is it solely because our identities have meshed with technology; distinctively and superficially, merging with the GI's, blackberries, playstations, xboxes, and ipods, how tasty;

"I've asked you over and over again not to answer your cell phone while we are having dinner, or out with the family. It seems we are never able to spend any quality time together without being interrupted by your cell. And you continuously refuse to turn it off. With every free moment that you get, you're spending it with your blue tooth. You are up at all hours of the night playing the Wii, surfing the net, engaging in unacceptable chat room behavior. And our children are processing these negative manners of conduct."

She continues to journal: "No longer second to God, or third to the job...go long and catch this. A relationship will not stand on its own. We transfer our thoughts, our hopes, and our dreams to Microsoft. But in the real world we are not fully protected and we will become infected with a virus that Norton can't fix. 5 + 2, you've exhausted me; my strategies, my ideas, have all been depleted. You've left me with no other alternative but to desert them and take on new ones. The views and the plans that I once had for myself and my family were apparently not the same plans and ideas that I should have had for myself. I used to be a story book but now I am a blank page. How do I begin again?"

"When I think back over my life, and all the trying times; the times I could've chose your way, but instead I chose my own. You lifted me out of the maw and the clay, you've been my protector all along the way. I know there is no pit so deep, that you, oh God aren't deeper."

Cadence had come to grips with those things and those people that had come and gone, in and out of her life. But the one thing that has always remained constant, was her passion. "Why won't my passion leave me?" she questioned. They have overtaken her since conception and she could never escape them. When she thought of them, her eyes well up, her heart begins to flutter, her psyche becomes restless, and she'd become uneasy within her soul. No, I am not easily swayed. Her thoughts would belong to her and her alone. She owned them. She was neither weak nor naïve. Yes, she weebled and she wobbled but she didn't fall down.

Cadence had been attacked on all sides, surrounded by that which aimed to take her life, but grace had defeated it. So why was she so passionate about the natural world and the injustices that subdued it without bond? Why was she concerned with vegetation and animal life, and the suffering of those all around the world? Why does she allow these things and their circumstances to influence her mood? Cadence found long ago that they were all a part of the same story; her story, my story, our story. And they were all a part of the same circle of life. Their lives and deaths were contingent upon hers, and hers theirs.

She found that she could see a glimpse into her own life; only if she could step outside of it. As she saw what it looked like to be on the outside looking in; the warmth of her tears streamed down the sides of her face in awe. It wasn't within her character to just look at the question at hand, but the origin of the question in relation to the history of the matter.

She saw her life as it use to be and as it is now. She saw the lives of her future grandchildren and theirs. She saw the value system of the existing generations and those that will proceed, and its diminishing factors.

Cadence became cognizant of the belief that love didn't live anywhere anymore. But what did it all have to do with seven? Well 8 − 1 is the year that Cadence, like so many others, came to an end of an era in which they had succumbed under the scrupulous and immoral plague that had infiltrated country, community, homes, and their very lives.

Seven was the year where so many things that had burdened her and held her in confinement, by law would now release her. For Cadence, she understood the seven Pillars of Wisdom to be virtue, knowledge, temperance, patience, godliness, brotherly kindness, and charity. She understood that they would provided her with support and a foundation to uphold her. She understood that without them she would be crippled for life.

Cadence felt the misdirection, the hurt, and the confusion, that was a great part of the environment in which she lived. She understood that trials built character, paying homage to all who paid the ultimate sacrifice. The quality of her life would span far greater then theirs, not because of who she was, but because of who God made them to be. So yes, she was passionate about the fact that so many had forgotten that there was definitely a struggle with human kindness that was very much alive and that its principles had become subtle and complacent.

She lived in a time where committed relationships were almost extinct. Because the world will not embrace what their minds will not allow them to believe. So they can not believe in unity if all they see is division. They can't identify with love if they've only experienced conflict and dissension. But the world was created in such a way that it was intended that no one aspect of it could operate independently without the others.

A great author wrote, "If I speak with the tongues of men and of angels, and have not love, I am become as sounding brass, or a tinkling symbol. And if I have the gift of prophecy, understanding all mysteries, and all knowledge. And if I have all faith, and could remove mountains, but have not love, I am nothing. Love bears, believes, hopes and endures all things. So where faith, hope, and love abides, the greatest of these……..is love." 1 Corin 13 But oh how predictable is the world.

"So if I wake and rise one day, and no longer like what I see, I have the freedom to abandon you and live without penalty. I loved you yesterday, I did, and loved you the day before. But I woke up early one morning and found that I didn't love you anymore. So I'll be leaving now, and you don't have to worry, and don't you wear a frown, I'll be gone in a hurry. I may be passing through you know, I mean from time to time, my brand new life gets all my money, and the old one can't get a dime."

Chapter Thirty-Six

Identity

"CC" recalled the rainy nights she'd lay awake listening to all creation; the winds thrusting against the outside of her home. Droplets of rain formed a unique pattern against the siding amidst the stream of air. She'd listen until it began to sound like a symphony; the irrigated drips assimilating the whistling wind, musically drumming every other beat upon the worn siding. She lay there until the winds were finally exhausted; until everything became still and the calm emerged.

Her index fingers from both hands rose to meet her ears, smothering any chance of hearing even the smallest sounds except the sounds from within her. Candace's life had never been a torch, but a flame. She never desired to be seen but had the gift of lighting a room. She could never understand why those she came into contact with were always somehow drawn to her. She never wanted them to, and it was sometimes burdensome because she had so many concerns and unresolved issues of her own. Why couldn't they see that? Why couldn't they see that she had nothing left to give?

She'd had a gift for motivating and encouraging others, but had grown weary of it. She'd been encouraged and motivated by those close to her as well, but it didn't quite seem to be in the same aspect. She knew in her heart, that she couldn't stop being whatever she was to others because she felt insufficient. But she had to admit, that lifting someone else's spirit always seemed to lift hers. It permitted her to take her mind off of herself and her situation for a while. And it would be just what she needed.

It is definitely easier said than done. She sat inside her car in front of the Lincoln Middle School, on the corner of Seventh and Poplar, waiting for Kote and Zauria to be dismissed from school. As she studied the crossing guard, she began to think about all her shoulda, coulda, woulda's. It was the middle of May, temperatures were in the mid seventies and the weather was in comparison to a lovely fair day in early June. She quietly studied the expressions and body language of the children as they were released from school, one class after the other.

Cadence particularly noticed the children who were off by themselves and walking alone. It was clear that they were not a part of any particular group. They probably came to school alone, and most likely, that's how they would leave. But what were they thinking? Their eyes told a story of misplacement. They wanted to belong, but where did they fit? All the other children seemed to be content and well adjusted in their relationships with their peers, and also with their lives. Cadence knew better then anyone that it's not always as it seems.

She knew the children that were pretty much a part of a group, were even themselves divided within the group. There were those who drew people to them. There were those who were drawn to other people. And there were others who just slid in wherever they could, on the premise of being recognized through the affiliation of both groups.

The eyes of those who drew people imaged confidence, buoyancy, and self assurance. The energy that illuminated from them was also absorbed by those drawn to them. Those who were drawn, reflected the admiration of those they were drawn to; fighting for their own identity and wanting in some ways to be like those whom were drawing them. There was a combining of their own energy with that of the energy that they were absorbing from those they were drawn. There was a merging of the two identities. Those who were affiliated by association only, used none of their own energy, but sought the energy from those around them, allowing the world to create identities for them.

As a youth, the world saw Cadence as belonging to the first group. During most times, she would agree. Those that belonged to the first group definitely had a magnetic strength. They exhibited vigor and drive. They produced a powerful force from within that was natural and could be seen by most. But as time went on, those belonging to the first group, during any course of their lives, would have spells where all sources of power and strength had been depleted; and those depending on their energy would be left out to fend for themselves.

There were many times in Cadence's life where she grew weary of not being able to replenish her source of energy and it got the best of her. When she needed to revive and rejuvenate herself, she often found that she was alone. She found herself wanting at times to be like those of the third group. She'd wanted so much to use all the energy from those around her, thus reserving her own. But who would she be?

She concluded that those of the second group wanted to please those of the first group; wanting nothing more than to prove to them that they too were operating off of a source of ability and strength and would be great successors. They wanted to be recognized as equals but they would settle for the next best thing.

They wanted what they thought the first group had; popularity, reputation, stability, and admiration, which was their definition of success. It would take them almost forever to understand that in order to want someone else's life, you had to become an heir to everything else in their lives. Their joys and pains would become yours. Their heartaches and short comings you would also adopt. And if you changed one thing about your life… you will have changed everything.

Children are the greatest mimickers on the face of the planet. They become so many people and so many things before they actually become themselves. They know they've been given something special because so many people throughout their life times have assured them of it. They knew that for some reason people were fond of them, and when people liked them, they tended to experience more opportunities then the average person. And how they used their talents would say everything about who they were on the inside.

From the very start, they'd use their talents in whatever capacity they saw fit. It meant that consequently, depending on who they really were deep inside, would dictate how their skills would be used. When Cadence looked into those children's eyes she could tell which of those belonging to the first group would lead by their instincts and the second group would lead by doubt.

Cadence had a feel for those who could draw people, but had chosen to be led by their instincts rather then their doubt. They would head in a direction of manipulation, which would capitalize off of all those who wished to be in their presence. They would use them to feed their egos, meet their needs, and take from them what they were already willing to give.

Cadence saw her associates and herself in those children that day; even down to the very clothes that they were wearing. Fashion had reintroduced itself to a new generation, and though there was really nothing new under the sun that had been created, it was exciting to see it all again. She began to reflect back on her living and how it had brought her to this place where love, laughter, and order no longer resided; if it ever did.

Cadence was defiant at times, but for the most part, would be led by her heart. She was different that way. But her way was painful because she wore her feelings on her shoulders as a badge of honor. She spoke of misdeeds and felt very strongly about injustices against anyone and anything. She was probably very much the activist or politician in a previous life; standing up for the rights of others and against all those who violated those rights. She was liked by most and hated by few.

She was motivated and driven by the passage of her grandmother and mother. She was determined that if her journey were to bear a resemblance to theirs in any capacity, she would make it count for something other than heartache. Cadence promised that it would not be in vain. It wasn't for sure why the world grieved her so or why her highs always became her lows.

Cadence was institutionalized like many she'd known. She wanted to escape her circumstances but fear of failure and the unknown held her captive. Her relationship with Halstead began with great uncertainty and its ending would be improbable.

Chapter Thirty-Seven

||||||||||||||||||||||||||||||||||||||||||||||||||||||||||||||||||||||||||||||||||||||||||||||||||||||||||||||||||||||||||

The Stranger

Growing up was anything but a walk in a park where Halstead was concerned. The circumstances surrounding his birth would prove to be a most challenging one, and so it would seem to dictate the unfortunate events that would follow him throughout the rest of his life.

Halstead was born to Tracey Jean Walker, T.J. for short, and entered this world when his mother was just the tender age of sixteen. As the story goes; one night T.J. had gotten permission to stay the night with a very close friend of hers, named Gracey. T. J. and Gracey were both the only children born to their parents. Their parents had known one another and grown up together, and so it was only befitting for T.J. and Gracey to follow suit.

It was three months after T.J.'s fifteenth birthday, at about 9:15pm. She and Gracey were walking home from the Saddie Hawkins Day Dance at the school. The weather outside was pretty mild and Neither T.J.'s or Gracey's parents drove; and so it was common for the girls to walk home together. It was a little after dark and they'd just gotten finish saying their goodbyes to friends before they started their seven block walk. They lived only one block away from each other, and were about three blocks away from their homes when a stranger in a Taxi Cab drove up slowly as they walked.

The lamp post on that particular block was out, and from what they could see in the darkness, the stranger looked awful big and grizzly. His head, lips, and face were covered with mounds of dark hair and he had a pair of dark beady eyes to match. They were very close together atop a rather large nose.

As he pulled up, they noticed an arm that was dressed in red plaid, out stretched from his car, with hair shown on his wrist as he held something in his hand. He inched along side the curb until he came to a complete stop. He rolled down his window, and asked the girls politely if they new the person that was on the flyer that he had in his hand. He said that the girl on the flyer was his daughter and that she had been missing for two weeks.

T.J, concerned over hearing this, moved in a little closer toward the car to get a better look at the flyer. She advanced to the car door's window in an attempt to study the flyer. The expression on her face changed dramatically when she realized that the flyer had only a picture of a silhouette. There was no face and there was no body—only a shadow of a person.

T.J. began to question the makeup of the flyer when she heard a clicking noise. She recognized the funny shaped cold piece of metal that the stranger held beneath her chin. He said to her in a voice that only she could hear, "Just act normal and calmly ask your friend to come closer to look at the flyer. T.J. was paralyzed and was unable to say a word. "Do it," he ordered. "Or I'll shoot you right here and now."

T.J. called out to Gracey in a trembling and unstable voice. "Gracey, come see this." Gracey came over slowly to the cab when she sensed something was wrong in T.J.'s voice. "What's wrong, what is it?" she asked as she approached the car. She was instantly stricken with fear, when she got close enough to the car and saw the stranger who resembled a lumber jack. He had a black barreled gun pointed at T.J.'s neck. She too, had become paralyzed, and was unable to move or say a word.

The stranger instructed Gracey to get into the back seat of the cab or he wouldn't hesitate to shoot T.J. Terrified, Gracey slowly opened the door and climbed in. He then commanded that T.J. open the passenger side door and climb in quickly. T. J. had only a second to think. She looked at the stranger, then looked around and thought of making a run for it. But she saw that there was a plexi glass partition separating the back of the cab from the front, and the stranger had locked Gracey in the back.

T. J. was petrified. Something deep down in her stomach told her that if she got into that cab, they would probably never see their families or even each other again. She looked at Gracey crying uncontrollably in the back seat and saw that shear panic had overcome her. She opened the door very cautiously and looked around in hopes of seeing someone who could help them.

The stranger became irritated at T.J. as his voice began to anxiously escalate, "Get …in… right now or I'll drive off with your pretty little friend and we'll have a party without you." T.J. shook her head no and then got in.

T.J. got inside the cab. The stranger then handed her a pair of handcuffs and asked her to put them on. "Please mister, why do you need two of us? You can keep me, you don't need Gracey," T.J. pleaded. The stranger observed how protective T.J. was of Gracey. And he knew that she would probably do anything to defend her.

Cynically, the stranger responded, "Gracey huh…what a lovely name. What's your name?" he asked. T.J. became silent. "What's your name girl?" he growled.

"T. J.," she said.

"T.J., what kind of name is that for a pretty thing like you?" asked the strange man as he brushed his hand across T.J.'s cheek.

"It's short for Tracey Jean," she answered nervously.

"Tracey Jean now that's more like it," the stranger smiled as he handed her a pair of handcuffs. "Well Tracey, be a doll and put these bracelets on for me and attach them to the handle on the door. Can you do that for me doll?"

He saw an ocean of tears filling T.J. eyes and said, "Come on now, there's no need to be afraid. I'm not gonna' hurt you or your friend. I just didn't feel like being alone tonight and I wanted a little company. There's nothing wrong with that is there? We're just gonna take a little ride down the road a ways, and we'll be back before you know it…I promise," the strange man stated in a peaceful, almost genuine voice.

"You promise?" T.J. asked naively.

"I promise," the stranger repeated. T.J. refused to put the handcuffs on.

"I wanna sit with Gracey, mister," T.J. said. The stranger's expression became cold and he began to talk with clinched teeth.

"Put the bracelets on now." When T.J. looked into the stranger's face, she frantically started to put the handcuffs on and was unable to hold back the tears.

The stranger drove for about an hour or so down a dark and deserted road that led to a remote place in a wooded area. Gracey had been crying the entire time, while T.J. just sat silently, trying to remain calm, as not to insight violence from the stranger.

The car finally stopped. They weren't able to see much as the stranger got out, went to the trunk of the car, and removed a small lantern. He lit the lantern, walked about five feet from where they were, and hung it from one of the branches of the tree. He came back to the cab and opened the back door where Gracey was. "Please," Gracey begged. "Don't hurt me. Please mister, please let us go." The stranger continued to reach in to pull Gracey out. Gracey scooted herself all the way over to the other side of the vehicle, as far away from the stranger as she possible could.

The stranger, emerged his body, mid-way into the back seat of the vehicle, reached in far and pulled Gracey out by her feet, dragging her out the cab and over to the tree. Gracey began to scream and was hysterically trying to free herself, kicking and punching wildly at the stranger. The stranger punched and slapped Gracey until she was too tired to fight anymore.

The stranger unfastened his pants and pulled them completely down to his ankles. T. J. watched from inside the cab while the stranger proceeded to sadistically violate Gracey. He silenced her screams by holding one hand over her mouth. T.J began to viciously kick at the car door window, trying to kick out the glass. With no success, she tirelessly looked up to see the stranger towering over Gracey as he engaged in an up and down motion. T.J. began to die inside when she realized that she was not able to help her best friend.

Gracey became semi-unconscious as the stranger continued to get his fill. When he finished, he got up and let go a big sigh of relief. He turned around, bent over and picked up a large stone from the ground, and held it up above his head. As T.J.'s eyes grew larger, she pleaded from inside the Cab. The stranger turned to look directly at T.J. with a crazed and smug look on his face, turned back and plunged the stone down onto Gracey's head, smashing in her skull.

He stood there for a moment, gloating on what he had done. He walked slowly back to the Cab and opened the door. Right away he punched T.J. and knocked her out. When she came to, the stranger was upon her, committing the same sadistic acts, that he'd committed on Gracey. With a bloody and pounding head, ringing in her ears, and blurred vision, T.J. was unable to stop the stranger from humping about her body and grunting like a wild animal.

She tried to scream once. And then she tried to scream twice. On the third time, she felt her lungs fill with air that was concentrated with the aroma of farm animals. All of a sudden, T.J. let out a scream that shook heaven and pierced the atmosphere. And just as she was about to give into her demise; she looked up with surprise and her scream became silent. It was Gracey. Somehow she managed to will herself to survive, when she heard T.J.'s screams.

The stranger turned to see what had startled T.J. Just as he turned, he slightly lifted his body off T.J.'s. Quickly, a shaky and unsteady T.J. rolled from under the stranger, as Gracey threw the lantern towards the stranger. The stranger jumped up as he saw Gracey aim the lantern at him and then release it from her hand. But he was not fast enough to escape the fateful inferno. The stranger became engulfed in flames. He yelled and screamed as his clothes began to melt like plastic upon his body as he ran off into the darkness of the night.

Moments after the stranger ran off, Gracey collapsed and became unresponsive to T.J.'s desperate appeal. "Wake up Gracey, wake up. Help is coming, okay. T.J. assured her. T.J. dragged herself back to the cab and picked up the radio that was attached to the dashboard. She had never operated a car radio before. So she began to twist knobs and push buttons as she called out for help over the intercom. Suddenly she heard someone asking what her position was.

Overcome with emotion and weak from the blows to her head, T.J. began to speak sluggishly, "I don't know what position we're in. My friend and I have been kidnapped, beaten and raped. "We're in the woods," she went on to explain. "I don't know where we are, about an hour from where I live. We're on some type of farm. Please come quick," she begged as she began to sob. "Gracey", she said as she began to fade. "Gracey..is hurt.. real bad and she won't wake up. Please somebody. Please."

"Keep the line open please, hello", the voice from the radio responded, "Stay with me OK and keep the line open while we check for all the farms on the outskirts of town. Can you hear me? Help is on the way. Please respond so that I know that you're alright," the voice from the radio said. There was no response. The line went dead as T.J. slipped into unconsciousness.

There was an all points bulletin issued throughout the county. Twenty five minutes later the girls were found across city limits. Federal, State, and Local authorities were notified in addition to the paramedics—and arrived promptly. T.J., Gracey, and even the stranger were taken to the hospital. The stranger was found about a half mile up the road, suffering from third degree burns.

Once they arrived at the hospital they were met at the emergency room's entrance by several cars of family members and friends. Both T.J. and Gracey's parents were there. Also present were a couple of teachers, a few neighbors, and the pastor of St. Luke's Church.

T.J. was drifting in and out of consciousness and could only hear stifled voices. Her vision was blurry and she really couldn't focus on any individual's faces. Her parents were walking closely to the gurney as they transported her to examining room #7. The doctors explained to her parents that they had come as far as they could, and that they would have to stay in the waiting area.

T.J. who was suffering from shock had to be slightly sedated. She no longer felt the excruciating pain in her arms and shoulder that she suffered when the stranger held her arms partly over her head. The pain that was throbbing from both of her upper thighs and her pelvic bone as the stranger inflicted pain as he forced her legs apart and placed both his knees on her thighs, immobilizing them—was no longer there. Her insides no longer felt as though they were yanked from her body, T.J. thought to herself, "Whatever they just gave me is working just wonderfully."

She felt a hand holding her hand. She could hear her mother's soothing voice saying, "I'm right here baby. Everything is goin' to be just fine. We love you T.J. We love you sweetie. Mommy's gonna be right here when you come out. Okay? We'll be right here." But T.J. had no idea that her mother was up the hall and in the waiting room. All she wanted to do was sleep.

She was examined by three different doctors. They took blood samples, x-rays, and ultra sounds. They did a rape analysis on her and a series of other test for sexually transmitted diseases. There were officers from the Special Victims Unit on standby to question her about the events that took place that evening. They were informed that she would not be in any condition to answer questions until the morning. She suffered extensive internal damage, a concussion, a fractured pelvis, and the blow to the side of her head caused her to lose some hearing in her left ear. That night her parents spent the entire evening at her side.

Morning came rather quickly. T.J. awoke and saw her parents asleep in her room. She realized it wasn't the room she was used to waking up in. She realized that her worst fear had come true and it wasn't all just a dream. The stranger was real. The cab was real. She began to get agitated. She wanted to see Gracey to make sure she was alright. "Where is Gracey?" she started to ask as she cleared her throat from the sedatives. She looked over at her parents and called out to her mother. "Mom, mom." Her mother awoke to her voice.

"T.J., thank God, oh we worried so. Don't try and speak right now, just rest."

"Mom," T.J. continued, "Gracey, I want to see Gracey."

"It's important for you to rest right now. They'll be plenty of time for that," her mother explained.

"I'm fine mom, I just need to see Gracey, just for a minute. How is she?" Her mother looked down at her as she ran her fingers through her bang.

"Gracey hasn't awaken yet baby. But I'm sure when she wakes up, you'll be one of the first to get a chance to talk to her as much as you like."

Two Detectives from the Special Victims Unit came in to talk to T.J. All T.J. could think about was Gracey. She was a bit cooperative in the beginning, but as her mind kept thinking back on the terrible things the stranger did to her and Gracey, especially Gracey, she could no longer continue on with the questioning. Every answer from that point on was; I don't know. I don't remember.

Four days had passed and Gracey had been placed on life support. During the attack she suffered severe head trauma which caused bleeding and swelling to her brain. The doctors informed Gracey's parents that she had no brain activity at all, and that there was nothing more they could do for her. The family and doctors met and agreed that she would be taken off life support on the very next day. She breathed on her own for a couple of days and then she stopped. T.J. was absolutely distraught. She found it difficult to even think of a world without Gracey in it, especially hers. T.J. immediately shut down emotionally and ceased speaking. It was decided by the doctor's and the parents of Gracey and T.J., that it would be in the best interest of T.J.if she not attend Gracey's services.

Chapter Thirty-Eight

||||||||||||||||||||||||||||||||||||||||||||||||||||||||||||||||||||||||||||||||||||||||||||||||||||||||||||||||||||||||||||||||||||||||||||||

Halstead

Almost two months or so had passed, and it was time for T. J. to go back to the hospital for a follow up visit. It was at that time that the doctors found a change in T.J.'s condition. After more tests were done, they discovered that T.J. was seven weeks with child. The doctors were astonished. They immediately spoke with T.J.'s parents and the church council in regard to her sensitive predicament. Her parents were mortified at the news as they wept. Her parents automatically suggested that it would **be** best if T.J. would relocate until the baby was born. It was mutually agreed upon that the baby would be put up for adoption because abortion would never be an option.

T.J.'s parents and the doctor would now have to make known and discuss the matter at once with T.J. But the question was how would they approach this very delicate matter given all that she had already been through? How would she react to the news? They had a couple of doctor's on standby in case they needed to restrain or sedate her. Doctor Smalls and T.J.'s parents came into the examination room where T.J. had just finished dressing and was now sitting on the table as she waited to be dismissed. Her mother and father knocked and came into the room with a solemn and sober look on their faces. The doctors entered next and said, "There is something that we need to talk to you about T.J.", said Doctor Smalls. With everything that you've been through this past month, I just want to commend you on how well you're doing. Your progress is absolutely astounding.

During your examination, as he paused, we found something that um"…and before he could finish the sentence, T.J. interrupted. "I'm pregnant right? I know." They all looked at each other in amazement with their mouths open, first of all to hear her speak for the first time in months. Secondly, they were over taken by the fact that she knew.

T.J's mother immediately held and comforted her. "Don't you worry about a thing, everything is gonna be fine." We thought that it would be a good idea if you could go stay with grandma for a while, you know, just until all of this is over. We'll make sure the baby finds a good home and good parents to love it."

A home,...parents", T.J. snapped. "I'm not giving my baby up mom." Her mother leaned back in shock.

"What are you saying? You can't possibly be considering keeping this child T.J.?" her father stated.

T.J. began to get very upset. She began to speak with tears in her eyes and determination in her voice. "Yes… I am going to keep my baby. She began to talk solemnly, "Gracey saved my life", she stated as the room became silent. And I don't know why I'm still here and she's not. I wouldn't be here if it weren't for Gracey. And for some reason she died, and now I have this life growing inside me. Can anybody explain that to me? All I know is, instead of looking at this baby and remembering all the horror, I'll look at it and I'll think about Gracey."

"Erum," Doctor Smalls said as he cleared his voice. He saw that the situation was escalating and felt that he would intervene. "Ok, I think we should pick up this discussion at a later date. Right now we want to try to be as calm as possible. T.J., would you please have a seat in my office dear. I just want to have a few words with your parents, and then we'll be right out." T.J. got down from the table and proceeded out of the room with the assistance of another doctor. As the doctor closed the door behind her, her mother started expressing her concerns right away.

"There is no way we are going to raise that demon child. She is not capable of dealing with all of this and neither are we." T.J.'s father, saw that his wife was clearly upset. He came closer to his wife and placed his hand on her shoulder. "Doc, this is an impossible situation. What exactly do you think we should do? We want to do what's best for T.J., but as you can see, she's not thinking clearly. She wants to have the baby of the man who killed her best friend, and raped, beat, and almost killed her. We will be willing to get her all the help that she needs, but we cannot raise that man's seed," he said firmly.

"You can't or you won't?" Doctor Smalls asked. At this point, I don't think any of us should be making any hasty decisions," the doctor responded. "We must remember that T.J. has experienced a great loss. Her best friend was savagely beaten to death and raped as she witnessed it. But she also witnessed her friend's heroism and successful attempt to save her life. For T.J., this baby doesn't quite represent all of the pre-existing horrors that we understand it to be. To her it is a representation of yes, both good and evil. But In her mind she can offset the transgressions of the offender with the honorable and loyal actions of someone she loved deeply. And it will be through the birth of this baby that she tends to pay homage to her so that she will forever be reminded of the ultimate sacrifice that was given—her best friend's life.

"But is that normal doctor?" her mother asked.

"I'm afraid that under these extraordinary circumstances, I believe it is. If T.J. is to fully recover from this devastating ordeal, then we need to assist her in every way possible in finding her way back to normalcy. It is our job to help her put everything in its prospective place. If nothing else, the thought of having this baby has brought T.J. from out that dark place that wouldn't allow her to speak. T.J. hadn't spoken a word since Gracey's death and I'm not too sure she would've ever spoken again. It's quite possible that T.J. would have continued to separate herself from the world never again returning back to you completely as she once was. In my line of work I see a lot of things. And I tell you, from the injuries that she has sustained internally from her attacker that night, there is no scientific way that anyone can explain this pregnancy. Her uterus had incurred significant damage and had to be reconstructed. So when I tell you it is a sheer miracle that she is even alive, let alone that she could conceive with so much damage to her reproductive system, I'm being modest."

"Well what do you suggest we do?" her father asked.

"I suggest the both of you give this a lot of thought. And remember that it's not necessarily what we want that matters, but what's important for T.J. We have to be open to her needs and what she's feeling… and God will do the rest."

Needless to say, T.J. did go to live with her grandmother. And eight months later she gave birth to a seven pound seven ounce baby boy. Unfortunately, she never did finish school because there weren't many options for an unwed mother during that time. T.J. had given her baby boy the name Halstead. A name derived from a town in Essex, England—Hal (meaning given above) and stead (a place). She felt the name befitting him as she hoped with all her heart that he would rise above the stigma of his conception and overcome the obstacles of this world and be placed where God would have him. From the first moment that T.J. laid eyes on him; his skin as soft as cotton, and eyes so convincingly pure—she knew without a shadow of a doubt that she had made the right decision to keep him.

T. J. now twenty one years of age and officially legal, decided to leave her grandmother's and come back up North to her home town. There weren't many jobs in Canton, where she lived with her grandmother, and T.J.s only hope for employment was to relocate. It was hard for a girl in the 1940's to find a decent job, especially an unwed mother.

Nobody in Fayettville really knew her whole story, and that's how she liked it. People speculated about her, to the point where they began to make their own stories up about that night with their own versions of what happened. Because of the degree and the nature of the crime, it was not made public knowledge about her pregnancy. But people had assumed especially, when she came back into town five years later with a child around five years old. There were all sorts of rumors circulating. The one that she'd heard involved she and Gracey hitch hiking to some hole in the wall hotel, where they would turn tricks. Their pimp was suppose to be the one who killed Gracey and got T.J. pregnant.

Although the rumors weren't true, they were still very hurtful because people believed them. And if they believed them, people would assume that both Tracey Jean and Gracey got what they deserved. T.J's grandma would always tell her that there were always gonna' be people afraid of what they really couldn't understand. And that it was O.K. to be afraid at times, as long as the fear you had didn't inflict pain or hurt onto anyone else.

T.J. new that she had been away long enough and that it was time she and Halstead came out of hiding and went home. She needed to find a school for Halstead to attend since he was old enough to start Kindergarten. She thought it would be pretty cool for him to go to the same elementary school that she and Gracey attended. She wondered if some of the teachers that taught her were still there. She wanted them both to be accepted into the community but she knew that there was a possibility that they would not be. She wanted Halstead to have a chance at life. She knew that he was a child wise beyond his years, and a blessing to anyone that was in his presence.

T.J. moved back in with her parents whom had never seen Halstead until then, but welcomed the two of them, even though T.J. could sense some distance between them. It took quite some time for them to warm up to Halstead, but eventually they came to accept him and they loved him the best they could.

T.J. wanted to give Halstead a chance at living a normal life. She was concerned that she didn't acquire the skills needed in order to land a job. And she desperately wanted and needed a way to meet their financial needs, if she was ever to get out and find a place of her own.

T.J. had been unpacked for about a week when she decided to go into town to seek employment. There were plenty of stares and whispers, leading T.J. to believe that they all knew who she was. She was told day after day that she would be called if an opening became available. It had been two months and nobody called. T. J. was at her ends wits. Her parents had worked at the same generic bread company for years. The company had just sent out notification of a lay off that was coming near the end of the month. They were losing customers to competition by the new Wonderful Bread Company that opened one mile east of Godfrey St.

It was 2:45pm, one year later, and it was time to pick Halstead up from school. T.J. hadn't quite gotten use to picking him up towards the end of the day yet, since his last year's kindergarten class would let out at 12:30pm on a half a day schedule.

As she proceeded to wait out in the school yard for Halstead and his class to be brought out by his teacher; a gentleman with a somewhat familiar face came over to her and spoke. "Hi, I think I know you. I believe we went to school together. My name is Blake, Blake Saunders," as he extends his hand during his introduction. "And your name is," he waited for T.J. to help him remember.

"I'm Tracey Jean, but my friends call me T.J.," she replied.

"Well Tracey," he replied in a very deep voice, "I hope you'll consider me a friend of yours one day," he continued, "I haven't seen you in a long while. Where have you been?"

"I've been out of town"

"Yeah, I heard that you left town and was like, somewhere in California, never to return. What brings you back here?"

"California, pwew! not hardly, try Canton."

"Really?"

"Yes, really," they both chuckle. "Actually, there weren't many jobs in Canton. And besides that, I missed my folks. I needed to come back to try and make a life for me and my son." T.J. answered as she anticipated a negative response from Blake.

"Woe....your son? I had no idea you were married," Blake being very careful in how he chooses his words.

"I'm not, T.J. interrupts, it's just the two of us."

"Oh," well, what's his name?"

"Halstead,... his name is Halstead." Pointing to the building, "You here to pick him up?"

"Yeah, he started a couple of weeks ago."

"How is that working out for the both of you?" T.J., shocked at the fact that he was still standing there showing such kindness and seemingly legitimate concern, "I-I-I," she stuttered, Its working out okay."

"So you goin' to be in town for a while?"

"Possibly, if I can find a job."

"You mind if I ask you a question?"

"You're asking a lot of questions. I don't know if I want to answer anymore." She pauses for a moment as she looks down. "Okay, I'll answer one more."

"Is he the reason you left?" T.J. looked at Blake and reluctantly responded by nodding her head, "Yeah."

Blake thought it was a good time to change the subject. "Well I'm here picking up my little nephew, my sister works long hours. Anyway, um, I'd really like to continue this conversation later when we're not pressed for time. You think that might be possible?"

T.J. was almost speechless. She stood there for a moment and just looked at Blake. She glanced at his flawlessly shaped hairline, trimmed mustache and side burns. His skin, the color of black walnut, and his lips were plump and even darker. "If that's a problem, I won't trouble you, Blake responded to T.J.'s distraction.

"No, I think that would be fine," she finally responded.

"Great, what are you doing tomorrow, if that's not too soon?" T.J. shook her head as to answer, nothing.

"Your over at your parent's right?" he asked.

"Yep, that's where I'll be."

"O.K. then, I'll see you tomorrow around 7:30pm."

"7:30pm sounds good," T.J. confirmed. Both Blake's nephew and T.J.'s son were brought out with their class by their teachers. Blake and T.J. said goodbye.

Like clockwork, Blake arrived the next evening promptly, with desert in hand.

"Hi, what you got there?"

"Oh nothing much, just my famous Red Velvet cake with cream cheese frosting."

"Wow, who made that?"

"You're lookin' at em."

"No, you bake?" T.J. asked in disbelief.

"Why yes I do. You got something against a man who bakes?"

"No, I don't, I'm just a tad bit jealous. I have a hard time just boiling water."

"Well, I guess we'll have to fix that now won't we? You'll have to allow me to give you a few lessons."

"I'll look forward to that."

It was a beautiful night in early September, still officially summer. The night was quiet as the crickets harmonized. The atmosphere was soft and airy as the stars were in sync and illuminated the sky. T.J. took the Red Velvet Cake inside and prepared a nice cold pitcher of lemonade and a couple of turkey and cheese club sandwiches. Blake and T.J. spent the entire evening on the porch talking for hours.

Through their conversations, Blake and T.J. became very comfortable with one another. Blake brought up the crazy stories that he'd heard about T. J. and Gracey, but admitted that he wasn't the kind of person to listen to gossip and that drawing his own conclusion was his way. He told T.J. that his parents did attend Gracey's funeral, and so did a lot of kids from the school. Upon hearing this, T.J. became silent as she was taken back almost six years ago. Slowly, she began to share with Blake the horrors that took place that night.

Blake saw how difficult it was for T.J. to open up to him. He held her hand as she sobbed while explaining the petrifying events that had taken place. When she finished, he reached into his pocket, pulled out a handkerchief, and began to wipe her tears. Blake was blown away by the accounts of that evening, and how T.J.'s best friend lost her life, and how T.J. almost lost hers. He felt privileged that T.J. would even trust him to the point that she would share such a intimate part of her life with him. He was magnetically drawn to her, her strengths and the power of her mind had convinced him that he had fallen madly in love with her on that very night.

December had come again and the whole town was preparing for Christmas and all its merriments. T.J. had been volunteering at Halstead's school, when the Principal notified her one day that there was an opening in the Cafeteria if she was still interested in a full time job. T.J. accepted the position and was obliged. Within five months of serving breakfast and lunch to the elementary school kids, she became head dietician.

Blake and T.J. began seeing a lot of each other for about eight months when Blake asked T.J. to be his wife. They were married on the same September day as their first date, one year later. T.J's parents were ecstatic for the two of them. But Blake's parents didn't share in their sentiments. They were sympathetic to T.J. and tried not to hold Halstead against her. But their main concern was their son. They were having a problem with the fact that their only son had married a woman whom they considered tainted. They weren't happy that Blake would be taking on a ready made family. They were concerned about what people would say.

But unlike most guys in that town, Blake was led by his heart and not by the convictions of others. He loved T.J. and he would rather die than to be without her. Two years into their marriage he landed a full-time job at the lumber yard. It was great because it gave him full access to all the lumber he needed, and so was able to build a house for his new family, moving them from their one bedroom apartment to a three bedroom home.

Nine months later, T.J. gave birth to a beautiful baby girl. It was most appropriate that they name her Gracey. Halstead was smitten with little Gracey and was proud to be a big brother. He couldn't wait to get home from school to hold and play with his new baby sister.

It wasn't until Gracey's second birthday, that Halstead began to show signs of detachment. He had always been the picture perfect child. And although Blake had never shown signs of favoritism between the children, because he loved Halstead just as if he were his very own. But by age eleven, Halstead had urbanized misplaced feelings. He did know that Blake loved him; but he also knew that Blake loved Gracey and he was her father and not his.

Halstead began to wonder about his real father. He was always told by T.J. and the rest of his family, that his father died in a bad fire before he was even born. But that is all that they ever told him. Why didn't they discuss him, who he was, or his accomplishments? He was my father and I am part of him," Halstead thought to himself.

But the truth be told, the stranger had been badly burned from head to toe, only he didn't die. He survived his injuries, and after many surgeries that were necessary to sustain him, he was tried, convicted, and sentenced to life in the Maximum Security Prison just outside of town. Blake and T.J. promised that Halstead would never find out about him until he was grown.

By the time Halstead was twelve, Blake and T.J. had another addition to the family—a boy. They named him Gaines. Halstead had picked up a very bad habit of disappearing. He would go off alone to find ways to amuse himself, while Blake and T.J. were preoccupied with his little brother and sister. He was pretty much shunned from the kids in school for reasons he didn't understand. He was never included in any activities. Most days he would sit alone in the school yard at recess and would be off to himself. It was as if the other kids were all afraid to be around him. Halstead was really unhappy at his school and he often thought of how much he missed his great-grandmother. He wished he was back in Canton where people were nicer. In Canton he didn't have to fit in and he never felt alone. His great-grandmother had a special way of making him feel unique and different in a good way, and he missed that.

Halstead spent a lot of time down at the tracks. He loved collecting bottle tops and pieces of metal. He would make all kinds of creations out of the metal. The one mirror that Blake and T.J. had in the entire house was too high up and Halstead wasn't quite tall enough to see himself in it. He enjoyed looking at his reflection in the pieces of scrap metal that he found. He would admire himself in the windows of parked cars and business shops. He was told by most people he met that he was very easy on the eyes. Every where he went, that seemed to be unanimous.

One rainy day, Halstead decided that it was too gloomy outside to be in school. He'd already made up his mind that school was already gloomy enough. He decided to skip school and spend the day down by the tracks. He ran into a couple of older boys who had also decided to ditch school. Halstead saw them from a distance but wasn't ready to introduce himself.

He sat off to the side and watched them for the next two weeks as they drank Roll and Rock's, smoked cigarettes, and often entertained the company of females. They too were watching Halstead as he transformed the metal and bottle tops that he collected. Halstead had a very social personality. He didn't even have to convince the boys to let him hang out with them. They invited him too. They practically adopted Halstead and made him their mascot.

Halstead began to skip school, sometimes three times a week. He felt comfortable enough to ask Frank, the oldest one of all the boys, and the first to befriend him, about something that had been troubling him. "Do you know anything about my family? "Anything like what?" Frank asked."

"Do you know what people are saying about me?" Frank, sixteen, became serious for that moment when he saw that Halstead needed him to be. He took his time to answer.

"Things like what?"

"You know…things. The kids at school don't like me very much and I don't know why. You would tell me if you knew why, wouldn't you?"

Frank paused for a moment. "I mean I've heard some things," he said…but you can never worry about what people say about you man. People are going to always talk. That's what they do, they discuss other people's lives." Halstead paused. He looked down for a moment as he drew faces in the earth with a stick. Then he looked back up at Frank.

"What do they say about me?" he asked.

"It's not important little man. None of it is important."

"It is to me."

"Well I'm not sure I'm the one you should be talking to about this," Frank responded.

"Did you know my father?" Frank saw how important the truth meant to his little buddy.

"I was just four when it happened," Frank told him.

"So you know about him dying in the fire? Who was he?" Halstead got more aggressive with his questions. Frank stood up and took one more tote from his cigarette before he plucked it.

"Look Stead, you should be asking your family these questions." Halstead looked desperate.

"Nobody will talk to me about anything, Frank. I've tried. Why won't anybody talk to me about him? The kids in school are saying awful things. They don't even want to be around me. I have no friends. Even the adults, for the exception of Mr. James and the Petersons, treat me like the plague. I wanna know why Frank."

Frank looked at Halstead. He knew that Halstead had a right to know what happened that night. He felt that it was his right to know. Frank thought highly of Halstead. He believed he was one the brightest and smartest people he knew. It was obvious that he was missing something in his life, something that he needed desperately. And if he was able to help him with that, then that is what he wanted to do.

He grabbed a few beers from the cooler. He handed one to Halstead. Halstead looked at the beer, looked at Frank, took it, cracked it open, and began to drink. Frank drank and began to tell the story of that night as he heard it. Halstead looked on starring with blank eyes. Finally, Frank stopped talking. Halstead hung his head low, got up, walked over to the cooler, reached down and took two cans of beer and put them in his pocket. He shook Frank's hand, and thanked him for giving him the piece of his life that was missing. "See you tomorrow buddy," Frank called out." As Halstead began walking, he stuck his chest out, with an air of maturity about him that he didn't have before. Halstead didn't know how he should feel about what he had just learned. It was too early to tell. He went home and hid out in the shed where he finished up the other two beers. Three hours later he decided to go inside the house. Blake and T.J. were worried beside themselves. He stumbled up the steps leading into the house smelling like a brewery.

T.J. and Blake met Halstead as he came into the house. T.J. was livid. "Where have you been?" she questioned. "We've been worried sick about you, do you know what time it is?" as she looked into his eyes with disbelief. "Have you been drinking? Oh my God Blake, he's drunk," T.J. reacted. She began to cry, "He's drunk." Blake moved in to get a closer look at Halstead. In disappointment he responded, "Well there's nothing we can do about this tonight. He's wasted. We'll put him to bed and we'll deal with this in the morning.

The next morning Blake and T.J. were up early. They barely slept a wink as they were up all night discussing Halstead and his recent behavior. Blake went to work. He instructed T.J. to call him when Halstead got up, so he could come home to be there to talk to him. T.J. waited as half the day went by. Then finally, around 1:00pm, she heard Halstead moving about in his room.

T.J. called Blake, who worked right down the road. "Yeah, he's up."

"I'm on my way." By the time Halstead came out into the living room area, both Blake and T.J. were sitting on the sofa patiently. "Won't you come over here and have a seat," Blake, suggested. Halstead came in and sat down. "You know we need to talk about last night. I think you owe us some answers" Blake stated. Halstead looked away.

"What's wrong?" T.J. asked. "Whatever it is, you can tell us. You've changed so much over the past year. Your teachers tell us that you haven't been attending school. Where have you been? Where do you go? You've become so distant from your father and me. You barely play with the children anymore. What is going on? And now, we find out that you're drinking. Halstead that's not like you. You're thirteen years old. You're gifted. You can do anything you put your mind to. I don't understand any of this."

"Well I didn't understand either until yesterday," Halstead commented. Blake and T.J. looked at each other in confusion.

"Everybody knows Mom. Everybody." Blake and T.J. felt that their worst fear had come home to roost.

"Everybody knows what?" T.J. questioned, hoping that Halstead had not found out the truth.

"Everybody knows the truth about me." Blake and T.J. remain silent. "Do you know that nobody wants to be around me? I have no friends in school. People treat me as if I'm infected with something that they can catch," Halstead continued as he looked at T.J. with tears in his eyes. "Why mom…why would you even bring me into this world? I would have been better off dead," he stated as he got up and walked toward the door. "I'm better off dead." He ran out the door and down the road.

"Oh God," T.J. called out as she grabbed her chest with her hand and ran out onto the porch calling for him.

"Halstead," she shrieked as she reached out for him and held on to a column on the porch, "Halstead!" Blake, right behind her, held her as he helped her back into the house and onto the couch. He tried to console her. T.J. looked up at Blake, "He knows, oh dear God he knows," she continued to break down inconsolably. Blake pulled her in to his bosom and held her tightly.

"Shh shh shh," he sang. Everything is gonna be alright," he told her as he grabbed her face and held it gently with both his hand. He spoke to her in the only voice that could calm her down. "I'll find him. I'll find and I'll bring him back and he'll understand. Once he hears it from you he'll understand" T.J. nodded her head, believing and hoping in her husband's words. "We'll make him see," he confirmed. Blake had never seen T.J. overcome by such fear and grief as she was that very moment. He witnessed her whole world being shaken right down to its very foundation. He felt her anguish as though it belonged to him. He knew that it was solely up to him to rid her of her agony. In minutes, he'd gotten up and put on his jacket. But before he proceeded out the door, he stopped, got on one knee, and placed both hands gently on T.J.'s shoulders. "You trust me?" he asked tenderly.

"Yes," T.J. responded with teary eyes. Blake kissed her forehead, and with that, he was off.

Blake began to ask all around town whether anyone had seen Halstead. He questioned some of the kids that went to his school if they knew where he liked to hang out. It had been seven hours. The sun had set and it was extremely dark out. He was two doors from an old girlfriend of Franks, questioning an elderly lady that lived there. The girl stood in the door of one of the apartments and saw how desperate Blake was to find Halstead. "Hey mister," she called out. "You lookin' for bottle tops? You can find him down at the tracks," she told Blake. Bottle tops, Blake thought to himself. He knew that Halstead liked to collect bottle tops, so the girl in the door must be referring to him.

He looked in her direction to see who the voice belonged to. "Thank you…thank you so much," he said as he took off. Blake made his way down to the tracks in complete blackness where he found Halstead sitting alone. He slowly walked over to where he was and sat down next to him and began to speak. "Regardless of what took place, I've always loved you. You're my son and I never looked at you no different. You, your mother, Gracey, and Gaines are the best things that ever happened to me and nothing can ever change that. Not the past. Not the present, or the future.

We can't dictate how we come into this world. And we can't dictate how we leave it. But we do have some control over what we do with our lives while we're here, and that's what counts. Now, your mother is hurting real bad over this. I've never seen her like this before. I know that it's hard for you to take all of this in, because it's a lot, it really is. But its no fault of your mother's and it sure ain't no fault of yours. She loves you more than the air she breaths, and she's not gonna' be able to move pass this thing until she knows that you're alright and she makes you understand. She's lost a lot and she's been through a lot, and she won't be able to take losing you. So please, for all of our sakes, come back to the house and hear her out. Listen to her side of the story." And with that, Halstead stood up and Blake stood along side him. Blake put his arm around him as they proceed to walk home together.

Blake and Halstead approached the porch of their home and entered in. There they found T.J. anxiously waiting. Her hair was frazzled, her faced flushed and swollen, and her eyes were bloodshot, as evidence that she had been crying the entire day. "You hungry? I fixed you some ox tails. I know they're your favorite," T.J. said, trying so hard to break through the tension that filled the room and the heavy cloud that hovered over their home. Blake and Halstead came in, washed their hands, and sat at the dining room table. Blake took a seat at the table on a three hundred and sixty degree angle to Halstead's left.

T. J. nervously sat at the same angle, but to Halstead's right. They all sat and waited until T.J. got up the nerve to speak. She hesitated and prayed that the words would come. She dreaded that moment since the day Halstead was born, and now it was here. He was only thirteen. He was still a baby. She prayed that He would be mature enough to understand what she was about to tell him. And then finally, she opened her mouth and the words began to flow.

"When I found out that I was pregnant with you I didn't know what to think. After my best friend Gracey died…my voice was taken away from me for about three months. I couldn't speak. The doctors…they all said I was in shock and that I had given up on life. I didn't want to live in a world where people could go around hurting other people, the way Gracey and I was hurt.

But then I found out that I was carryin' you. I couldn't understand why Gracey died and I was left alive. I couldn't understand why there was new life growing inside me. I was fifteen years old, I was scared to death, and I was alone. I had people around me who loved me, but I felt abandoned and discarded inside.

I didn't know what to feel. I was confused. I was angry at the man who did this. And I was mad at God for allowing it to happen. This man killed my best friend. Why was he living and she was not. Many people talked against me having you. Nobody really understood. I didn't even understand. They were saying awful things.

Halstead they don't treat you different because they hate you. They treat you different because of what you remind them of, and they're afraid of it. But what I know is that you have to face what you're afraid of or you'll never be whole. Remembrance can be good if you understand what it is that you're supposed to get from it.

I've come to accept that nobody has to understand me or my decisions. You're my son and that's all that needs to be understood. Nanna understood that nobody will ever know what that man took from me that night. I never thought that I would ever have a normal life again or know what love felt like. That man took my innocence, my virtue, and my self esteem. He even tried to take my life.

I was supposed to die that night, but I didn't. Can't you see that you are not a curse, you are a miracle? When I felt you growing inside me I knew that you were sent by God. And through you, he gave me back my voice. He made me want to live again. I wasn't alone anymore because I had you. So when I look at you right now today, I don't see the ugliness of this world or what the stranger did to us that night. I see Gracey. I see Nanna. I see ice cream, and long walks in the park. I see rainbows in the sky, and fresh squeezed lemonade on a hot summer day. When I look at you Halstead, all I see is love.

There is a difference between the people in town and me. They can only see that which preceded you. And they are remiss in seeing the beauty that came afterwards." T.J. placed her hand under his chin and lifted his head gently. "That's what you are to me…beautiful." T.J. wrapped her arms around Halstead's neck and Halstead wrapped his arms around T.J.'s waist and they cried. With tears in his eyes, Blake came closer and wrapped his arms around the both of them.

"Why is everyone crying?" Gracey asked. "They're tears of joy sweetie," T.J. said. "They're tears of joy."

Six months later, Blake received a call from his uncle Jake who resided in Philadelphia. His aunt had become ill and Uncle Jake needed help running the mill. Uncle Jake didn't have any children and Blake was his only nephew. So Blake packed up T.J. and the children and they moved to Philadelphia to help out his uncle. Two weeks after the move. Halstead was enrolled in Austin Meehan School. There he laid eyes on Cadence for the very first time.

Chapter Thirty-Nine

||||||||||||||||||||||||||||||||||||||||||||||||||||||||||||||||||||||||||||||||||||||||||||||||||||||||||||||||||||||

Halstead and Cadence

Although Halstead was secure about the genuine love that Blake and T.J. showered him with, he wasn't sure about the love that he had for himself. He knew what his DNA consisted of, and that T.J. was the best part of him. For as much as he tried not to think about his biological father, something within him would not let him forget. A voice would always remind him that he would forever be his father's child.

At age fourteen, Halstead was introduced to his sexuality and began to live promiscuously. He lost his virginity to a seventeen year old female that lived around the corner from his home. But Halstead had been smitten by Cadence as he watched her gracefully walk through the halls of Austin Meehan. And even in his promiscuity, he endlessly pursued her, as she refused to give him the time of day because of his reputation. Every girl in the school wanted to get to know Halstead, and he never turned down an opportunity to get to know the ladies.

Cadence, a couple of friends, and myself were in Center City at the Arcades at thirteenth and Market St., getting our pictures taken, when we ran into Halstead. He had been sweatin' Cadence something fierce and it didn't look like he was gonna give up anytime soon. He walked up behind her as she and I were admiring the photos that we'd just taken inside the photo booth.

"Can I get one of those pictures?" she heard a voice from behind her ask. Cadence turned and saw it was Halstead.

"I think not," she responded as she began to walk off. Halstead began to follow her. "Boy where are you going?" Cadence snapped.

"I'm going wherever you're going," he answered

"No, I don't think so," she cut him off short.

"Why not?"

"Why not?" she repeated. "Because I'll tell you today, like I told you yesterday, and the day before, I don't want to be bothered, can't you see that?"

"No, I can't. You don't even know me."

"I don't have to know you, I know of you. And from what I know of you, I don't want to get to know you."

"Damn, for you to be so fine, you mean as hell. Why you gotta' be that way?"

"Because that's just the way I am."

"OK, I can live with that."

"Nobody's asking you to. Come on Shelly," she said to me as we left the Arcade to go next store to the Pizzeria. Halstead is left standing there.

"Come on Stead man, stop chasing that girl," Tee Pee said. You don't wanna mess with her anyway, she's one of them bougie girls. You can't do nothin' with her. If you do happen to get her, she ain't goin' allow you to have no fun. Hey come on let's go up in this new flick, Caligula. They say that movie is wild. It's all types of sex up in this piece."

"It's X-rated. They not goin' let us in to see that, and what you know about sex anyway?"

"Who said anything about them letting us in? I'm talking about going through the back door. And for your information, I know plenty about sex.

"The only time you've seen sex is in the movies."

"You can believe what you want. I don't have to prove myself to none of y'all." They all laughed as they left the Arcade.

As they passed the Pizzeria, Halstead looked in. "Hey, I'll catch up with y'all later, I'm goin' run in here for a minute."

"Come on man", lil' man yelled. "Leave that alone, she ain't even on your level,"

"Yea, yea, I heard what you said, but I'm not listening."

He walked into the pizza shop and began to walk over to where Cadence was standing waiting for her order. "Halstead is walking towards you, girl don't look," I whispered in her ear.

Cadence slightly turned her body so she would not be able to see Halstead when he walked over.

"Yea, give me what she ordered", he told the man behind the counter.

"You got enough," he talked to the back of Cadences head. She felt his hot breath on the back of her neck, and turned.

"What?"

"Do you have enough for whatever it is you ordered?"

"Yes I do, thank you. I wouldn't have ordered it if I didn't have the money to pay for it. That's something you woulda done. You probably don't even have any money in your pocket to pay for your own order?"

"What?" Girl first of all, it's rude to inquire about how much a man has in his pocket. And second of all, you don't know me well enough to even be talking to me like that.

"A man, Cadence and I laughed heartily. "Let me see what's in your pocket, Man."

"Not until you show me some respect."

"Just like I thought, you don't have any money."

"Girl, why you so hard on a brother? Have I done something to you that I'm not aware of? I mean all of this attitude and hostility is so uncalled for."

"Stop tryin' to change the subject. Let me see." Halstead and Cadence looked at one another as he reached in his pocket and pulled out one dollar and ten cents. It was just enough for his slice of pizza and canned soda.

"I knew it," then they both started to laugh as they found a seat in one of the booths.

"Hey, I'm spending my last dime just to be up in here wit' you. Don't that count for somethin'?

"I'm not impressed." Halstead became serious for a minute. "Well what can I do to impress you?"

"Leaving me alone would impress me."

"Naw, I can't do that. You goin' to the dance?"

"Maybe."

"Well maybe I'll see you there." He got up and left without taking so much as one bite of his pizza or a sip of his soda.

Two weeks later Austin Meehan held its annual end of the year dance. Cadence and I were about an hour late to the festivities. The music was blasting, there were colorful streamers and balloons everywhere. I must admit, the place really looked nice. When we walked into the gym about an hour late, we were met by a couple, who told Cadence that Halstead was looking for her everywhere.

Cadence began to freak out. "Awl man, what does that boy want with me? Come on, let's hide out in the locker room." As we made our way across the floor to the locker room entrance, we saw Halstead dancing with not one, but two girls. He couldn't have been that focused on them, because as soon as he saw Cadence making a "B" line to the locker rooms, he left those girls dancing by themselves, slid across the floor out of no where, and began to dance with Cadence as she continued to walk. "Go head with that now I'm not dancing with you. Can't you see that I'm busy. Come on Halstead stop it."

"You stop," he said playfully. "I'll leave you alone if you give me one dance. You might as well…the locker rooms are locked, he grinned"

She tried to walk in the opposite direction, but Halstead slid that way too. He finally took control and grabbed Cadence by her hand. At the instance of the touch, she was troubled as she was able to see pieces of his life flash before her eyes. It startled her in such a way that, when she tried to pull away from him, she fell backwards and landed on the floor. Halstead immediately helped her to her feet apologetically.

"Are you alright?" he asked as he helped her to her feet. I stood by and watched how gentle he was with her. I didn't bother to try and help her because Halstead had it all under control. He brushed her dress off and walked her over to one of the tables while everyone stood by and observed a more tender side of him.

He went and got her a glass of punch and pulled up a chair. "I'm sorry about that. I was just messing around." Cadence was quiet. "You mad at me?"

"No" she said. It wasn't your fault, I'm clumsy like that." Halstead noticed that Cadence had drifted off to some other place. "You sure you're alright, I could walk you home if you're ready to leave?"

"I'm fine, you go ahead, you don't have to sit here with me."

"I know I don't…I want to."

Just the three of us sat alone at the table until Tee Pee came over and joined us. Cadence now knew so much more about Halstead and his life. She'd seen the rape and the violence. She'd seen the funeral and the move to nana's house. And she'd seen Halstead's pain; but she never saw herself anywhere in his life. The DJ was playing "Firecracker" one of Cadences' favorites. "That's my song," she hinted.

"So what, you wanna dance or something?"

"Yeah."

"Oh, so now you wanna dance? Again I ask, are you feelin' OK?

"Just come on boy," she said as they approached the floor. They danced for about six songs straight including the slow ones. Nobody asked me to dance not even once. Halstead and Cadence became the hottest couple at Austin Meehan and all through high school.

Cadence tried harder than anyone I've ever known to keep her relationship in tact. But Halstead just couldn't be faithful. Every time Cadence found out he had been with someone else, she'd breakup with him. He'd go around pleading his case to anyone and everyone who would listen; her parents, sisters and brothers, and even me. We would all convince her that he was truly sorry for what he did, because we believed him. She would feel guilty and he'd charm his way back into her heart, joking and making her laugh as only he could do.

But finally, none of us tried to convince her this time because we saw the toll that the seventeen plus years relationship had taken on her and their family. We recognized when she hadn't laughed in a very long time. And we too, realized that Halstead wasn't willing to change his behavior, no matter the cost; because he couldn't change what he didn't recognize. And for that, we were all saddened.

I do believe that Halstead did love and care for Cadence and the children, as much as it was in his ability to do so. In his struggle to be completely opposite from how he presumed his biological father to be, day by day he began to resemble him more and more.

His father would often visited him in his dreams and in an attempt to escape his father's hauntings, as well as the idea that his father's cold and demonic blood ran through his veins; he turned to every drug on the market and counted on them to help him forget who his father was and who he was. As a result, he would never be able to appreciate or cherish the very things that were in front of him.

Chapter Forty

||||||||||||||||||||||||||||||||||||||||||||||||||||||||||||||||||||||||||||||||||||||||||||||||||||||||||||||||||||||||||||||||||||||||||||||||||||||||||||||||||||||||||

A Change Is Coming On

Cadence came face to face with the notion that being a part of Halstead's life may not have helped him as much as it may have hindered him; as she continued to enable him. She finally came to the conclusion that Halstead was as much a crutch for her as she was for him. Neither had been strong enough to do what they knew needed to be done.

She knew that she had it in her to do what she never thought she could; that which used to be unthinkable. The doubts crept in like age on an old house. Her thoughts told her that she couldn't do it and that she would never succeed without him. But she had already been for so long now and she hadn't even acknowledged it.

It was important that her children witness her strength of mind and her transformation. Cadence made sure that they knew with all certainty that they had all the ingredients of greatness within them. And if there ever came a time when they would doubt it, they would be reminded of the exceptional reserve that they were made of and how they would depend on that very element to get them through even the toughest of times.

Although Cadence had taken the first steps in the resolution of her relationship with Halstead, she still walked but with one foot still dragging behind. She was zapped of all eagerness and willingness to try new things and take risks because she was reminded of the chance that she took when she married Halstead and her poor decision making skills. She was skeptical of moving forward yet she wanted desperately to find her purpose of life.

"I looked at the blueness up in the sky.
My wings got clipped, so I couldn't fly; high above all my adversities, I cried out lord,
come see about me. I'm injured and I'm caged and I
can't get out. I'm planted but
never watered like a seed of
doubt; stumbling in the darkness where I can't hear or see. Come quickly, oh my Lord.
Come see about me."

But late one Friday evening when the children were sleeping over Mom's, she was at home in her small apartment trying to wind down after a pretty long day at work. As she started to clear the dining room table of two weeks worth of mail; she came across a complimentary issue of Black Enterprise Magazine. She kicked off her shoes, popped a bag of Orville Redenbacher, added a bit of Cajun seasoning, opened the magazine and began to read.

There were two articles that stood out and ministered to her and her predicament. They were stories of women, who had found themselves in unhealthy relationships and they descriptively gave an account of how they journeyed through. As in most cases, they endured a painful and lonesome hardship. But through their courage, fortitude, and their determination, as time went on, they were finally able to find a place for themselves in the world and were beginning to gain new ground. Their relentless refusal to be defeated by the trials of life and the crap that happens to you during your travels through it, brought about a different meaning to the term valiant.

There was one woman who Cadence could particularly relate to in her dilemma. Her name was Jessica. Previously, she managed to vacation in St. Martins and other popular islands at least twice a year. She was salaried at six figures with one of the most reputable advertising agencies in San Diego. She had become accustomed to fine living and dining and she rarely cooked a meal in her entire career and her taste in clothing and shoes were exquisite.

Up until that point Jessica thought that she was prepared for anything; that is until the bottom fell right from underneath her. The company had made quite a few bad investments. They paid out close to seven billion dollars in lawsuits in that year alone. They were forced to downsize considerably if there was even a remote possibility that they could pull themselves out of the hole that they dug.

Rather then terminate the position of just one of the CEO's who made an astounding salary, they opted to terminate seven members of staff who had less than ten years on. Jessica was given a two weeks severance package, a thank you for your services, and was politely asked to clear out her office by the close of the seventh day.

To pour salt on a wound, she had met and fallen in love with someone. They had been dating for four years and they were one month away from their wedding date, when she discovered that her fiancé' had a secrete relationship with her sister, who was younger by two years. They say when it rains it pours.

She had gotten behind in all of her bills and her home had gone into foreclosure. She was fortunate enough to sell her house in just under seven months. The house was sold as is with most of the things that were in it. She down graded from a five bedroom house to a two bedroom house and didn't have any room for a lot of her things. She sold her car and brought a used one to escape a car note. Depressed and dismayed, she found herself having a hard time getting up in the morning and leaving the house to look for a potential job. Her social life no longer existed and she became an omen to those she thought were her friends.

After about eight months of melancholy she found a book of inspiration behind her waste basket. She began to read a page every day. She became stirred by the verses that spoke to her about believing and speaking to her mountains; those obstacles and stumbling blocks that had been placed in her path to deter her progression. She began telling them to get out of her way. She was tired of feeling sorry for herself and bad about the situation that she found herself in. She was tired of blaming and hating everyone for how they hurt her. She decided to get up, shower, and get dressed. She had little experience in doing her own hair or nails, but she did the best that she could do. She began to go to job fairs and seminars, attempting to recreate herself.

And as fate would have it, her new found attitude and motivation paid off. She landed a job at a Marketing firm as a clerk typist. She knew that it was a long way off from an Advertising Consultant, but she was willing to start over from the bottom. She mimicked a financial planning report that she had seen in Black Enterprise as she was determined to work her way back. She ate tuna, potted meat, baked beans and hot dogs; inexpensive and sometimes unhealthy meals that would allow her to save as much money as she could.

Prayer and meditation became her therapy. She saved enough in two years to put a substantial amount of money down on a small piece of property that she had her eye on for some time. After building her credit back up, she applied for a small business loan through one of the special programs that President Obama had implemented through his stimulus package and opened up her very own Advertising Business.

Once Cadence was finished reading Jessica's story, she had been inspired like never before and had been given a new lease on life. She was moved and enthused; provoked to look for great things to begin to take place in her life. Her trials were no different than the trials of Jessica and the other women that she read about in that magazine.

They had all too many things in common with one another. Cadence too was hurt and deceived. She too had worked long and hard to build a quality life, dedicating her time to long hours at work, striving for a better future in order to offer her family the best of her. She was always taught that if you worked hard and invest now, then the payoff would be substantial. And although she had lost practically everything and had virtually nothing left, she was careful to be reminded that she was spared her job and thankfulness was still due always.

That night was mystical for Cadence. She lay still in her bed with the television on mute. She closed her eyes as she meditated and tried to get in tune with the heavens. She sat up suddenly and as she began to think about faith and what its true meaning was. She hit the mute button and restored the sound back to the television, only to hear a revelation given by the voice of a prominent minister.

His words were soft, but they were clear. He spoke to all those who were engulfed in hardships and had been down so long that they had forgotten how it felt to be up. He looked out into his live audience as though he were speaking directly to Cadence, as he said, "There is only one of three places in life that any of us could be in. You are either in a storm right now, coming out of a storm, or you are about to enter into a storm. He reminded everyone to take heed that every setback was actually a setup for a comeback."

Those words became etched in Cadences mind. When she heard them, she felt such an electrical, exhilarating force run through her body. She was sure that she wasn't alone in her suffering and she felt ease and simplicity. She knew that those words were maybe some of the most significant words that she had heard in her life. She would imagine that those words were probably meant for others, but they were definitely meant for her too. She began to do something that she had never really and truly done before, and that was to believe. She started to believe that she could really come out of this thing better off than when she went in it. She figured that if those women that she read about could muster up the strength to move forward, then so could she.

She decided that she would not lie down anymore, even if she had to crawl. She began to tap into her analytical self. Revisiting her past was awkward for her, but she had grown weary of running from it. Facing it allowed her see just how far God had actually brought her, and to appreciate where she was right now in her life despite its appearance. She decided to embrace all the bad choices that she made and make them count for something bigger and better.

Cadence felt like she had been in a boxing match all those years. She felt beaten up from life because she hadn't been properly trained. Her opponent was good, but she knew that God was better. She practiced her stance. She learned to shift her body and use the appropriate combinations. She had to get in tune with her opponent as she learned when to duck and when to dodge; when to step and when to slip.

It had taken a lifetime for Cadence to realize that she had to be broken down before she could finally break out. She believed that where she was, was exactly where she was supposed to be. Her love and life experiences had opened up a whole new world to her in which she was able to see a different perspective.

> *"I went back and I took a look around. I wasn't really surprised at all the things I found. Although I had never begged and was blessed to never borrow, I had no hopes and had no dreams, not even for tomorrow."*

During her suffering, Cadence often wanted to drift off into an abyss of dejection and hollowness, never to ever feel again; becoming numb and insensitive to it all. But what she really found was that out of every misfortune and unpleasant thing that has happened to her, there was an increase and an opportunity for her to grow.

With all that had over shadowed her life and the fear of doom that had befriended her, somehow she knew that those trials weren't given to her as a mechanism to destroy her; but instead, they were given to her as tools to build her up.

Seven challenged and defied her. It threw her into water without a life jacket, expecting her to use the survival skills that she had learned in order to stay afloat. She found that with each test there would be more difficulties; but the greater the test the greater the triumph.

Chapter Forty-One

||||||||||||||||||||||||||||||||||||||||||||||||||||||||||||||||||||||||||||||||||||||||||||||||||||||||||||||||||||||||||||||||||||||||||||

Loves Proof

A door had opened and Cadence was not afraid to walk through. The agony of yesterday slowly faded, but it had an unyielding determination to hold fast to her. She halted as it gained on her heels. Quickly, she stepped aside as it passed. She stood by and watched as it continued to run on; without realizing that she was no longer in front of it, and therefore could not pursue her any longer.

Cadence rarely heard people speak about love and all its proofs. She's almost never heard tales of an enchanted and improbable love; that which she only understood to exist in the imagination of minds and hearts. She thought of a world where love could really reach the leaps and bounds of all of its expectations. She believed that the world could never offer her that which she could only envision in the estimation of her own views.

Her decision not to inflict the whimsical impulse of love that could only subsist in a place far beyond what was true for her; upon anyone, as it would eventually prove to be such cruel and unusual punishment as time and history for her has demonstrated. But true love... is a love evident of a selfless and unconditional state governed by the spirit of God—that which humanity alone has yet to grasp.

Needless to say, Cadence never did go back to Halstead that last time. She never even took the time to look back. She embarked upon a new business venture that had taken off like the horses at Church Hill Downs. She'd done exceedingly and abundantly well for herself and for her children. She moved from her apartment and had a home built from the ground up, somewhere near California. She finally made it. Wow!

Chapter Forty-Two

||||||||||||||||||||||||||||||||||||||||||||||||||||||||||||||||||||||||||||||||||||||||||||||||||||||||||||||||||||||||||||||||||||||||

Michelle

For me; I guess it just wasn't in the cards. Because I wasn't quite that fortunate; not even enough to see my babies grow into the fine adults I know they've become. Jim received fifteen to twenty five years for Non-Negligent Manslaughter. I was two days shy of my thirty-eighth birthday. Cadence came back in town to see me one last time as I lay in a beautiful mahogany box, all shiny and polished. Just as fast as her salty tears dropped from her expressionless face, she wiped them dry. She whispered to me that I was finally at peace and that I didn't have to worry about the children. She took my fourteen and sixteen year old back with her to Pasadena and finished raising them. My parents respected and honored my wishes. They agreed that the children needed to move and get away from all the bad memories. Although they lived with Cadence, my parents shared in their custody and there were daily phone calls and plenty of visits.

My two oldest were already out on their own, but they made sure to keep close ties with their younger sisters. It was supposed to be just until the trial was over. But after Jim was convicted the girls never wanted to come back to Philly again. Cadence made sure that my girls were taken care of. She saw to it that they graduated high school and got college educations, just like she did for her own children—just like I knew she would.

You might wonder how it is that I came to know so much about Cadence and her family's history. I thought you might. It just so happens that my parents weren't my parents at all. It seems that my biological parents weren't in the position to care for me—and so my mother lent me to a family who's last name was Heally and never came back to claim me.

Ironically, there was a Heally family who lived in Greenville around the same time as the Anderson's, Cadences grandparents, Blue and Gama. They lived on the land that the Anderson's and four other families resided on and sharecropped—Mr. Calloway's land.

The oldest boy, Jacob Heally married Rosalie Mcconnell and gave birth to a little girl named Petrice, whom they called Peatty. Peatty married her long time Bo, Xavier Parker, X for short. The Heally's along with the Parkers migrated to Philadelphia, as everyone on the Calloway farm eventually did. Unfortunately, Peatty and X were never able to have children of their own. That's were I came in.

My real mother's name was Serenity, and she was a runaway from Up State New York. She left her home with a tragic set of circumstances. One day her father, Malcolm, had come home for lunch to retrieve some important papers that he'd left and needed for an afternoon meeting at the office.

He unlocked the door, came in, and picked the mail up from the doorway that had been delivered earlier. He headed for the kitchen as he began to look through the mail, when he thought he'd heard noises. He paused with caution, in order that he might hear more clearly. He walked slowly toward the stairs as the sounds became more intense. The grunts, moans, and heavy breathing drew him up the stairs to he and his wife's bedroom. He became over heated and nervous as he neared the door.

Malcolm had a history of working sixteen and seventeen hour days frequently. His wife Jai was a very sensual woman who had an undying quench for intimacy. For some time now, Jai has expressed her feelings of neglect and rejection to Malcolm. Malcolm flashed back to the conversation they had the previous night, as he placed his hand on the door knob.

"There are all kinds of people in the world. There are those people who are in need of much. And then there are those who don't need much at all. Well I belong to the first group, Malcolm," Jai explained. When I married you, you knew this about me. I can't continue on in this type of relationship where I'm all by myself," she went on .

"I know, and I hear you", Malcolm responded. "But just as soon as I get this promotion, I'll be able to secure the money that I need for the new contract, and we'll be able to get back to living our lives, I promise."

"No, Malcolm. How many times have I heard you say that? You'll get that promotion and the contract, and there will be some other thing that you need to accomplish. Four nights out of seven, when I close my eyes at night, you're not here. And the other three nights that you are, you're down in your office until midnight, and so I'm alone whether you're here or not. I'm tired of being alone Malcolm," Jai communicated. "I'm tired."

"I know that I've asked you to be patient with me. I'm just asking that you bear with me just a little longer," Malcolm pleaded with Jai.

"How much longer; a week, a month, a year?" she asked.

"I don't know," Malcolm raises his voice. "I just don't know."

"Well I do know. I know that this house isn't big enough for the three of us", Jai responded.

"The three of us?" Malcolm questions.

"You, me, and your ambitions. All I wanted was a simple life with you. The kids are growing up before our eyes, and you're not around to see any of it. You will never be able to get any of that back. You do understand that, don't you? You have the kids where you want them and you have me on a leash and a time frame," Jai reveals her heart. "I want you to look me in my eye and tell me you know exactly what you're doing." Malcolm didn't respond. "I can't hear you Malcolm," she waited for a response. "I need someone to keep me warm at night. I will not be kept at bay any longer," Jai stated with assurance.

The present noises cut through his body like a knife. Malcolm removed his handkerchief from his pocket and wiped the beads of sweat from his forehead as he proceeded to turn the knob, enter the room and expose his wife's tawdriness. He stood there for a moment as he gathered his composure while hearing the two bodies under the bedding exhibiting passionate, contouring, sexual performance with fiery exaltations. His eyes began to fill as he called for her. "Jai," before he burst into the room to witness the bodies heavely gyrating.

All of a sudden the movement in the bed ceased. The two frantically emerged from the flaming pit of ecstasy in a world wind. Malcolm couldn't prepare himself for the confrontation before him. His mouth…his eyes….his heart….all victims of shock as he watched his children emerge into plain view and run pass him like the devil's wind.

He was over come with thoughts of anger. His mind instantly grew cloudy as he became disorientated, and paralyzed; feverish even. "Oh wake me now."

Once it settled into his mind that he wasn't sleep walking; he got his legs to move and he ran after them. "Blizzard," Malcolm called. Serenity ran into her room and shut the door. Blizzard, who was three years older than his sister fourteen year old Serenity, grabbed Malcolm's car keys, left the house and drove off.

"Open this door right now Serenity. Open it before I break it down," Malcolm hollered at the top of his lungs. He realized that Serenity was probably frightened; he tried to calm down. "Open the door sweet heart, I'm not mad at you, I promise." After about one minute later, the door slowly opened. Malcolm stepped in with caution. He didn't know what he would or wouldn't say.

"Are you okay?" he asked.

"Yes sir," Serenity answered.

"Did he force himself on you?"

"Daddy we love each other," Serenity stated with conviction.

"Love?" Malcolm cringed. "How long?" he asked. "How long has this been going on?" he silently wept. Serenity gave no response. "Love has no place in any of this, you have to know that."

"I know what love is daddy."

"He took advantage of you…and I don't suspect you'll see that," Malcolm interrupted. "You haven't a clue as to what love is because if you had this would have never happened. Do you have any idea what this will do to your mother? Do you have a clue as to what you've done?" he asked.

"We knew you wouldn't understand," Serenity said.

"I understand that Blizzard can never set foot in this house ever again. He's no longer my son and he's no longer your brother," Malcolm said.

"What kind of son does this? What kind of brother does this?" he asked.

"You don't mean that, take it back," Serenity began to unravel. "Take it back."

"You're never to see him again, do you understand?" Malcolm insisted as he left the room. Never."

"You can't mean that," Serenity yelled as she shut the door. "You can't keep us apart."

Blizzard left that day and didn't return. Two days later, the police fished out Malcolm's car from the ravine with Blizzard's body strapped in it. The police were pretty convinced that it was a deliberate action that led to his death. After his funeral Serenity packed her bags and ran off. Malcolm and Jai put a missing person's report out on her as they frantically searched. The lost of both of their children caused them to disregard their previous quarrels and to see what was really important in life—family.

Serenity boarded a bus headed for Philadelphia. She walked the streets of downtown Philly where she met a couple of undesirables who helped her pick up a small habit for methadone. She slept in the bus depot for a couple of weeks, using its bathroom to keep her clean. She met a lady whom she befriended, named Peatty. Peatty was a volunteer at a homeless shelter in Center City where she prepared meals and a cot for those who were hungry and needed a place to stay. She invited Serenity to come back to the shelter with her. Serenity took her up on her offer and became a regular.

She was back and forth for months, and after a while it became apparent that she was with child and would soon deliver. She trusted and confided in Peatty. Peatty was very motherly and authentic. Serenity sensed the goodness about her. One day Serenity broke down and told Peatty her secret. She revealed that she believed that her behavior with her brother led to his death and that her pregnancy was her punishment. Peatty listened without judgment. She assured Serenity that everything happens for a reason, and what was done, was done. Serenity told Peatty that she was staying with some people who weren't really privy to rules, regulations, or even decency; but that things would be different once I was born.

I was born the next day. Serenity was delighted that I had all my fingers and toes and that I wasn't mentally challenge due to my blood line. Three months after my birth, Serenity took me to see Peatty. Peatty greeted her with a long hug and even a kiss. "Serenity, oh my God you had the baby," she said in a surprised fashion. "I've been so worried. How have you been getting along, with the baby and all? What's her name?"

"Michelle," Serenity responded. Her name is Michelle. We've been fine. Yep, just fine."

"Have you been eating? Does the baby need anything?" she asked with much concern.

"Awww, look at her," Peatty remarked as she gazed into my eyes. "Can I hold her?" she asked.

"Sure," Serenity replied as she handed me over to her. "Um look, I need to talk to you about something" Serenity said.

"Sure, what is it?" Peatty said in a soft and comforting voice.

"I was kinda hoping you could watch Michelle for me." Peatty listened attentively. "Just for a couple of weeks.

It's not safe to have her in the environment that I'm in. I checked myself into a center that helps girls with my back ground, but they won't take my baby. They say they can get me clean and teach me some skills so I can find work and a place to stay. But then I'll come for her, I promise. She has a fresh bottle, and few diapers in the bag. I'll bring you money just as soon as I can," she stated.

"No, No," Peatty said. "Don't you worry about anything, I'll take care of everything. You just go do what it is you have to do to get yourself well and we'll be waiting for you. I need you to bring me back pass the address of where you'll be so I can check on you and make sure you're OK."

"I'll bring it to you tomorrow. Can I just hold her for a second?" Serenity asked.

"Sure you can." Peatty handed me back over to Serenity and she began to talk with me.

"Mama's got to go away for a while," she told me. "But I'm gonna come back for you real soon. I have something for you." She reached in her pocket and pulled out a necklace with an angle on it. "This was given to me by your grandmother on my last birthday. It's yours now. I won't be needing it anymore. It's the only thing that I have to remind me of her. It'll watch over you and keep you safe until I come back for you," she said. "I love you, Michelle."

Peatty said that she kissed me one last time and handed me back to her and she said goodbye. Weeks had gone by and not a word from Serenity. Peatty and Xavier went to the address where Serenity said she would be and they were told by the Supervisor that Serenity checked in on a Sunday, a few weeks back, but she left three days later. She never completed the program. Peatty never saw her again.

Cadence and I have known since we were young, that our family's had come from the same hometown and shared the same land. And no it wasn't by chance that we met. It was our destiny. Maybe deep down inside I never really expected much from my life. I never expected to know anybody like Cadence. And I was blessed to have a mother like Peatty and a Father like Xavier.

Cadence and I shared our stories and compared notes over the years, as it was told to us. Our connection was strong and fervent throughout our lives since the very first time we met. Like I said; we were always more than just friends; we were family.

Chapter Forty-Three

||||||||||||||||||||||||||||||||||||||||||||||||||||||||||||||||||||||||||||||||||||||||||||||||||||||||||||||||||||||||||||||||||||||||||||

Forgiveness

Halstead never took a real interest in the lives of the people who really loved him. He zig zagged throughout the next ten years of his life. But one day without warning, he showed up at Cadences door step, almost two thousand miles way. His conduct was unfamiliar. He was strangely sincere and remorseful. He apologized for all he had put Cadence, the children, and his parents through all those many years. He told her that he was a new person, changed in all of his ways. He had a legal job now working as a counselor in a rehabilitation facility; the same one that rehabilitated him.

"What are you doing here?" Cadence asked in shock.

"I was in the neighborhood and thought I'd stop by to tell you something," Halstead began as Cadence was caught off guard and remained silent. "You were right.", he confessed. You were right all along…I am not my father. He was a ghost that haunted me and I was terrified of being anything like him. I was afraid and so I ran. I ran so long that I chased everything that I truly loved and that truly loved me away, and for that I'm sorry.

I want you to know that as unbelievable as it may seem; I did love you CC. I took out the contempt that I had for myself on you. Not because I didn't love you, but because I couldn't see how you could love me," he continued as the water began to stream down both their eyes. "I guess I never thought that you would actually leave me," he pauses. "That kinda took me for a loop you know. I was mad about it for a long time—just blaming everybody except myself. You know I waited for you. I waited a long time for you to come back, but you never came. But I'm not mad anymore," he stated humbly. "I was wrong and you had every right to leave and to wanna' make a better life for you and the kids. I know it had to be hard on you. And then you turned around and took Shelly's kids as well. But look at you now. You came up. I knew what you were made of the first day I laid eyes on you and I'm proud of you. You deserve every bit of it," he continued. "I just wanted to come by and say thank you. If it wasn't for you leaving me, I would have never found the courage to find help for myself.

I didn't come down here to manipulate you or mess with your head or anything like that. You were my best friend and I miss that. I need to ask you for your forgiveness." Cadence held her tongue for a moment, still shocked at his presence and all that he acknowledged.

"You came all this way to ask my forgiveness?" she asked in disbelief.

"This was something I couldn't do over the phone. I had to do this in person," he explained.

"Well it really was no need for that. I forgave you the day I left." Halstead looked at her for a few seconds and dropped his head as if a weight had been lifted from off of him. Cadence could see that he was grieved by who he used to be. "You coming in or not?" she asked as she swung the door opened invitingly. Halstead looked up at Cadence with an expression of thanks and a spirit of gratitude. "Come on, I wanna hear all about how legal you are now, I gotta' hear this," she said as they entered into her home laughing heartedly.

"Okay I'm gonna' tell you." Halstead and Cadence laughed and then they talked for hours on end. From that moment on, they remained close as a new friendship developed and a new allegiance was formed.

"Seven is the exact point in your life when you feel it's at its worst. It is the last inning; the final lap. It is the point where you have been stretched so far beyond your limits that you know within yourself, that you can't possibly be stretched any further. But it is also the point where you'll find a life force outside of any thing you've ever experienced and you'll witness for yourself just how much the human spirit can bear.

The windstorms and tempests of seven taught Cadence things that only seven could. It taught her to love hard and to cry out loud. It taught her to embrace her pain as it would surely pass. It taught her to let go hate, disappointments, and ill feeling of guilt; as the lessons of life guided her to acceptance and reassurance.

It taught her to trust forgiveness and to look to the heavens in faith. It taught her to always hold the unimaginable close to her heart and to believe that all things are possible. Seven is the end of a trying and wearisome season, which in due course would ultimately lead to the beginning of a greater era and new and better things...... if she only dared to believe..

Thank you seven. For all the disappointments and for all the wrongs that were never made right. For the apologies that were never sincerely given, and the confessions that were never made. Those things hinder us only because we feel we cannot go on without them. But it was not the truths that were never disclosed, confessions that were never divulged, or apologies that were never made that really mattered, but the mere fact that we are able to forgive, love, and go on to be better – in spite of them.

This book was inspired by my mother, Rose M. Lassiter Sheppard and her mother, Bessie Taylor Lassiter. Through their lives, lessons taught, and unspoken words; I was able to capture the true meaning of love, family, and the sum of all things. They........ are my unsung heroes.

The number seven is associated with those things that have been completed as it was with the natural creation of the world. It is associated with mystery and prophesy alike.

There were **seven** sorrows – Luke 2:34 / 2:43 / 23:36, M 2:13 / 25:57, J 19:25 /
Seven deadly sins – pride, envy, gluttony, lust, wrath, greed, sloth
Every **seventh** year was sabbatical
Six days shall work be done, but on the **seventh** day there shall be
rest. Ex; 35:2
Seven natural wonders of the world – Mt Everest (Nepal), Victoria Falls
(Zimbabwe), Grand Canyon (Arizona), Great Barrier Reef (Australia), Northern
Lights, Paricutin Volcano (New Mexico), Harbor of Rio de Janeiro (Brazil)
Seven years of abundance are coming…
Gen: 41:29
But **seven** years of famine will follow Gen 41
Seven years until the missing can be declared dead
Elijah sent his servant **seven** times to look out for rain 1
Kings 18:36 / 43
Samson's wedding feast lasted **seven** days
"**Seventy Seven**" are decreed for your people and
your holy city to finish transgression. Daniel: 9:24
Nebuchadnezzar was a beast for **seven** years
Daniel 4
Seven keys of music (A B C D E F G)
The were **seven** churches of Asia (Ephesus, Smyrna,
Pergamum, Thyatira, Sardis, Philadelphia, Laodicea.
seven candlesticks, **seven** stars, **seven**
trumpets, and **seven** spirits were before the
throne of God
Forgive **Seventy** times **Seven**
Seven Kings of Rome